THREE
YEARS
DEAD

A. D. DAVIES

Copyright © 2015 A. D. Davies
All rights reserved.
ISBN-13: 978-1508539506
ISBN-10: 1508539502
Cover by Adrijus at www.rockingbookcovers.com

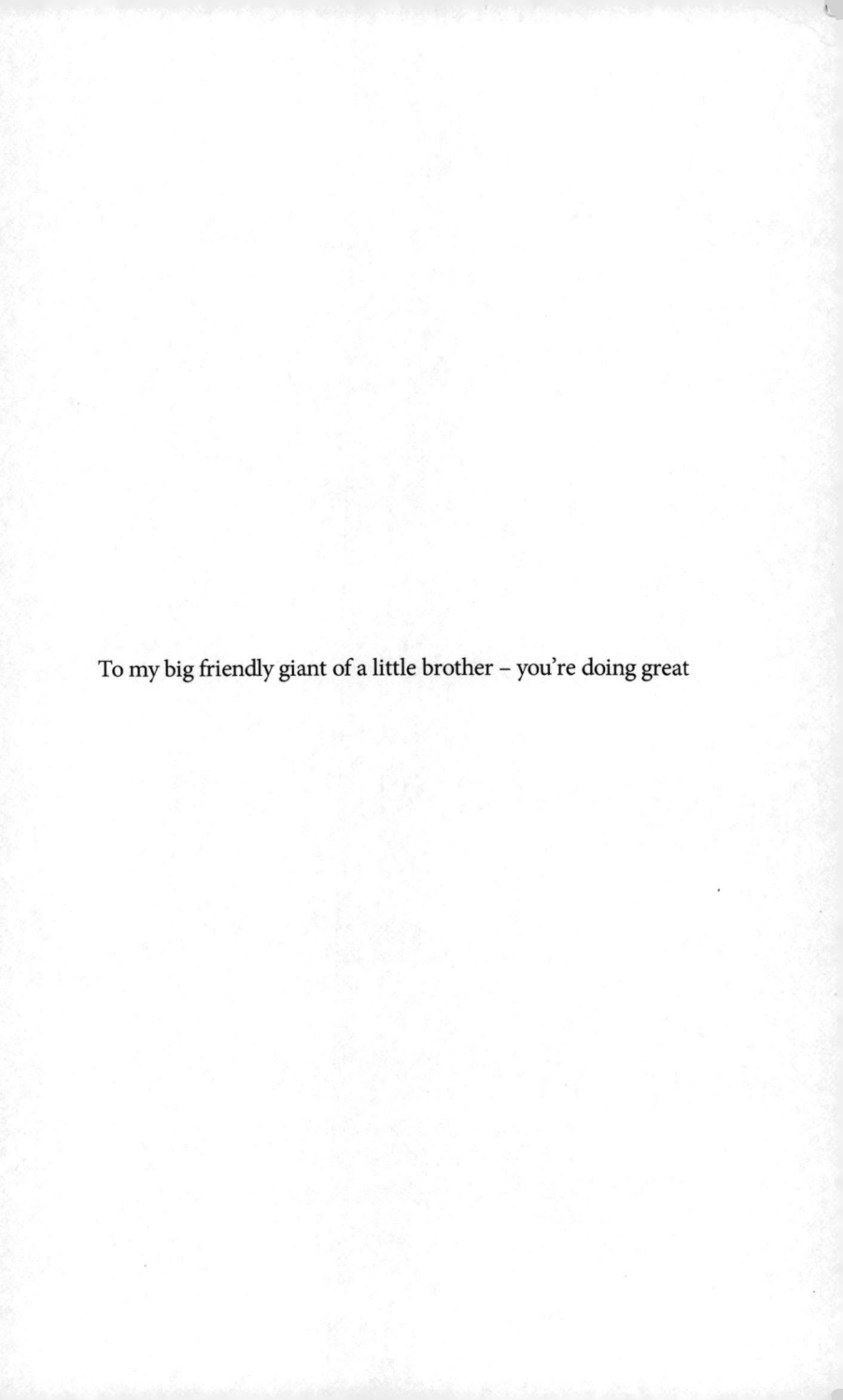

To my big friendly giant of a little brother – you're doing great

NEWS

I want to give you free stuff.

This is only my second book, but over the next 2-3 years I will be growing my list of titles and if you enjoy this one – or my debut novel, His First His Second – you might be interested in forthcoming work too, plus any freebies that will be exclusive to subscribers. When I've written them, of course.

I am planning a number of short stories over those years, and even some novellas, which will cost money on retail sites, but will be free to those who sign up at www.addavies.com/newsletter

I guarantee not to pass on your details anywhere ever, and I won't spam you constantly with sales pitches or irrelevant nonsense. Thank you for taking the time to read this, and I look forward to talking to you later.

I hope you enjoy Three Years Dead.

CONTENTS

Beginnings 7
Looking Back 31
Looking Ahead 55
First Day Back 71
History 113
Out of the Fold 132
Progress 155
Almost there 181
Losing Focus 196
Trying Hard 241
Drugs and Art 273
Everybody Lies 287
The New Time 322
Endings 340
Redemption 349

BEGINNINGS

The Before

The spinning was the worst. No—it was the hope. Hope I might survive, might crawl out of this when, really, I was underwater, hurt, wrapped in wet ice. My arms and legs shot into spasms, and then the water...

Inside me.

I tried to cough. More water sluiced into my mouth, my throat, my chest.

I tasted mud and copper.

My nose stung, as what little air inside me leaked out, the bubbles razor-sharp...

Then darkness.

My feet hit the sludge at the bottom of the River Aire, and plumes of muck swirled. The current gripped again, and the spinning resumed. I tried to pivot, but swimming up, swimming down, it was all meaningless, even if I could have taken a breath.

Spinning.

Up...

Down...

Gulps of muddy water...

Fighting on was futile. Only pain lay ahead if I did.

So, to end it all as quickly as possible, I simply opened my mouth, breathed in hard, and—

Awake

—Martin Money opened his eyes to a bright light. Instead of filth, he tasted plastic. Plastic and disinfectant. He gagged on a pipe; thrashed at the object lodged in his throat. Gripped it. The extraction grated, each ridge bumping over his flesh, but it had to come *out*. As he pulled, his shoulders creaked, throbbing to a numb beat.

There!

The tube came out fully. He vomited something clear and viscous onto the sheets covering his legs.

My legs...

He couldn't see his legs, just the lumps where they should have been, and when he tried to move them, they didn't work. He beat the mounds with one limp fist. He felt nothing.

"No!" The word was agony.

It was white everywhere. Tight sheets; the *beep-beep-beep* of the monitor; wires suckered to his chest; a *hiss-fffffff* from a machine, the one attached to the tube that had been inside his mouth.

Bleach, disinfectant. Another smell. Something... *hospitally*.

Okay, so he was in hospital.

But *alive*.

His gut ached. Sitting up hurt. Moving his arms hurt. Turning his head... well, it hurt, okay?

But his legs. He still couldn't move his legs.

And what about sight? He could see the bulge under the sheets representing his legs, but not much past there. Blurs of light flashed—left, then right. But little else. If he had neighbours he couldn't see them. It could have been a private room or the middle of ITU.

The water came straight back to him now. Drowning tends to stick in the mind. But after that?

No.

Nothing.

That morning, he rushed out the door without breakfast, stopped by his wife who tried to push a bowl of porridge on him. A kiss, a nice kiss, and he told her not to worry, he'd grab something—probably. He found a cereal bar on his car seat, a Post-It note attached with a love-heart drawn in biro.

Ah, Julie. Nice one, honey.

Martin's stomach had settled since the up-chuck, but now a hollow ache told him to fill it. He had never been a patient in hospital before, not even to extract his appendix or tonsils. On TV shows or films, the patient always wakes up and starts stabbing at some button next to their hand.

He could locate no such button.

Instead, he gripped the cords stuck to his chest, ready to dramatically yank them off.

Stopped himself.

Instead of yanking, since he had something of a hairy chest, he forced his heavy thumb and heavier finger to pinch the first sucker, and peeled it gently away. His elbow served as a counterweight, making the effort akin to lifting barbells.

The machine blipped and squawked.

He peeled off the next one. Two more to go.

With the third, sweat prickled on his brow. He dropped his arm, leaving the fourth until he could get his breath. However, it seemed three was enough for the *beep-beep-beep* machine to trigger an alarm somewhere.

"Oh my God!"

The voice belonged to a fuzzy, dark-skinned form in a blueish tunic. Thick-hipped, round, she entered through a door to his right.

A door! So it was a private room, not a ward.

Martin said, "Hey." He tried to, anyway. It came out as one long croak.

"You're awake!" she said, and ran away.

It was not the reaction he was hoping for.

Doom

It took them half an hour to find a doctor. To find *his* doctor. Vasilas. Martin didn't catch his first name. Polish perhaps. Eastern Europe for sure. A definite accent, but his English was clear.

He asked, "Do you know your name?"

"Martin Money," Martin said.

"What city do you live in?"

"Leeds."

"Your profession?" Dr. Vasilas rolled his 'R's, almost seductively.

"I'm a copper," Martin said. "A police officer. Detective Inspector. I work out of Sheerton station with the expanded DOMU initiative."

"DOMU?"

"The Drugs and Offender Management Unit." Martin's throat grated every time he spoke, but the nurse who ran away had returned and fed him iced water and patted his hair and told him what a good boy he was. Mostly. She was the ward sister. Emma Coombs. A big lady, with soft hands and a smile like sunrise. A light Jamaican lilt to the way she talked, more diluted with Yorkshire-ness than Dr. Vasilas.

The doctor asked, "Your mother's maiden name?"

"Carter," Martin said.

"Next of kin?"

"Julie Money. My wife."

He referred to a note on a clipboard that appeared from somewhere, and asked, "Who is the prime minister?"

"David Cameron."

Nurse Emma stroked Martin's hair, tilted her head. "You're doing so great."

Dr. Vasilas said, "And the president of the United States?"

"Obama."

"Ukraine?"

"I don't think I've ever known the answer to that." When Vasilas made a note, Martin said, "Come on, what is this? I know you have to do these tests, but shouldn't you be talking to me? How did I get here? What the hell happened?"

"Sir, I will tell you everything in good time, but for now—"

"NO, TELL ME NOW!"

Emma Coombs snatched her hand away and both of them backed right off. More than out of arm's reach. Vasilas held the pen like a knife, his clipboard a shield.

Martin said, "I'm sorry. I don't know why I did that." He tried to chuck a laugh out. "I can't reach you anyway, look at my legs." He used his hands to lift one leg through the sheets and let it drop.

Both watched his hands return to his lap.

The door opened and a uniformed police officer entered at pace. "Everything okay?" He was young, fit-looking, taller than Martin.

"I think everything is fine," Dr. Vasilas said. "You were very slow."

"Want me to wait here?"

Vasilas shook his head and the young PC returned to the corridor, leaving the door ajar.

Martin asked, "Why is he here?"

"Protection," Vasilas said.

"Why do I need protection?" Martin looked at each in turn. "What happened to me?"

Vasilas sat next to Martin's bed and lay the clipboard beside his useless legs.

Nurse Emma sat the other side, this time not touching his hair or his hand.

"Okay, listen," Martin said. "I'm fine. David Cameron is the P.M., Nick Clegg his deputy, they formed a coalition government two years ago and straight away began jiggering around with police budgets and basically shafting everyone in the country. Bin Laden's been killed, Prince William is married, the peasants rioted cos bankers are rich or whatever shitty excuse they used. I know all this. I need you to tell me why I can't move my legs and why I'm in the hospital."

"Sir," the doctor said, "someone stabbed you just beneath your right kidney, close to the spine. The blade made a cut in the connective muscular tissue that runs down your back. It did not result in serious damage, but you will need to go through a period of physiotherapy."

"And they dumped me in the water?"

"I heard from your colleagues that you fell in trying to escape. I cannot say if this is true."

"Do they know who did it?"

"I believe they have a suspect in custody, or are questioning someone, but then I do not have all the details. You were pulled out and you were resuscitated. But you lost a lot of time, a long time without oxygen to your brain. If you were to recover, I predicted some mild brain damage, perhaps serious."

"But I don't have brain damage, do I? I'm me. I know who the P.M. is, I know who I am…"

Vasilas's deep breath made Martin pause. He'd attended enough interrogations to recognise a suspect about to crack, about to grass up his mate, about to *confess*.

Vasilas said, "There are some… inconsistencies with my notes."

"Incon— what? What do you mean 'inconsistencies'? I got them right, didn't I? How long was I out for?"

"Only a few days, a week. But, sir—"

"What inconsistencies?" Martin was suddenly so tired he could barely keep his eyes open. "I need to sleep. Just tell me. *Please*."

"Sir, your rank in the police. According to my notes—and I will check these—it is not detective inspector. It is detective sergeant."

"No, I— I'm a DI. Detective Inspector Money." Martin's words slurred. Earlier, there'd been a needle embedded in his arm. He checked: still there, a wire snaking to a bag of clear liquid.

Emma Coombs held her thumb and forefinger around a square of plastic—some sort of flow control. With that head-tilt of hers, she said, "To calm you down."

Martin flailed at the line. "I don't wanna *relax*!" His fingers missed and he slumped sideways. Vasilas helped him up. Martin grabbed him by the neck. "Where's my wife? Where's Julie? I need to see her. She'll tell you."

The young buck of an officer stormed in, pulled Vasilas away and Martin's arm dropped dead again. The buck PC was about to strafe Martin with pepper spray but Nurse Emma shouted, "NO!" and the kid paused long enough for her to say, "He's out of it. Don't worry."

Vasilas stood over Martin, rubbing his neck. Martin tried to say sorry, explain this wasn't like him, that he was one of the most chilled-out funky cool guys anyone could hope to meet. In place of comforting words, though, he drooled onto his shoulder and eked out a groan.

Vasilas said, "I'm sorry, Mr Money. But Mr Cameron and Mr Clegg are approaching an election now. Those events you mention, all of them, were three years ago. And your *ex*-wife is no longer listed as your next of kin."

Gloom

Martin woke up again. Hungry. And the thirst had returned with a vengeance. The lights were out, machines glowing quietly. His hands shook. He lifted one, but it was cuffed to the bed rail. This time someone had positioned a call button in his left hand, so he pressed it. He wasn't sure what to expect. An acknowledgment of some sort maybe. But if it rang at a nurse's station up the corridor, why would it be acknowledged?

He tried to relax, but the doc said 2011 was three years ago. So that made it, what? 2014 now. Pretty much the future. He'd been here three years?

No. Dr. Vasilas said it was a matter of days.

Blurred Christmas lights.
Street slick with rain.
Biting cold.
Pain in his back.
Anger.
A scramble on all fours.
Must get away, must get away.
Water, rushing up.
Bubbles.
Filth in his mouth, his lungs…

"Fuck," he said.

"Happy new year to you, too." A man's voice. Somewhere in the room. "So, how you doing, Rosie-Boy?"

"Rosie-Boy? Who is that?"

A figure rose from Martin's left side, where Nurse Emma had sat. An outline, a bald scalp silhouetted against the heart monitor, pointy ears and sloping shoulders. "Hey, you gave us quite a scare."

"Who's 'us'? Who are you?"

The figure reached a long, thin arm to the wall and flicked on a side light. It flared in Martin's face, and when he twisted away, the world blurred and something cut through his brain like cheese wire. His gut cramped, but he couldn't double over, couldn't press his hands into his soft belly. He retched but nothing came.

The man said, "Easy, Rosie. Easy."

Rosie. A new nickname? Ginger hair attracts nicknames like nothing else. Rusty, Red, now Rosie. A new one that had cropped up in the period he'd forgotten. He would have to get rid of *Rosie* pronto.

Martin said, "Get the light off. Or move it, or something."

"I heard your memory is a bit sketchy, Rosie."

The man's shadow fell over Martin, who clicked the call button. "Who are you? Where's my guard?"

"PC Wadaya? He's outside, of course. No need to keep me out. We're friends."

"Who—"

"Here." The man slid in front of the light, but the brightness behind cast him completely as a silhouette. He held something out for Martin. "A little pick-me-up."

A thin object, the length of a finger.

"I can't," Martin said, and rattled the cuffs.

"Bastards. Treating their own like this, it's fuckin' criminal."

The man held Martin's left wrist just above the binding. Held it hard. Martin gasped. The man tapped the arm several times, gave a 'hmm', and nipped out the drip feed. Tied it up.

Martin said, "What are you doing?"

"I told you. Pick-me-up."

As he shifted, Martin now saw the object as if illuminated in a spotlight: a syringe.

"Hey," Martin said. "Are you a doctor?"

The man laughed. "You're really playing this card, huh?" He rested a hand on Martin's chest, leaned his face close and Martin still couldn't see him clearly. From what he made out, the man had small eyes and a squashed nose, a crooked mouth surrounded by a thin line of hair.

Calmly, he said, "Look, Rosie, this is *me*. I'm not wired, and I'm pretty sure it would be against your human rights or some shit to bug a hospital room. It's okay."

He patted Martin's shoulder and moved to insert the needle into the plastic valve already in his arm.

"Wait!" Martin thrashed at the man but was too weak to push him away.

"It's okay," he said. "It'll help you."

"What is it? You're not a doctor."

"No, Rosie, I'm not a doctor. I'm your *friend*."

"If you're my friend, tell me what's in it."

He lowered the syringe, stood back so Martin was again dazzled by the light. "That feeling in your stomach, that ache? It's withdrawal. Your body should've dealt with the worst of it while you were out, but this stuff gets inside you, in your head. You're going cold turkey, and if you say the wrong thing while you're having a fit... well, it'll be bad for all of us."

"All of who? Cold turkey? What are you talking about? *What*... is in... that *needle*?"

"Your cocktail of choice, of course." Now he held Martin's arm firm, fingers like talons. "Just be a minute, then you'll be ready to face the world." He positioned the needle in the drip's aperture.

"No!" Martin yanked his arm away.

"Hey!"

Martin threw the call button with as much strength as he could muster. It landed on the cabinet, its wire snared the glass next to the jug of iced water, and knocked it to the floor, shattering in a hail of noise and shards.

"Twat." he man said.

He dropped the syringe into the gap between the mattress and side rail, and stood up straight. The door opened within five seconds. The main light came on and PC Wadaya entered alongside a suited gentleman who Martin recognised as Detective Chief Superintendent Daniel Black.

"Sir," said the syringe man.

"Detective Constable Essex," DCS Black said. "You're not supposed to be here."

"He's my friend, sir." DC Essex looked at Martin as if for support. "Come on, Rosie. Tell him."

It was all Martin could do to keep from staring at the syringe, from drawing attention to it. He said, "I don't remember you."

"Well you need to fucking remember."

Black said, "That's enough."

"You drove your wife away, Rosie. Your colleagues don't trust you, and pretty much everyone you ever met now hates you. That Arab they got guarding you? Revelation time: he's not there to keep the bad guys *out*. He's there to keep *you* in."

"*Essex*," Black said. "Go. Now."

The detective constable sighed hard through his nose, eyes wide. "I'm not just your friend, Rosie. I'm your *only* fucking friend. Here. Remember this." He tossed a business card onto the bed. "When you're ready to chat."

With DCS Black eyeing him all the way, Detective Constable Essex departed. The large man dismissed constable Wadaya, and turned crisply. "So, Martin. You must have a lot of questions."

Politics

Memory," DCS Black said, lowering himself into what was quickly becoming the dedicated visitor chair. "It's a funny thing."

Martin said, "Not so funny right now, sir."

"No. Not funny at all. You know what today is?"

"That man wished me happy new year. So January."

"Correct. January first, actually. You were pulled out of the River Aire on Christmas Eve. Nice symmetry, don't you think?"

"It wasn't my first thought, but I suppose it has a nice ring to it."

Christmas Eve. Presents, shopping, mulled wine at the Christmas market.

Martin said, "The doctor told me there was a suspect?"

Black shook his head. "No, I'm afraid he was mistaken. We questioned a lot of people, but nothing came of it. No CCTV, no witnesses. Like many of these types of assaults, it's a bit of a dead end."

"Who pulled me out?"

"A woman walking her dog saw you washed up on a mud flat a mile from the bridge. Believed you were dead. Called three nines and waited. She isn't a suspect."

Martin's stomach growled. It bubbled inside. "Sir, do you think someone could get me a bit to eat? A drink?"

Black rubbed his hand over his mouth and stroked it slowly to the end of his chin, the gesture a staple of his. He would be weighing up the choice of being strong and forthright, but ultimately heartless, with being thought of as a waiter. He completed his mental risk assessment, called Wadaya in and gave him the order to send refreshments.

Martin took the opportunity to move the syringe out of sight, under his sheet. Not easy, still being cuffed, but even in that brief moment of pinching it between his fingers, he somehow knew that it contained a high-quality blend of one part cocaine to three parts heroin, a mellow wave backed up by just enough kick to keep the brain working. He could *taste* the drug in his veins.

"So," DCS Black said. "DS Money. This bit is tricky. But I think you'll like it."

"I'm not a DI anymore?"

"No, I'm afraid not."

"Why?"

"An... investigation. It ended badly. For you. And DC Essex back there. I can go into it in full later, but for now, we have to look at options."

"Options?"

"Options, yes." He took a notebook from his jacket and spent a couple of seconds adjusting the distance from his eyes. Wearing glasses was an admission to ageing. "With the injuries you sustained it is highly unlikely you will pass a police medical, and therefore you are eligible for a generous payout and full pension."

The syringe rolled on the bed, stopped by Martin's bare thigh.

"What do you think, DS Money?"

"Sir?"

"Disability. It's unlikely you'll pass a—"

"Yes, sir, I heard all that. Don't I have to go through some tests? The doctor mentioned physiotherapy."

"Indeed, but if we get the paperwork signed off straight away, you don't need to worry about fitness tests or police politics. You just concentrate on getting well, and maybe when you're up to it we can organise a leaving do."

Paperwork.
Politics.
A leaving do.
Martin said, "You're forcing me out."

"Not at all. Simply making the process as smooth as possible."

"What if I wait until I've gone through the physio? Maybe I'll want to return to work."

He put his notes away and stood. Straightened his jacket. "Martin, if you fuck with me on this, I'll make sure the PSD complete that investigation you scuppered."

"Professional Standards? Why are they investigating me?"

Black pressed his fists into the mattress, supporting his bulk. "This is all a lot of fun, Martin. But it won't stick. You got away with a slapped wrist last time, but now your choice is simple." He shifted slightly and, under the sheet, the syringe rolled into the crevice forming near his hand. "Either our Professional Standards Department reopens every investigation they shelved—and I mean including the allegations by your missus, by DS Cartwright, the complaints from Tug Jones's scrotes, even those irregularities with your timekeeping—or... and I want to make this offer very clearly. HR told me to step lightly but you don't seem able to take the hint. Either PSD investigates the living crap out of you, or you accept the ridiculously over-generous disability payout, and fuck off."

His reddening face eased as he stood back up to his full height.

Martin's hand found the syringe and held it. "Sir, I—"

"No need for formalities, Martin. Think of it as a new start. Not many people get that. Be grateful. Sign the paperwork when it arrives. There's a good lad."

Before Martin could say another word, the man who ran his station left. Martin was alone with nothing but a suffocating feeling of... he didn't know what it was. *Unfairness?* Just him, the beeping machines, and a tiny plastic tube filled with liquid pleasure.

Suspicion

Jerry Baxter, Mitul Singh, even Helen Cartwright—they had all at some point made a prank phone call to Martin, or taped a fish to the underside of his car seat, or filled his shoes with confetti that he didn't notice when putting them on after a shift, but spread all over his hall floor when he got home. If it were one of them delivering this sermon, he'd write it off as a joke. But DCS Black treated practical jokes between colleagues as formal notice that they had decided against any promotion opportunities that year. Helen Cartwright could even have roped Julie in, but the fact that Martin had been awake for over a day now, and he still hadn't heard a thing from his wife, meant he had to believe at least some of what they were saying.

His wife was gone.

None of his former colleagues had shown up, except one he didn't want.

He held the tube of plastic with his thumb and forefinger and rolled it between them.

That ache in his gut surfaced again. His mouth was dry.

One simple prick, one instant, and all this would seem so much better.

The door handle turned.

Martin stashed the narcotics under his pillow and sat upright. Wadaya concentrated on the tray—a platter of NHS gourmet nutrition: plastic cup of orange squash, a banana, an apple, two rounds of toast, and a red-top newspaper.

Wadaya said, "Doc wants you to keep it simple." He laid the tray down and turned.

Martin said, "Hey, why don't you wait a moment?"

"I have to stand outside."

"I'm sure you can do your job just as well in here. Besides, I need you to uncuff me if I'm going to eat."

He needed to look at the door and back to Martin twice before making the decision to plant himself in the dedicated visitor chair. He unlocked Martin's left hand, which was fine since he was a southpaw. Martin polished off the toast in seconds.

Wadaya patted his knees, feet tapping as if he held a tune in his head. He was in his mid-twenties, a serious kid, probably held ambitions to climb the ladder.

Martin had to reach over to his bound right hand to peel the banana. He asked, "Do you know me?"

"No." Wadaya tapped his leg faster. Glared at his hand. Forced it to stay still. "I work out of Sheerton too, but we haven't met. I've *heard* of you, though."

Martin sipped the juice intentionally slowly. "What have you heard?"

"You beat up your wife."

Julie. Nine stone soaking wet. Emerald-green eyes, a thin nose that bent up slightly at the end, a kindness that sometimes bordered on taking the piss. No one would want to hurt her. No one.

Martin finished the banana in a final big mouthful, mainly to prevent himself from issuing another denial.

Wadaya added, "You threatened colleagues. You made sex workers do you for free. I also heard you're a member of the OTT club."

"OTT club? What's that?"

He snorted. That, and DCS Black's comments, clearly meant people believed Martin was faking all this.

"Did I go undercover or something? Get smacked up?"

Occasionally, to maintain their cover, Martin heard of officers forced to take drugs, and some became addicts as a result. Even without the vices inherent in that line of work, it meant living with the constant threat of discovery. More than a few marriages had shattered because of it.

"No," Wadaya said. "You were part of one of them DOMU teams the commissioner set up. Guess you mighta got involved that way."

Martin bit into the apple. "Involved? In what?"

"The OTT club. The gangs, the drugs."

OTT club. Why would anyone say Martin was *Over The Top*? Was it an actual club? Who would be in that?

Martin said, "So, what, we beat up suspects?"

"Suspects, yeah. I heard other stuff too. Other coppers who wanted you to calm it down, witnesses, that sort of thing."

Martin swallowed. "Beating suspects. Intimidation. I fought against it. More than once."

Shit, another denial. Makes you sound crazy. Or dishonest.

"Why am I a DS, not a DI?"

"Demotion, I suppose. Not enough evidence to sack you, but—" He stopped talking abruptly.

"What?"

"Nothing."

Martin had almost finished the apple. The pieces swam in his stomach.

Wadaya said, "I don't want you thinking I'm falling for it."

"Don't want it getting out that the bad detective sergeant fooled you, eh?"

"Right." He pushed out of the chair. "Can I go now?" As he stood up, Wadaya handed Martin one of his pens from inside his stab vest. "I heard you liked crosswords."

Martin shuffled the newspaper to the crossword section, folded it over to make it easier to manoeuvre one-handed. *The Sentinel.*

Piss-easy general knowledge and celebrity gossip. Barely a challenge.

"I like the cryptic ones," Martin said. "The brain is a muscle. Puzzles are exercise. List, observe, conclude."

"Sounds like police work."

"Exactly. List what you know, observe the effects, form a conclusion." He completed two clues before Wadaya reached the door.

Before leaving, Wadaya said, "Other thing I heard? You been offered a cushy way out. It's a kick in the teeth to the rest of us, but it'll be for the best."

"You really don't think I can be a good copper again?"

Clue three. Celeb stuff.

Wadaya said, "I think sometimes there's no going back."

Martin wrote: *Amal Alamuddin*. "I think you're wrong."

He stepped up to Martin's bed. Picked up the newspaper. "How'd you know that?"

"Know what?"

He unfolded the paper so it lay flat. "See, like I said, I heard you liked crosswords. Even when you were going mental, you always had one on the go. So I picked one with things you couldn't know."

Martin glanced to the little black and white boxes. More pertinently, the title above it: *Sentinel Crossword Quiz of the Year*.

Wadaya said, "George Clooney got married like three or four months ago, but you got it down. Clue two, Ebola hit western Africa *this* year, and for clue one, you shouldn't have even *heard* of True Detective, let alone know who played the lead."

"Wait, what?"

"So come on, six down. Rapper caught on camera fighting a woman in a lift."

"I don't know."

Wadaya said, "Right. And I suppose you think Ukip got no MPs and Frank Lampard isn't playing for Man City."

Ukip with MPs? Frank Lampard leaving Chelsea for Manchester City? More hilarious pranks from friends. If it wasn't for the heroin so close to his veins...

Martin reached under the sheet and took out the syringe. "Detective Constable Essex was going to inject this into my arm."

"Wanna press charges?"

"No. I want to inject it into my leg, the way I have dozens of times before."

"So you gonna quit playing this dumb game? Come clean?"

He could have pretended to remember. Take the payout, no charges. Far easier. But he said, "No. I'm going to rebuild the trust I had. Get my friends back, my wife if I can."

Another snort.

"And since no one else seems that interested in solving my stabbing, maybe I'll take a look into that too."

Wadaya said, "They haven't got any physical evidence, and you can't remember anything. You won't even get close."

"I will." Martin depressed the plunger. The sweet, sweet narcotic squirted into the air, arcing to the floor where it splashed and pooled into tiny puddles. "There. Step one."

"Right." Wadaya took himself toward the door. "Enjoy your crossword."

LOOKING BACK

Confirmation

When treating heroin addiction, the prescription drug methadone takes the edge off, tricks the body into thinking it is still being smacked by the dragon, albeit with boxing gloves on. And yet, for two days after PC Wadaya submitted his notes to DCS Black, Martin retched almost constantly. He yelled, he begged for relief. Every minute burned every inch of his body, and the convulsions threatened to tear open his sutures, but still, even when the doctor prescribed methadone, Martin rejected it. Refused the long road. Could not wait a month to be weaned off, living in a daze, craving the good stuff every single moment.

Methadone keeps you addicted.

Methadone reminds you of what you really want.

Methadone was not for him.

Within forty-eight hours, Martin's body was free of the physical need. His mental state was another matter. Instead of food, he wanted smack. Instead of water, he wanted smack. Instead of breathing, all he could think of was bathing in smack's soft, all-encompassing pool, the fluffiness surrounding him and easing him into a world of light and glitter.

Instead he remained stuck in the grey tomb of a private hospital room.

Over the next five days, despite the near-constant craving for liquid love in his veins, he didn't lose his temper once. The bed baths got colder by the day, and the third one occurred without a smile from the nurse and bare minimum conversation, observed each time by one slab of Yorkshire beef in uniform or another, hovering nearby with a can of spray ready to launch. One particularly rough-handed male nurse, when bathing him, exposed his legs, which appeared normal but for two things. Two identical things. Flames. Circling his thighs, blazing yellow and red tentacles looped once under hair that had since grown back. At Martin's behest, the clean-shaven, skinhead nurse investigated further, and after turning Martin slightly he advised his patient that the flames actually commenced near his buttocks, giving the impression of a massive fart having been ignited.

The only person in the room not pissing themselves with laughter was Martin Money. Martin Money, who told his wife-to-be on their first candlelit dinner-date that even the smallest of tramp-stamps was tacky tacky tacky, then cringed as he waited for her to reveal she'd got drunk one night in Ibiza and allowed some guy on a beach to brand her. Fortunately, she actually agreed and Martin breathed out so hard he extinguished the candle. Martin swore he would never ink himself, no matter what. No Julie-stamp, no hitherto-non-existent baby names, no skulls or dragons. All unnecessary blights, and he and Julie promised a tattoo could be grounds for divorce if the other ever succumbed. So, no, Martin did not laugh that day.

Not at all.

Fifty hours after seizing Dr. Vasilas by the throat, Martin persuaded the ward manager to free both his hands, which she agreed to only after Dr. Vasilas consented.

Martin now tried several more crosswords, and answered the general knowledge ones fine, took some time to get back into the cryptic ones, and found himself stuck on anything relating to the years missing from his brain. Dr. Vasilas specialised in spines not brains, but said if he had to guess he'd say the memory-loss was more psychological than physical. It might well have been the drop in oxygen that facilitated the initial problems, but it was Martin's reluctance to accept what he'd done that prevented the barrier from dropping fully.

"Meaning what?" Martin asked.

"Meaning," Vasilas said, "that, if you are not faking, information you have learned might be accessible by your subconscious, but not if you try too hard."

Martin still couldn't move his legs. The blade had sliced into the tissue below and to the left of his right kidney, which suggested a right-handed attacker. No one stabs you in the spine from in front. It damaged both the thoracolumbar fascia—a long muscle directly connected to the spine—and into the erector spinae nestled beneath. Either the assailant twisted it intentionally or Martin fought back. Whatever happened, the resulting damage was the same: shredded muscle tissue close to the spinal column, rupturing a nerve-ending or two. The plunge into the River Aire may actually have helped, slowing the blood-flow and numbing the muscles. If he'd been able to struggle or tried to squirm his way to a hospital, the injuries could have been far more severe.

With some tough physiotherapy, Dr. Vasilas was confident Martin would be upright in a matter of weeks. He might retain a limp, and cold weather would likely bring aches and pains, but he would be mobile. Then, on day eight, the phone arrived.

Wadaya had been delayed by mysterious car trouble, so a short, blond community support officer relieved Thompson for the hour. The beefcake constable offered to stay, but the PCSO—a different one to the pair who normally took over for lunch breaks—insisted she was perfectly capable of watching over a crippled drug addict. Fifteen minutes after Thompson departed, the PCSO read a text message and slipped into Martin's room.

"You got half an hour," she said. "Make the most of it." She tossed a large black mobile phone, protective case, and a charger onto his bed, and said, "Don't forget who your friends are."

Martin pleaded with her to stay, but she ignored him and returned to her post. It was possible she was risking her job willingly, rather than coerced by Dave Essex, but a bribe or some form of blackmail seemed more likely.

He located the 'on' button and the phone flickered to life. The Apple logo materialised on the screen, but the OS wasn't familiar. He owned an iPhone 4 in his old life, cutting edge at the time. This screen was far more colourful, with garish icons. It worked pretty much the same way as the old phones, except it was bigger. Martin learned from the settings that it was an iPhone 6. The network claimed to be 4G rather than 3G so it didn't require a manual to understand networks had sped up considerably. The phone book was empty. He only remembered a handful of numbers off by heart, but that was true before his attack, that time of his life he now referred to as 'The Before'. The one number he wanted to dial was his own. From The Before. To hear his wife's voice, to explain to her that whatever sort of man he'd become, that wasn't him anymore. He didn't even *want* the memories back.

In the absence of anyone to talk to, he Googled himself.

Several vague reports of a police officer stabbed while off-duty. A bit of follow-up due to the tragi-Christmas angle. But when it came out that he had no family, and the hospital confirmed his survival, the press lost interest almost entirely.

He was named in a couple of arrest reports, court cases, and statements requesting information from the public, but always the provider of information rather than the subject of the story. Some of the cases dated from The Before, some he had no clue about. He read one in detail, from just over a year ago, to try and jog something loose.

Devon Carlisle was a habitual burglar, residing in jail as often as out of it. According to the Yorkshire Evening Post's court reporter,

Martin acted on an anonymous tip. He arrested Mr. Carlisle and after his team obtained a court order to search the scrote's lockup, he confessed. A truly mundane case, notable for one thing: Martin didn't work burglary. He had been assigned to the drugs initiative DOMU since The Before, and at the time he took a dive into Leeds's key river he was still working for them. Nothing in the article explained it. Nothing in the article even questioned it. He could only guess it was a snout who tipped them off.

Them?

The team from the article, his unnamed colleagues, did it include DC Essex, or had it still been DS Cartwright? Helen and Martin came up together through uniform, endured firearms training together, sharing patrols and sharing friends. Martin even met Julie through her. Helen was Julie's bridesmaid and Martin ended up pairing her off with his best man Alan. In The Before, the pair were still married and trying for a child. Handy thing was, Helen's number was one of the rare ones Martin knew by heart.

"Cartwright."

"Helen," he said. "It's me. It's Martin."

No reply.

He said, "I know I haven't been myself lately—"

"Martin?"

"Yes?"

"I heard about the tale you're spinning."

"It's not—"

"Well, in case it isn't a lie, in case it's real and you don't remember the past two years... do you remember us? Our friendship?"

"It's three years. And of course I remember that. It's why—"

"Then you trust me, don't you?"

"Yes. Always."

"Martin, if this is real, if you can't remember, take the money and run. Don't probe it. Don't go back there."

"Can I meet you? Can I see you?"

Outside, Wadaya had arrived and was handing over with the PCSO. He glanced inside, saw Martin with the phone. Martin wasn't under arrest, though, and nothing was stopping him from owning a phone.

"Martin," Helen said. "If you really do only remember how things were in, what, 2011, use the trust we had. Use that and remember these simple words. Take the money. Go live your life. And most importantly, never, *ever* try to contact me again."

F.O.I.

The Freedom of Information Act is a piece of legislation designed to enhance transparency between public bodies and the public. It means that if you want to know something specific about finances, such as how much the BBC spends on taxis in a given year, you can submit an FOI request and expect to receive the information within six weeks. Hobbyist journalists or those experiencing a slow news day now have an outlet. Submit requests that might result in a salacious headline to various places and hope something bites.

How much did Leeds Primary Care Trust spend on homeopathy?
How much was spent on the failed youth initiative in Chapeltown?
How much did this or that lunch cost the taxpayer?
How much does the BBC pay Jeremy Clarkson?

That latter question, of course, gets shot down under data protection laws, but these, and others like them, are submitted on a regular basis.

However, one wrinkle in the Act that not many people are aware of is the right of every member of the public to know every morsel of information being held about them by any business, public or otherwise. It is a criminal offence to withhold anything. The level of detail includes emails that remain on servers, of printed correspondence, even text messages referring to a person.

Want to know what your bank says about you?
FOI.
Want to see how your complaint to Northern Rail was handled?

FOI.

Want to see your complete and uncensored record of everything your employer has on you?

F.O.I.

Martin submitted it using the phone during a lukewarm morning bed bath. By tea time, DCS Black eased himself into Martin's dedicated visitor chair with a thick manila file bound with several rubber bands. "This is everything we have."

"All the emails?" Martin said. "Everything?"

"All the documentation. You want a thorough sweep through the servers, we can do that. But if you really need to know what you got up to, it's all here."

Martin said, "I'll accept that file and withdraw the rest of it. Just let me come back."

"You'll get the rest within six weeks. Happy reading."

His latest pitch failed, he left Martin alone with his three dead years.

List, observe, conclude.

Helen Cartwright was admitted to the Leeds General Infirmary at two A.M. in early December 2014. Her injuries were not specified, but the doctors kept her in for three days, then released her into the care of her mother. Not Alan, her husband.

Her statement consisted of a series of escalating incidents in which Martin confronted her about betraying him. The order of her comments were garbled, moving back and forth in time between incidents. He got them straight in his head, listed them in one of the notebook functions on the phone.

June 2013: Helen and Martin dissolve their relationship as unofficial 'partners' in the DOMU section known as 'Street Level Informant Trading', or 'SLIT'. Martin didn't know what that was.

Probably an initiative spun off from one of DCS Black's umbrella task forces.

July 2013: Martin hooks up with DS Dave Essex. He's still a DI at that stage, so nothing too bad so far.

November 2013: Helen joins PSD full time. It specified 'full time', so she'd been seconded there prior to this appointment. Then there was a big jump in time.

April 2014: Martin confronts her in the parking lot of Glendale Station, accusing her of betrayal. The announcement had been made to close the station and incorporate it into Sheerton and Chapel Allerton. Apparently, Martin accused Helen of trying to force him out to impress her bosses, add to the 'natural wastage' required to balance the books. She called him crazy and he got within inches of slapping her. He received an official reprimand.

July 2014: Martin is arrested in a pub after an altercation with Alan Cartwright. Alan made a complaint about Martin earlier in the week relating to some sort of harassing phone calls. The pair had spent almost every day together in high school, bought their first pints together, Martin even loaned Alan money to set up his painting business. For Alan to start a fight that ended so nastily—both spent the night in hospital—must have meant he was absolutely positive Martin was responsible.

September 2014: Helen is assigned a case involving Devon Carlisle, the burglar, making a complaint against DI Money and DS Essex. This took place around nine months after Carlisle's arrest for fencing stolen goods, an encounter that resulted in Martin and Dave Essex being disciplined for unprofessional behaviour, but

PSD lacked the evidence to sack them completely. Demoted far below their experience level.

November 2014: Julie experiences a tumble, breaking her arm, nose, and somehow burning her hand. Helen helped Julie to a place called Sanctuary, one of those loftily-titled refuges meant to inspire a sense of safety for the abused spouses of the scum of the Earth. Helen also launched an investigation into Martin's conduct. A wife-beating police officer is enough to bring the West Yorkshire Police into disrepute, and therefore grounds for dismissal.

December 2014: PSD suspends their investigation as Julie Money withdraws her statement. But in Helen's statement against Martin, she alleged that Julie made an offer: because she was so desperate to get away, she said she'd withdraw her statement if Martin granted her a quickie divorce.

December 2014: Shortly after the investigation is shelved, Helen Cartwright is admitted to LGI with extensive injuries and suffering deep shock. She said Martin came to her place, drunk or high or something, thanking her for getting the investigation overturned. But Helen wanted him gone. No mention of Alan here, either. She tried to get rid of Martin, and although the scuffle was minor, she managed to cut herself on the sideboard as they both fell over in a heap. Martin was arrested, but the charges were later dropped when Helen decided she was equally responsible for the assault.

Helen was a strong woman, mentally and physically. There was no way she would 'blame herself' for anything that a man did to her. As for Martin, he wanted to take this guy they were writing about and subject him to a serious bag-nabbing. Only the worst subjects underwent a bag-nabbing, such was the seriousness of the consequences if caught, but this bastard deserved it.

This guy, he assaulted Martin's wife.

His partner too.

His best friend in the world.

Even though these acts were committed by the hands holding the file, it wasn't *him*.

He read the paperwork relating to earlier cases. All sounded solid enough, but in every case people either changed their minds or evidence disappeared. Yet, the Devon Carlisle thing stuck, and he was someone Martin had arrested before, so he assumed the motivation for some of his claims was brought into question.

In between the dates in Helen's complaint, he had been found to be not following correct evidence-handling procedures (read: caught snaffling drugs but no one could convict him), conducting overly-robust interrogations outside of a safe environment (anything from a slap to a bag-nabbing), running off-the-book informants (okay, he'd done that prior to his Before period; a lot of coppers do), and reached the top ten in class for sick days. On top of that, the PSD interviewed him on no fewer than twenty-three occasions relating to poor procedural conduct, twenty of those since he partnered with Dave Essex.

Twenty-three.

Martin's clearance rate was up from seventy-three percent during The Before, to ninety-two percent at its peak in the summer of 2014, coincidentally in the middle of what appeared to be unjustifiable behaviour, and just before he went off the edge of a cliff. A cluster of PSD interviews occurred at the same time as a cluster of high-profile arrests. They'd tailed him and, on six occasions, photographed him meeting with a chap called Tug Jones. They traced Martin's personal finances to show he withdrew two hundred pounds each time he met Mr. Jones, and he finally admitted to running Mr. Jones off the books a confidential informant. Valuable intel had led to the arrest of five on-the-up drug dealers on the notorious Bankwell Estate, and Martin paid him out of his own account.

It wasn't a positive thing in terms of the inquiry, but it was a positive thing counting it *ethically*. He hadn't gone entirely rogue.

The other stuff was more of the same: shady dealings with low-lifes; suspicion of drug and alcohol abuse; vanishing for days whilst 'off sick'; insubordination; domestic abuse complaints… with a glimmer of hope; he was still doing his job.

The file on his own assault was almost empty. Interviews, door-to-doors, known associates; CCTV scoured and turned up nothing but fuzzy images that 'might' have been him. Virtually no follow-up whatsoever. They would have spent more time investigating a paedo who got a bottle of piss thrown at him.

Martin closed it all up and secured the rubber bands, and noticed four hours had passed since DCS Black left. Martin checked through the phone numbers on the accompanying forms, and dialled Sheerton Station. He got put through to Black's office, but his PA said the man himself was, regrettably, unavailable.

Martin said, "Tell him I don't care what he does. He can lock me in an interview room for days, he can drill everyone I've ever spoken to, he can search my house every day if he wants. Bring on the investigation. But no matter what, I'm going to get back to where I was. If he doesn't care who stabbed me, tough. I'm coming back to work."

Not So Fast, Kid

Except he wasn't. The next day, the West Yorkshire Police officially suspended DS Martin Money pending a mental and physical assessment, and by the afternoon he had met Illyana, who may have sounded like a Russian honey-trap but was actually a bloke from Glasgow the size of a Land Rover. He announced himself as Martin's physiotherapist and told him, "My parents wanted a cool name, but got confused about boy-girl ones, so no fuckin' cracks about it, 'kay?"

First up, that afternoon, was a massage on a proper table. Not a Russian honey-trap massage, but a professional medical massage akin to getting beaten up by a bear. Half an hour in, Martin felt Illyana's thumb press in between two muscles in his thigh.

For the first time in—what was it, two weeks now?—Martin's feet responded. He moved the big toe on his left foot. Technically, he moved three toes, but the other two were pulled along by the first.

"Well done," Illyana said. "Tomorrow the hard work starts."

The physio suite was like a padded open school gymnasium, with clusters of machines and support furniture to aid those learning to walk again. Amputees, twisted humans, mentally-disabled, and those like Martin. They all came and went. The next week, he learned the names of some of the regular faces.

Anne Orvil would never walk again following a car accident, but she could cope with that as long as she could work her food mixer at home.

A soldier called Gav lost most of the right side of his body to an IED in Iraq. *Iraq? I thought we were out of there.* Illyana later explained the situation regarding Syria and the terrorist insurgents calling themselves ISIS.

Martin found himself in regular conversation with a twenty-year-old girl with spina bifida, whose fully-fit boyfriend brought her along twice a week.

On a Thursday in late-January, using his upper body to support himself on two parallel bars, Martin took his first steps. Right leg, off the floor, advance six inches, place down. The effort ripped a shard of glass up his back, past where he was stabbed. He shuffled his other foot forward, and when he put his weight on the heel, his knee buckled. Illyana caught his arm, but he shook him off. The next step turned his knee one way, his ankle the other, and this time Illyana took no shit.

The next day, he took five steps. The day after that it was seven. Then ten, then twelve. When he made it to fifteen, he called DCS Black's PA with an update. She promised to pass on the message.

The assigned psychiatrist was as helpful as most psychiatrists. They talked mostly about Martin's time from The Before. Occasionally the shrink would refer to something Martin did during the Dead Time, and after three sessions he pointed out that Martin often referred to his actions in the third person. 'That guy' or 'the person I became' or 'the other fella'.

All the shrink did was ask questions. 'Why do you think you did that?' and 'What do you think motivated you to...' and of course 'Relax and focus on X, Y or Z... can you see these events?'

Nothing jiggled loose. No montage of memories. Not even a brief flash. He'd been expecting things to rush forth at some point, unleashed like a dam bursting. He would convulse for a few minutes as his brain reassembled the jigsaw of violence, drugs, stress and, most importantly, the identity of whoever killed him.

The man who killed me.

Yeah, that's how he thought of it. He had died at some point, but was resuscitated en-route to hospital. Was it murder? Not technically. But he did die. As was the intent.

Because Martin was also, technically, the victim of a crime, the police allocated a crime number. A couple of detective sergeants called Cleaver and Ball took his statement and lied to him about how they'd do everything they could to investigate.

Everything they could.

Right. The fatter of the two, Ball, told Martin off the record that he was involved with so many lowlifes and off-the-book snitches that even compiling a list of suspects would take a whole inquiry team, but hey—they'd 'ask around'. *Cheers, boys.* He only saw them twice.

The second time, they demonstrated even less interest in the case, more impressed by the gossip that had now spread: that Martin was tattooed with two flames bursting from his arsehole that curled around his thighs. He declined their request for a viewing and they grumbled about how this was something of a come-down from last year's case that featured the death of a tattooist called Doyle. The taller one, Cleaver, told Martin that it was they who located him whilst attempting to track down a serial killer, but found him in his emporium with his throat cut and a bag of weed stuffed in the wound. The business provided a number of clues, not least a particularly detailed ledger, a cover for laundering his drugs money whilst administering what was, actually, exceptionally-professional artwork.

After they left, Martin's tattoos tightened on the skin he could barely sense, and he stared at the ceiling, for an hour. The day his mother sat Martin down, aged fourteen, to tell him his Uncle Thomas had passed away when a roadside bomb in Bosnia tore through his U.N. vehicle, he instantly sensed the void in which he never again received an unexpected (but always expected) chocolate gift from whatever country Uncle Mark visited most recently. His tattoos were forever. Ones that size, such a schoolboy image, would require months of surgery to remove. That Ball and Cleaver were more interested in a solved murder than in Martin's unsolved assault, it made the tattoos seem even more final.

Usually, no matter how bad a colleague is, no matter how incompetent or racist or drug-addled, when one of their own is assaulted, the police declare all-out war. Not this time. No one, Wadaya told him many times, wanted to be tainted by association.

So other than some union rep and a victim-support officer, with both parents now dead and no siblings, Martin received no visitors. Even DC Essex did not disobey DCS Black. Over a couple of weeks, PC Wadaya started bringing him newspapers and crossword books, and enquired regularly as to Martin's progress, offering an "Oh yeah" when Martin showed how he could circle the bed without crutches. He was soon replaced, though, and then they rotated Martin's guards on a daily basis. Some brought messages of support from Dave Essex and other nameless entities, but those people were part of a life he didn't recognise and had no intention of returning to. He sent no messages the other way.

What he did do, though, was start a Facebook profile under the name Jezza Blue, the name of the lead in in the first hardcore porn movie Alan and he watched together, aged fourteen. Alan found it in his dad's drawer, not particularly hidden from his mum, so the teen boys could only speculate as to whether the adults watched it together or if Alan's dad simply used it with her knowledge. As well as the athletic intercourse with multiple partners, Jezza's finale was to ejaculate into the faces of three hungry naked women. It didn't strike Martin at the time as a particularly sexy thing, but of course porn is a visual medium, and traditional climaxes don't translate particularly well to film.

He used the Facebook Jezza to contact a handful of friends, all the names he could remember from outside the force, and most of them ignored his friend request. Alan didn't, but he knew it was Martin. He accepted, sent a private message—*fuck right off*—and unfriended his old mate in what felt like one fluid motion.

Despite her warning, he called Helen again, intentionally not disguising his number. She did not pick up. Through various means, he looked up mates held over from his uniform days, and all of them either shunned him, told him to fuck off, or didn't remember him at all.

When the final Freedom of Information request information came through, he skimmed it, but nothing new stood out; some of the content was legally redacted, mostly witness statements given anonymously regarding small incidents, and the emails between DCS Black and the police commissioner contained no explicit premeditated decision to get rid of Martin, but the subtext was blatant.

By the end of February, he walked every day between his room and the physio suite aided by two walking sticks. But one day, instead of the suite, Illyana steered him to an office with a sign on the door saying 'Dr. Rupal Greer'.

The room was empty except for DCS Daniel Black, stiff and upright, his uniform pristine.

"Sorry," Illyana said, and stepped outside and closed the door.

Friendless

Black approached and stopped at an uncomfortably-close point a few inches from Martin's face. He said, "Last chance. Take the money."

"No. Sir."

"You will live comfortably. You enjoy reading don't you? Must have a shed-load of books on your list you never got round to. Get a job in a library or something, or Waterstones. It's an easy life, if you just stop with this nonsense."

"It isn't nonsense, sir."

"Isn't it?" His eyebrows shifted upwards. "You know you can't investigate your own assault."

"No one else will," Martin said. "And you can't stop me asking questions on my own time."

The eyebrows dropped. His finger pointed. "Use police resources for a personal vendetta and it'll definitely be the end of you."

"Then let me come back. If you have so much on me, why not let me back in? I'm going to pass my medical, I know I am."

Black threw his hands up, shook his head. "No one will have you."

"They have to. My rep says—"

"*I don't care what your rep says.*" He looked around as if the uncharacteristic outburst might draw attention. "I have followed every procedure I can think of. I asked every DI in West Yorkshire if they'd take a chance on you, take you back even on limited duties, paperwork, that sort of thing."

"You could order someone to have me."

"I could, but then I risk a dozen transfer requests from those teams. It isn't just political, Martin. None of the brass and none of the troops want you. I even tried people I know outside of West Yorkshire, but as soon as they get wind that none of my DIs will take you on, they want to know why. And you know what?"

"What?"

"I have to tell them about the PSD cases. The number of complaints by suspects that don't even make it to professional standards. And the wife-beating—that's also on your record. Because she withdrew her statement, the case is mothballed, not dead."

"So that's it? You can't do anything?"

"Once your physiotherapist says you are fit to return, we will run you through the physical and mental tests. If you fail we are within our rights to force you into retirement. If you pass, you will be dismissed for gross misconduct. You will sue us, and you will more than likely win a large sum of compensation."

"You'd rather pay that out than have me back on the force?"

"Correct."

Martin hobbled to the side. They'd been face-to-face long enough. He said, "Okay, fine."

"Hmm?"

"I said fine. I'll take the disability."

Reaching Out

In The Before, Martin and Julie regularly crowed about how much easier things would be if they both took jobs in a coffee shop or book store, or nine-til-five selling junk over the phone in a call centre. Awful jobs, but a great home life: box-set marathons, staying up late for *just-one-more;* quiet sunny Sundays taking brunch, maybe reading hand-in-hand; date night wouldn't need to be planned weeks in advance, then cancelled and rescheduled three or four times; and of course, lots and lots of sex. Maybe children at long last.

In the grey empty hospital office, he faced all that minus his wife. Box set marathons alone in some two-bed flat; working his way through a Goodreads list that he wasn't sure he still maintained; dinner alone or, if he got lucky one day, opposite some new woman, but someone he would be forever comparing to Julie, both in and out of the bedroom.

He looked out the window over the city. Mist settled over the town hall's ridged dome, sunlight a blob of white trying to break through. New buildings he didn't recognise had sprung up, white and glass monoliths a signal that, maybe, the government was on the right track in terms of economic recovery. In the 90s and early 2000s, he recalled Labour doing a great job on that front. Leeds changed so much for the better. By 2010, things had stalled, and people needed a change. Right up to the fringe of The Before, though, the Conservative-Liberal Democrat coalition seemed to have convinced the public that council workers, teachers and poor people were more responsible for the economic collapse than the bankers and the financial elite, and for Martin—and the police in general—he saw the effect most days. Petty crime going up; retail managers demanding they do something about the shoplifting 'epidemic'; even the quality of drugs was on the decline, as small-time dealers sought to squeeze their profit margins as the street value dropped.

Martin's city. Leeds.

He bent the rules occasionally, sure. Allow a smack-head a quick hit in his presence if it meant he sold out a crack dealer, let off single mothers and young dads who happened to have a couple of grams more weed on them than constituted 'personal use', and even turned a blind eye to a father who committed GBH on the ecstasy dealer that sold his daughter the contaminated tab that killed her. It didn't make Martin bent. Every copper he knew would do the same, and frequently did. It was big-picture policing.

But his Dead Time had gone way beyond that. One weed dealer—a twenty-one-year-old single dad—accused him of torturing him while his infant daughter lay sleeping in the next room. He gave up his supplier, but in this case Martin could not justify what he did. *If* it was true.

His dressing gown sagged around him. He rested on the office window. On a good day he'd probably see Elland Road football ground, as well as any number of new office blocks and hotels. He balanced using only his head, leaned the walking sticks against the wall. He would soon have all the time in the world to explore his new city, reacquaint himself with this fine place.

Something bumped his leg. The phone in the gown pocket. He weighed it in his hand. To truly start again, he had to dispose of this. This gift from an old pal, a guy who'd clearly fallen as far as Martin had, maybe even further if he could persuade PCSOs to risk their jobs by bringing him such things.

A man of means.

A man willing to break the rules.

Down the back of Martin's neck, something prickled. Something that ran into his shoulders, his arms, his hands.

He'd kept Dave Essex's card. Kept it close, where no one would accidentally find it: inside the protective case that came with the iPhone, a junkie giving up their narcotic of choice, but stashing one more hit behind the loo, a safety net should things get bad again...

He fumbled the card out, wobbling on his legs, fingers suddenly unsure how to grip.

He was going to leave all this behind.

It was not Martin.

Martin Money did not do this sort of thing.

And yet...

He dialled Dave's number.

Dave. Not *DC Essex.* Not *Detective Constable David Essex*—oh, he just got that; named after the ancient pop star—but *Dave.* When did Martin start calling him 'Dave'?

"Hello?"

"Dave," Martin said. "It's—"

"I know who it is. Glad you've woken up proper. Guessing you need something."

"Yeah. Yes. I mean, if you can. I'm not sure, I don't want you to take any unnecessary risks, but... I need you to locate my wife."

LOOKING AHEAD

One Final Play

Dave took two days to establish Julie had sold the marital home and relocated to York, three doors down from her mum and dad. He texted her number from an unfamiliar phone, and Martin now owed him a hundred quid.

The conversation went like this:

Martin: "Don't hang up. I swear I'm not calling you for trouble. Hear me out. Two minutes, that's all. *Please,* Julie."

Her: *silence.*

Martin: "I know what I did was wrong. But you must understand that it wasn't me. Not really. I mean, it was... it was my body, my hands... I'm not explaining this very well. Are you there?"

Her: *a loud exhale of breath.*

Martin: "Okay, okay, look. I'm so sorry. Sorry for what I became. But I don't know that guy. I don't have that in me anymore, I—"

Her: *silence.*

Martin: "I get it—there's no way... this isn't me begging you to take me back. You shouldn't. You absolutely shouldn't. But you do remember me from The Before... that's what I call it, before my brain stopped remembering things... and if you remember that guy, that's who's talking now. I need to rid the world of that other person. I can't do that from a hospital or from a flat or whatever. I need to be a copper, Julie. I need it."

Her: *moving the phone.*

Martin: "I'm the last person who deserves your pity or your generosity, or whatever it is I'm asking for. Trust? Yeah, I think that's it. I need your trust. Not the man who hurt you, but *me*. The real me. If you remember *that* me, the person you married, maybe there's a part of you that *wants* to believe me. A part of you that wants that guy to come back to life. Even if he's not married to you. Please, Julie, give him one thing, one favour."

Her: *a softer breath than before*.

Martin: "You know our friends on the force. Ask one of them, as many as you can, ask them to remember the man I was… in The Before. And I'll never ask you for anything again. I'll never call you, never even *hope* to see you. I know we can never be together again, but please, do this last thing for me—"

Her: *click*.

Mechanical female voice: *"The other person has hung up."*

Martin wiped the tears from his face, and got ready for yet more physiotherapy.

Failed Play

By early March, Martin could waddle from his room to the physio suite unaided. He'd even been escorted outside a few times, aided by Illyana and a constable or PSCO team. They were here more for show now, to tick the protection box that HR insisted upon. Martin observed them jotting notes occasionally, contributions no doubt to the report DCS Black was compiling.

By the middle of the month, Martin was able to walk nearly a mile before getting tired, and it was time for them to discharge him. Illyana drilled him in a strict regime of exercises to maintain his progress, and he would report back here twice a month.

Suffice it to say, Julie did not make contact, and none of their old friends did either. Martin kept the phone, mainly for building up a new Goodreads list and doing crosswords and Sudoku. As his discharge date approached, though, he gave up on the crosswords. He originally took them up because of Inspector Morse, to keep that analytical side of his brain pumped, but his time as a police officer was all but over. With no need to keep that part of his mind active, he subscribed to Netflix and Amazon Prime, and caught up on a ton a of TV and incredible films released during his Dead Time.

Interlude: hey, how GOOD is *Game of Thrones*? Martin usually hated all that *Lord of the Rings* shit, but... *wow*.

A number of times he predicted the twist in one film or another, sometimes even envisaging it outright, which he classed as a sort-of memory flash, but it could have been his crossword-mentality being funnelled elsewhere.

On the day Martin was to leave the hospital, Detective Chief Superintendent Black delivered a change of clothes, smart-casual of course, and returned his possessions, still in evidence bags: pants, socks, a hat, house keys, a torch, notebook (dried out but crinkled) and a couple of pens.

Martin wasn't sure why Black was here until he broached the subject of retirement paperwork. Black brought it all with him, and Martin was tempted to sign it all just to get it out of the way, but worried they might be shafting him one final time, so told him a lawyer needed to look it over first. The Force was obliged to provide mediation counsel in these instances, so Martin took the opportunity to stall the inevitable for a tad longer. He reassured the superintendent he wasn't going to welch on the agreement, and took himself out of the building.

Into the light.

The brisk spring morning seemed to lighten the fumes from the passing traffic. New number plates, new cars, not quite futuristic, but the shapes had changed yet again. Fashion hadn't altered too much, although there appeared to be a propensity for puffed-up Elvis-type hair in the younger men.

Martin needed this stroll. To reconnect with this place. He grew tired quickly, though, and accepted he would have plenty of time for this later. In his new life.

Retirement. It was so... *final*.

But it was indeed a clean break. And, like the big man said months ago, not many people get those.

Martin headed for a taxi rank, the iPhone in hand, ready to dump it in the next bin. The one at the head of the line, next to the black and white cab, that one would do. He placed it in the opening, paused for a full five seconds. Then let go.

Feeling lighter already, optimistic even, Martin climbed into the cab, and sat down, jangling his house keys in his pocket.

"Where to, mate?" asked the driver.

"Oh, crap." Martin flung open the cab door and ran to the bin. He fumbled through the sandwich wrappers, cans and general nastiness, and pulled out the phone. Flicked a dollop of mushed tomato from the screen. It still worked.

He dialled.

When the person answered, Martin said, "I don't know where I live."

"Where are you?" Dave said. "I'll pick you up."

Homecoming

Dave turned up in less than twenty minutes. His goatee joined with his 'tache more thickly than it had before, and his hair was intentionally shaved rather than naturally-bald. He was about forty-five, and although he wasn't fat he had none of the athletic grace of a truly fit person; soft and middle-aged and annoyed. Martin thanked him and watched the city go by while Dave steered the Lexus into traffic.

When they'd been on the inner ring road for five minutes, Dave said, "Nothing, eh?"

"No," I said.

"It's okay, you know. I swept this car before borrowing it. No way it can be bugged."

"I'm not worried about the car."

He stared ahead, hands tight on the wheel. "You think I'd do that to you?"

"What?"

"A wire. You think I'd sell you out to those PSD fuckers?"

His narrow jaw tensed. The way Martin had seen a hundred scumbags express their indignation at being arrested, benevolent spirits passing through the lives of their victims.

"No," Martin said. "Of all the people I worry might wear a wire around me, you're the last."

"Good."

Instead of carrying on at the next roundabout, he swung round and headed back the way they came.

"A test?" Martin said.

He shrugged, bottom lip pushed out. "Yeah, kind of. Well, spot-on actually."

"Even you don't trust me."

"So what's the story? Retirement?"

Martin told him about the physio, about DCS Black pushing him out, the call to Julie, all his friends ignoring him

"Not all," Dave pointed out.

"No, not all."

They arrived at a tidy gated apartment block on the outskirts of Chapel Allerton, an expensive suburb with low crime, where when a shop closed down a bar or eatery bought it up within weeks. A plastic fob was attached to Martin's keys, and he guessed correctly it let them into the parking area. Dave found the spot for number 23 and killed the engine. Sat silently. Martin guessed why.

Martin said, "You want a beer?"

Dave led the way to Martin's first floor apartment, watching everything, more-so even than the constables in the hospital. Constables who HR deemed were no longer necessary now Martin was out in the world.

"Lack of common sense," Dave observed. "You're even more at risk now."

Up steel steps, their footsteps clanged along the external corridor, wire mesh keeping out the unwanted.

"I don't think they were protecting me, Dave. Observe and report, I reckon."

"Twats."

Martin inserted his key in the dark blue door and it turned straight away. He entered to the smell of a clean flat, not the musty odour of homes untouched for three months. It was pristine, in fact. Small enough for a single male copper to afford. At least he didn't buy it with bribes. Not that he'd seen any evidence of bribery, of course, just the rumours.

Down the short hallway, past the lavender-smelling bathroom, a kitchenette gleamed with polished surfaces and an empty draining board—Martin's draining board was rarely empty even when he was married. Straight off the kitchenette he ventured into a living room with a dining table in the corner, a deep couch on one wall and a matching recliner nearby, both aimed at a 50-inch flat-screen TV in an entertainment centre containing a Blu-ray player, stereo system, and some sort of games console with a large 'X' on it. The door to the side was a bedroom. Compact, but the bachelor pad of many-a middle aged man's dreams.

Dave opened the fridge and took out two Sols, clipped the tops on an opener he took from a drawer, handed one to Martin, who told Dave he couldn't get over the cleanliness.

"Effy," Dave said. "She's in twice a week."

Martin said, "I have a cleaner?"

"She's cheap. Does all the flats here, so she doesn't have to travel. Entrepreneurial spirit and all that." He sat in the recliner and held out his beer. Martin clinked it, and Dave sat back, one hand behind his head. "So what's next for you?"

Martin opened the patio doors to a balcony crowded with two chairs and a table the size of a Frisbee. He sipped long from the bottle. "I don't know. Take up golf?"

Dave laughed at that.

Martin lowered himself to the couch. "So what happened?"

"No one knows. List's pretty long. We banged up a lot of people, me and you. In between dodging your old mate Helen."

Martin ran his hand over his face. "Even if I'm not on the Force any more, I'm going to look into who did it. First thing I need to know is, what happened to *me*? To the man I was."

Dave said, "You mean with Julie? And the others who fucked off when you needed them?"

"Yeah, I mean them."

"You were a bit of a cunt, yeah, but you stuck by me. Stuck by Gordo too. Danni and Nick too. We got some serious bastards off the street, and you need to remember that. The drugs... me and you, we had some problems on that front. I'm a month and a half without now. I assume you got cleaned up in there?"

"Yeah."

Dave nodded. "The others never got as deep, so it was easy for them to walk away. We've kept our heads down since we banged up Marco D. He was the big fish."

"Marco D?"

"Right, sorry. One of those black working-class-kids-done-good. Cried poverty, racism holding him back, the usual crap. Started out on Curtis Benson's crew, but worked his way up from dealer on the corner to running twenty pushers and girls of his own. Gang initiations, the works."

"Like the Wire," Martin said.

"Huh?"

"I've been watching a lot of TV." Martin drank again. "Sounds like quite a team."

"Too fucking right." He held the beer aloft in a salute. When Martin clinked it again, he said, "Not just good police work either. Good times all round. Real good times."

"Oh yeah," Martin said, "what the hell is with this tattoo?"

Dave nearly choked on his beer as he laughed. He coughed until he could speak. "A bet. A bet you made with Gordo. You thought we could get Marco on a rape charge as well as the pimping, but Gordo reckoned the witnesses would buckle. He was right."

"Gordo?"

"A mate."

The beer slid down smoothly, but now Martin was so sleepy. Halfway down a beer. Sobriety will do that.

Still, and maybe he'd been watching too much TV, but he couldn't help wondering. He asked, "Did you do something to this beer?"

Dave said, "What the fuck, Rosie? What would I do to your fuckin' beer?"

"I don't know." Martin looked into his bottle.

"Why would I?"

A little addictive something in Martin's system would give Dave his needle-buddy back. Yet, Martin was off the force, so where was the upside?

"I'm sorry," Martin said. "My brain. It's all scrambled."

"Sure. Well, why don't you get yourself some sleep. We'll catch up properly later."

Dave downed the remainder and left the bottle in the kitchen sink on his way out. He didn't turn back or say goodbye. As soon as the door closed, Martin placed his half-a-beer beside Dave's empty and arrowed for the door, needed to explain why he said what he did, emphasise that he should know Dave would not betray him, the only person who wouldn't.

But the steel corridor was empty, and all Martin now had the energy for was a shower and to dig out some clean PJs and to slip into a cool, comfortable bed.

Almost as soon as the door closed, the doorbell rang again.

Dave, popping back to make things right?

Martin returned to the entrance, and opened it to a tall woman with dark hair and a year-round tan, carrying a brown leather briefcase, and Martin suddenly wasn't tired anymore.

"Hi, Cupinder," he said. "What are you doing here?"

One Final Chance

Cupinder Rowe was the offspring of a hippy girl who 'found herself' in India. Falling in with a dodgy-sounding Swami group (not a cult—this was an important point), she eventually fell pregnant and gave birth to a beautiful baby girl, who grew up with skin dark enough to identify herself as mixed race, but light enough to pass for Caucasian, meaning she was privy to many more *I'm-not-racist-but...* conversations than most darker-skinned British-Asians. Upon returning to the UK, her mum dragged her along on one protest after another, where the young Cupinder encountered those big bad men in darkest blue who corralled and kettled and beat the people around her as they exercised their democratic rights. Those experiences impacted her so much that, when she was old enough, and to her mother's eternal disgust, she joined the police, swore to change things from the inside, and conducted her career with that single goal in mind: to regain the public's trust in the police.

If that sounds like rather heavily-detailed account of a person's life, that's because Cupinder Rowe was the first detective constable that Martin Money mentored.

He was a new DI when they met, in love with the woman who would later become his wife, and had a partner in Helen who would have slapped him straight if he even looked at Cupinder the wrong way. DC Rowe studied everything Martin recommended, obeyed his instructions in the field, and where most recruits hid their shortcomings from their superiors, she even came to him in a panic one day over her firearms training, and he spent time with her on the range, providing extra tuition until she was confident of passing a course that was growing ever-more essential. Soon, Martin allowed her to make her own calls far more often than he would with other new detectives.

She was also one of Martin's 'old pals' that he tried to contact. She had ignored him.

Now, she said, "Julie called me."

Martin invited her in. She walked stiffly, eyes roving, checking the corners. Martin followed a good five paces behind. In the living room, she stood square in the centre.

"How are you?" Martin asked.

She said, "Ah. Small talk it is, then. I'm fine, thanks. Seeing a chap who works for Network Rail. I bought a cat and I moved house six months ago. My mum still refuses to talk about my job, and her new boyfriend is fifteen years younger than her. I drive an Audi, and the weather is damp. Does that cover it?"

He said, "How are the Rhinos doing?"

She squinted, and sighed heavily. Clearly, Martin was out of practice at jokes.

She said, "Tell me you're not faking this."

He adopted an expression he hoped was 'earnest', but worried he was trying too hard. He said, "I swear it. I don't know the guy I became. I can't remember him at all."

"What was your OTT mate doing here?"

"I…" This was one of those times where the truth might've sounded weirder than a lie. Also, he couldn't be sure how much she already knew. Asking questions she already knows the answers to… he taught her that. He said, "I couldn't remember where I lived. Dave is the only person who takes my calls."

She nodded. Yes, she already knew how he got home.

She said, "I'm a DI now."

"Congratulations."

She folded her arms. "I should be arresting you for breaking your court order against Julie."

"But you aren't."

"No." She slid two envelopes from her briefcase. "I just came from Daniel Black's office." She dropped the envelopes on the dining table. "One of these has your retirement papers in. Sign them and post them back, or drop them off, whatever."

"The other?"

"The other, Martin, exists because I got my sense of justice from you, my ethics on the job. Without you... I don't know if I'd be half the copper I am today. And it's because of our history together, because the... the man you *were* means so much to me, and because I hope he isn't lost forever... this other envelope is an offer of a transfer to MisPer."

"Missing Persons? Me?"

"That's my unit now. Has been for a year. We're doing good work, turning round a lot of lives."

"You always loved that part of the job."

"It *is* the reason the police exist, isn't it? When the public needs us, we deliver."

"Yes, but... missing persons?"

MisPer was scut-work at the best of times. Well-meaning, but ultimately the person who was missing usually either turned up dead or the unit couldn't make them go back. Sure, the odd teen runaway might get stopped at the train station or surface in London somewhere, but Martin had solved gangland murders, put away big-time drug dealers and—

"Fine," she said. "If you're going to turn your nose up at it—"

"No! I swear, I'm grateful. I'm so grateful. Thank you. I mean it."

She nodded, folded her arms again. "You still have to be passed fit to return."

"I know."

"Good." She headed for the door.

"I won't let you down," he said.

She paused. Without looking back, she said, "You already did, Martin."

And she left him alone, one final chance to rebuild his life. Not many people get one of those.

FIRST DAY BACK

Pariah

Martin strode into Sheerton police station on a sunny April morning, wearing all new clothes, including the most expensive suit he'd ever bought—£400 from Debenhams. His legs still tired quickly and his back ached if he sat in one position too long, but his body served him well enough during the physical. Also, other than that beer with Dave Essex, he was clean of alcohol and drugs for the last three months, and actually in better shape than in The Before; the physiotherapy had hardened the muscles in his upper body, and his mind cartwheeled around crosswords and sudoku and whatever mental exercise he applied. He even figured out how things worked on the movie *Interstellar*—he'd bought a lot of Blu-rays as well as the TV subscriptions.

There were no balloons welcoming him home, no surprise party, unless you counted DCS Black on the mezzanine balcony watching him cross the reception's polished floor. The best approach today would be to act as if his return was not a significant event. An impassioned speech would draw attention, making those who didn't know him in the Dead Time automatically distrust him. All the same, last night he wrote one, just in case, but when it came to missing persons, the focus—more-so even than drugs and murder—was on serving the victims and families. Martin's new colleagues would surely put any personal misgivings behind them if it meant locating a vulnerable person.

The civilian receptionist signed him in, and he waited five minutes for Cupinder to escort him through the station. He was familiar with the place, of course, his old task force being a cross-city initiative, but that was based out of the now-closed Glendale station near the city centre. The new corridors were clean and air-conditioned, notice boards protected by glass screens so no well-meaning plod could stick ads for their bake sale over persons of interest and union announcements. They passed a canteen that was functional and well-stocked. The old-timers here complained regularly about losing the subsidised bar at Glendale, but for Martin the other amenities made up for it.

Cupinder—*DI Rowe*—kept things all-business, and Martin didn't bother with thanking her and promising her things all over again. By the time he got done here, other departments would be desperate for him on their team, and DI Rowe would be begging him to stay. He would consider it. Maybe even wrangle a promotion back to DI, junior to Cupinder of course, but in time he would move on up into narcotics or vice or even DCI Streeter's team who seemed to get all the best murders.

If he could balance his official workload with assessing all the suspects in his own assault.

Their passes scanned them in through the double doors into the 'MisPer Hub' where eight desks clustered in batches of two, the DI's office a small cubicle of glass at the end. Six detectives worked between piles of paperwork and their computer screens—three women and three men.

DI Rowe said, "Okay, he's here."

They looked up from their work with the sort of weary expression people save for a toddler's 'watch me' tantrum.

Rowe pointed them out in turn. "DC Carol Henry, DC Lauren Gascon, DS Shirley Webster."

Once they'd offered wan nods they went back to work. Carol Henry aimed cold eyes Martin's way.

The men Cupinder announced as: "DS Dennis Albarn and DC

Gurdeep Khaira. And I believe you already know DC Wadaya."

Martin hadn't recognised the young constable in his suit.

DI Rowe said, "DC Wadaya passed his OSPRE exam but we have no permanent vacancies at Sheerton. He's here on secondment."

Martin leaned back and again, all offered the scant nods of greeting. Wadaya continued staring after Albarn and Khaira returned to their screens. Martin had called Wadaya correctly: ambitious.

He said, "Great to be here. I'm really looking forward to—"

"This way," DI Rowe said.

She led Martin towards her office, his new team members watching in silence. A couple of grunts followed and at least one grumble rode up his back. She stopped by a desk that was clear except for a computer terminal and a manila file an inch thick with papers.

"Your desk," she said, loud enough for the team to hear. "Try it for size."

He sat in the high-backed chair and the air hissed out of the bottom as it took his weight. He faffed with the pneumatic height adjuster and set the back rest to 'firm' and nodded. "Okay."

"Glad you approve. Any questions before I assign you the case no one else wants?"

"Only one. This is a fair-sized department. How come a new detective inspector is running it?"

The team turned almost as a single entity, a herd on alert.

Rowe said, "If it means that much to you, Detective Sergeant Money, I've been a DI eighteen months. And yes, usually a DCI would run this department, but almost a year ago they wanted to scale it back along with the savings closing Glenpark Station brought. I didn't want that, so I took my ideas to Superintendent Black. He agreed to let me run things in my own way. A DI's salary with no replacement for me as team leader. Means I have a caseload as well as management responsibility, and I answer directly to Black himself. Do you approve of that too?"

"Impressive, Detective Inspector Rowe."

The team returned to their work, the blood in the water too diluted to explore.

"Okay," Rowe said. "Time to talk about Simon Larson."

Si

It was an old-fashioned file because it contained so many photos and 'missing' leaflets. The details were scant, but clear.

Simon Larson of 22 Westbury Walk, eighteen years old, five foot-three, was last seen in Leeds city centre on the 19th December. It was a Friday, so many businesses were closing up for the Christmas break, and their various employees had knocked *off* early and knocked *back* more beverages than they were used to. By seven P.M. the bars were full, and people in Simon's line of work were making a killing.

"Rent boy," Martin said.

"Sex worker," DS Shirley Webster corrected.

"Just happens to be male," added Lauren Gascon.

"Right," Martin said. "But, terminology aside—"

"Terminology is important," Wadaya said. "Use an insulting term like 'rent boy' and your witnesses clam up. Parents don't trust you."

DC Khaira looked at Rowe and waved a hand in Martin's general direction. "He's been out of this too long. Shacked up with the drug squad. You sure you want him on Si Larson?"

Martin said, "Was this your case before?"

"Me and Carol, yeah," said Khaira.

"Annoyed I've got it?"

"Not really. We're pretty sure he's dead. It's a corpse hunt."

"Because rent boys are always in trouble?"

The team bristled again. It wasn't quite political correctness gone mad; Martin saw their point about correct word-choices, but 'rent boy' was a term the police had used for donkey's years.

Martin said, "Okay, so what makes you think he's dead?"

"Because," Khaira replied, "he's dropped off the face of the Earth. No sightings, no communication with his family. Even when he was on one of his drugs benders, he could be found texting his mum and dad, or partying with his boys."

"CCTV not showing anything?"

Rowe gestured to Wadaya. "DC Wadaya, how about you fill Martin in on that side of it?"

Wadaya briefly explained he was originally seconded to MisPer for this particular case. After Si's radio silence lasted four days, he'd taken the call from Si's parents and transcribed their original statements, and tracked down Si's CCTV trail on the 19th before referring it to Rowe's team. Because he was so familiar with the case and the images they were looking at, with his OSPRE results classed as outstanding, the brass allowed him to work on it. But with little else to go on but blurry images and the statements of drug addicts and sex-workers of both genders, the trail died.

I said, "These were the only pics you could get?"

Taken from up-high Si was filmed leaving the southern end of Lille Park at two A.M., and the screen grabs progressed from the gated exit to the rain-slick road, to him greeting and then kissing a man in the street. The second man wore a hooded top and was of a reasonably tall build, much bigger than Si.

"He was never positively ID'd," Wadaya said. "But we assume he is a client. They left together in the direction of the park."

"And no other sweeps throw anything up?"

Wadaya shook his head. "This isn't CSI or NCIS. You can't just program a computer to look for someone and have it magically clean up all the faces in the crowd. Not *our* equipment, anyway.

You need specific identifiers, like a unique logo on a hoodie, or an unusual walk, a hat or something we can scan for."

Rowe said, "What DC Wadaya is trying to express is that he spent two frustrating weeks scanning every camera feed in Leeds for any sign of Si Larson, and got nowhere."

Carol Henry made a point of holding up the final CCTV print and said, "If you don't know exactly when someone disappeared, or where they were, it's bloody impossible to get a clear image. This is a tool with nothing to build on."

The one clear photo of Si saw him posing with his parents Aamon and Becky. Skinny, freckled, with dark blond hair. Eighteen years old. Probably a hit with the girls at school, and now those same cherubic features treated middle-aged men to a glimpse of what their lives could have been had they not denied their sexuality in a youth where homophobia was not only commonplace but the norm. Martin often wondered if he would have been that sort of guy, had homosexuality come knocking at his own loins. Would he have tucked it away and forced himself to love a woman, or been brave enough to express his true self to the world?

"Good looking kid," Rowe said.

"Premium prices at first," Khaira added. "But his looks started to fade some as the drugs got into him. Pretty soon he was selling hand-jobs for twenty quid a go in the Shack."

Martin said, "The Shack?"

"Old storage space at the edge of Lille Park. Somewhere dry for the hookers and—well, y'know, sex workers of both genders, to take their johns. Details are in the file and on your email."

"So, he's a heavy drugs user, a *sex-worker* serving men, and he was last seen leaving a park renowned for prostitution. The 19th is absolutely the final sighting of him—on surveillance or from witnesses—for over three months? Is that right?"

"Right," said DC Carol Henry. "The *very* best of luck."

"You don't think I can do it, do you?"

Shirley Webster, the Detective Sergeant, flicked a sour smile. "Me, Gurdeep and PC Wadaya couldn't do anything on it when the trail was fresh. What are you going to do? You're here because the boss thinks you're worth a second chance so she gives you a case with fuck all chance of—"

"*Shirley.*" Rowe pointed at her sergeant.

"Sorry, ma'am. But you know he's only here because no one else would have him, and we know it too."

"He'll do fine."

"Until it's time to move out," Wadaya said. "Once he's convinced you and the brass he's turned over a new leaf he'll be laughing."

Rowe said, "PC Wadaya, I can end your secondment early if you want."

"No, ma'am. Sorry, ma'am. We just want it out in the open."

Martin stood up from his chair. "In that case, maybe I should get something else out there."

DC Khaira tossed his pen onto the desk. "Oh good. This going to be a long speech?"

Albarn piped up: "Lemme guess, you realise no one believes you and you know you've done a lot of harm, but you're determined to make up for it, and you'll start by solving this case or burst a blood vessel trying. Something like that?"

Almost exactly like that.

Martin said, "No. Actually, I was going to thank you for the information. Then I was going to suggest you all put your personal feelings about me to one side, and when I ask for help with this case, you think about Si Larson rather than getting one over on me. Can you all do that?"

She tried to hide it but Rowe cracked a smile. "I want daily updates, Martin, *in person.*" The team shuffled and looked away from Martin, then at each other, lips tensed.

Finally, DS Albarn said, "Fine. Get to work. You need anything, shout."

The others grumbled agreement and Martin spent the next hour setting up his I.T. gubbins, security settings and various passwords. Once he accessed MisPer's share drives he delved deeper into the files. He used the paper copy for statements and profiles, and the computer for photographic info, meaning he could zoom in and out, and make notes on the side. As he worked, the team paired off and made their way outside to various cases, to interview witnesses, and drum up interest from the community. Not an easy ask, but there's only so much you can do behind a desk. Two others were left behind: Wadaya—for admin work and any background research the others couldn't do out in the field—and Cupinder Rowe, who liaised with press outlets, concerned relatives, and a charity aimed at giving refuge to runaways.

Throughout the morning, he digested what he could, but needed to start putting physical faces to names. His plan was to examine those closest to Si, then move out step-by-step, examining everyone in order of the degree of contact they had with him, spiralling toward the person responsible for his disappearance. Because Martin was convinced this would soon become a murder inquiry.

The friends Si worked with hadn't seen him, his family hadn't heard from him, and more importantly his dealer hadn't sold to him since the afternoon of December 19th. Addicts don't simply drop off the face of the earth like that. He would either have OD'd in a concealed place that only he knew about (can't trust anyone around your stash, after all) or he'd been murdered.

With his list ready and sat-nav programmed, Martin threw a sandwich down his neck for a late lunch, and headed for the car park. However, he didn't quite make it that far.

Helen

Reacquainting himself with corridors that had appeared so familiar as he returned that morning, they now twisted and morphed, reshaped themselves into a tunnel system designed to flip the brain into confusion. Notices for new clubs, signage with new acronyms, and uniformed officers with HD cameras perched on their chests for stop-search evidence. The more Martin saw, the more the changes seemed for the better, although during his recovery he'd read a few blog posts from pissed-off constables ruing the politicisation of grass-roots policing.

Then he saw the sign for the Professional Standards Department. It pointed diagonally up a passage where a steep staircase branched off.

DCS Black had promised to bring them down hard on Martin if he returned, scraping away at scabs he didn't remember inflicting. Poking at them could well mean drawing blood faster than necessary. And, besides, Si's parents were waiting.

But that sign...

PSD so close...

He took the stairs, his thighs groaning under his trousers, but made it to the double doors of frosted glass, guarded by a keycard entry. When he swiped his own, it didn't work. Like a dick head, he tried three more times before pressing the buzzer.

A voice he recognised came on the intercom. "PSD."

"Hi, Helen," Martin said. "It's Martin. Can I have a word?"

The intercom clicked off. Martin waited for what felt like a reasonable time and was about to leave when the door opened revealing a tall, shaven-headed Caucasian man with a thin moustache.

He said, "She ain't got business with you." Northern Irish, a little nasal. "On yer way."

The door was swinging shut before Martin could speak. He jammed his foot in its way. Pleading and insisting he *only wanted to talk* wouldn't work here. Instead he said, "Give her a message?"

The Irishman said, "Get yer foot away."

"Please? Just pass it on."

"If it gets rid of you sooner, hit me."

Martin said, "Tell her I won't bother her. At all. If there are questions to answer I'll cooperate fully. All she has to do is come to me."

The man opened the door again and stood close, coffee-breath fogging the tight space. "You think that'll happen do ye?"

"Probably not."

He prodded Martin's chest. "Come near her, I don't care—even if it means my pals in there have to discipline me—I'll deck you. Touch her, I'll stick you back in that hospital—"

Then: "Derek."

'Derek' shifted aside and Helen stood in the doorway. She'd cut her dark hair short and put on a couple of pounds around the thighs and hips. Not that he should notice that sort of thing.

She said, "It's okay. I'll give him thirty seconds."

"Thirty more than he deserves."

"True," she said. "But I might have something to say too."

"Right y'are. I'll be inside." He ducked back in the PSD anteroom, but the door remained open.

Martin said, "Helen. I need to—"

"You need to listen."

"Okay, but—"

"I heard your message, so you don't need to repeat it. I'm going to tell you this once." She posed with a slant to her gait, harder on one hip than the other. She said, "Martin, you got back in through sheer bloody-mindedness. I'm sure you reached out in ways that should see you jailed but no one can prove that. Breaching a court order, speaking to your wife? Pfft." She always made that noise when dismissing something as inconsequential. "The union has been in on your behalf too, and my boss agreed not to reopen any old cases without new compelling evidence. Might look like a witch-hunt or 'bullying'. So that's your window, Martin. We are not currently investigating you. If you're serious about this fresh start, do what Rowe tells you. Do a damn good job. And pray no one digs up anything on all those complaints you walked away from, because we'll be right on it. Do anything new, we'll be right up your arse. Is that understood?"

"Stay clean," Martin said. "Piece of cake."

"Don't take this lightly, Martin. I don't care about our past. I'll nail you as quick as any crack-dealing scrote."

She moved to return inside, but Martin had to ask, "Are you hurt? You're walking funny."

Her back to him, she lowered her head. "You really don't remember?"

"Remember what?"

She raised her chin so the left side of her face was visible. The way she was standing was at an angle she was almost in profile to him. Now he saw what she was concealing: a spider web of raised scars spanning the area from her eye down her jawline, to just under her ear.

"I did that?"

"Yes, Martin. You did."

"How?"

"We fought. You won."

"How did I—"

"How did you get away with it? Because I refused to cooperate as a witness, and let you off the hook." Tears came to her eyes. "I shouldn't have. I wanted to do Julie a favour, but mostly I blamed myself. I told them it was my fault, and it *was*. In part, anyway. But you're responsible for this. You want to know exactly why, you'll have to grow that memory back yourself, because I'm putting it all in the past. But I'll *never* forgive you."

Martin stuttered, then managed to say, "How can you be responsible?"

"Go, Martin. Enjoy your fresh start." She stepped inside, and the door swung closed behind her.

The Family

DC Carol Henry had already called ahead on Martin's behalf, so the Larsons were expecting him. The father, Aamon, was the spit of his son, albeit turning doughy in the middle, and when he invited Martin in he spoke with something of an accent. In the hallway, he offered his left hand to shake and Martin took it.

"A fellow lefty," Martin said with too much jollity, then swiftly resumed his sombre demeanour as Aamon Larson led him inside.

Aamon's wife, Becky, was also blond and slim but somehow far more frail than her husband. They stood together in the large kitchen-diner of their four-bed terraced house as if awaiting some sort of verdict.

Martin decided to be direct. "Mr. and Mrs. Larson, DC Henry told you we are putting more manpower on your son's disappearance, but did she also explain that doesn't necessarily mean there's new evidence?"

Aamon Larson nodded. "Yes. We understand. I do not know why you need to come here, though."

"May I sit?"

"Of course."

Martin pulled a chrome-framed chair out from the glass-topped dining table and took a load off his already-aching legs. He'd driven out to the suburb of Roundhay, but there was nowhere close to the house to park, so trekked through the roads lined with modern semis and juice bars and even a refurbished Thai restaurant, until he found the street of tall sandstone houses.

He took out his notebook and poised his pen. "So, your son went missing on the nineteenth of December. When was the last time you personally saw him?"

Mr. Larson broke away from his wife to sit opposite. Her fingers nipped at his cardigan as he left her and she turned to the kettle and offered tea or coffee. Thinking it would do her good to keep her hands busy, Martin accepted a tea.

Mr. Larson said, "We saw Si the weekend before. He came here for Sunday dinner."

"We had roast beef," Mrs. Larson said.

"Yes, yes. Roast beef, potatoes, Yorkshire pudding. He loved that. But this week he was not quite right. Now we know it was probably drugs, but Becky worried it might be a girl. Or a boy, Si was never too particular on that front. But she thought maybe someone had broken his heart."

"Now we wish that's all it was."

"Maybe it is," Martin said. "I know at least one case where a nineteen-year-old went to Mexico for six months just to get back at her parents for dumping her marijuana stash."

Mrs. Larson thumped a cup on the counter so hard Martin was shocked it didn't break. *"He hasn't run away!"*

Aamon Larson was on his feet in less than a second, his sobbing wife in his arms. He enveloped her almost entirely as she buried her face in his chest and allowed the tears to flow. The woman was thinner than Martin first realised, clothes hanging off her.

Mr. Larson looked at Martin. "I am sorry. This has been hard on us. After so long with no news, we both agreed our son is dead. But you coming here... it has given us more grief. Hope, mixed with hopelessness. You understand."

Mrs. Larson freed herself and dried her eyes on her sleeve. "I'm fine." She resumed making coffee.

"When I was in the Army," Mr. Larson said, "we held onto hope in the worst places. I lost friends, but I did not give up hope. Now we have no hope. Except, maybe, justice."

"Tell me about Si," Martin said. "As a person, not what you've learned through this case."

"We are—*I am*—originally from Sweden, and my wife is from here, but we have a Scandinavian approach to life. To raising our child. When others are talking about race and sexuality and sex like it is something to learn and to tolerate, we just allow it to be a normal part of life. So when Si started to like boys as well as girls, he was not worried or ashamed. Even though others at his school had a less... *healthy* attitude."

Mrs. Larson delivered the tea to Martin and her husband. She drank black coffee made with some fine powder labelled 'Nescafe Barista'. She sat beside her husband and stared at Martin as they spoke.

Mr. Larson continued, "It was in sixth form that he started to become popular. When children think it is cool to have a gay or bisexual friend. He hung around with lots of girls and a few boys. We knew they went to clubs and they drank, and we knew about the weed. We were not averse to a little ourselves now and again."

Mrs. Larson squeezed Aamon's hand. "We were told you wouldn't take any action about that, DS Money."

"No," Martin said. "All we want is to find Si."

"Yes," Mr. Larson said. "Casual, minor drug use. All part of growing up. Experimenting. We already taught him about which drugs are dangerous, which ones are okay in small doses, so it was not much to worry about. Plus, you know, we watched for behavioural changes, mood swings, but we saw nothing. He got a job in a bar so he had money coming in, too. We didn't think for a moment he was..." His smooth, firm voice caught suddenly. "We want to be liberal parents, to give him freedom, but not...not that much."

"Summer," Mrs. Larson said. "It was summer when the worst started."

Martin noted this down, although he knew about it from the file. "His behaviour changed?"

"Yes." Mr. Larson had regained his composure. "He had more money, and he stayed out later. He refused to believe we should be concerned. We fought regularly. We never fought before. Even in his difficult puberty years. It was only later, after... after Christmas that we learned of his other activities."

"We had no idea," Mrs. Larson said. She had to sip at her coffee to fight back the tears.

Martin sipped his own tea. Mimicking body language and offering reassurance is one of the first things you learn when putting witnesses at ease. He said, "Parents rarely have a full picture of their children. My parents didn't know a tenth of what I got up to."

"He was a prostitute," Mr. Larson said. "He used heroin. The boys and girls from his school faded away and we saw him with older boys, usually boys, sometimes girls, but all of them painfully-thin and with tired eyes, and Si's eyes got tireder and he got thinner..." A tear streaked down the man's cheek. He wiped it away. "He was a stranger. Came to us whenever he decided to give up, but he'd always get a call. A friend needed help, or he was going to help someone else kick the habit, or they were all clean now and going out for coffee. Every time he received one of those calls he would be absent for several days, turn up on the doorstep, hungover or needing to dry out. One time we had to go to the hospital with him because we found him asleep in our garden and could not wake him. He wanted to give it all up, but with those friends, that lifestyle... he could not."

Martin tried to come up with something more reassuring than the platitudes already dished out. Heck, if he could reach into the ground and pull Si Larson out and present him to his parents, he would have. They'd taken weeks, maybe months, to come to the conclusion their son was dead; Martin had taken a couple of hours.

"I owe you more," he said aloud.

"What did you say?"

"Sorry, Mr. Larson. What I mean is, *we* owe you more. The police. If Si is alive, I'll find him, and if he's willing, I'll bring him home. If he isn't…"

Both Larsons nodded, gripping one another's hands.

"Thank you," Mr Larson said.

The Friends

Martin travelled from the affluence of Roundhay across the city to Bankwell, walking distance from the city centre and ostensibly a compact suburb, but in functionality it was a sprawling estate dotted with high-rises and wide swathes of council housing. Observing from the outside, the Bankwell Estate was a dumping ground of chavs and drug addicts and people scamming the tax payer out of their hard-earned money. Really, though, the majority of residents actively sought work, and worked in manual labour jobs, as shelf-stackers, as cleaners, or fast-food servers, sometimes several part-time ones, demonstrating the sort of old-fashioned work ethic people tend to associate only with Polish migrants. Those people, grafters, could do nothing about the skivers and the addicts, except close their doors at night and try to ensure their own kids didn't get involved.

But if the good people in this area were far nicer and more readers of various tabloids could imagine, the flip side was far, far worse.

The flip-side was best highlighted on Rose Grove, a cul-de-sac of eight semi-detached houses. When the former council tenants—who became home-owners—defaulted, the banks sold the properties to various landlords who didn't give one solid shit what their clients did to the property as long as they didn't expect to have it fixed, and that the government's welfare cash arrived promptly. Soon, the landlords sold their houses on to property developers, who had sat on the land ever since, hoping for a surge in its value.

The result was eight semi-detached houses with no official tenants, metal grilles over each doorway and window, and foliage taking over the front yards and rear gardens. The grilles, however, were soon dismantled with the right tools, allowing access to people like Callum Jackson.

"Fuck off," he said as Martin showed him his warrant card. He would have slammed the door if it hadn't been a wobbly slab of MDF.

Martin said, "I'm here to ask questions. No trouble for anyone in there."

"You can ask the garden gnomes." Callum sniggered at his own joke, backed inside, and replaced the MDF board.

Martin lingered out back at what used to be a patio door. The garden bloomed in a huge square of random weeds and grass, brambles and nettles. Beyond this, the city centre sprawled out in the late-afternoon haze, as well as Lille Park in which Si often plied his trade.

In the olden days, those currently occupying number 7 Rose Grove would have posted squatters' rights and Martin would've been required to treat the place like any other private residence, but one thing the Conservative/Liberal Democrats had done during his Dead Time was change the law on squatting. To evict such people, the owners now barely even needed a court order.

Still, what Martin did next wasn't exactly by-the-book: he shoved the MDF board and it fell inward, slapping to the once-tiled kitchen floor in a cloud of dust.

Every appliance had been ripped out. Sold for scrap most likely. Old gas pipes twisted out of the wall.

Callum played a handheld games console at a plastic table, three other lads with similar machines.

Martin said, "I just want to ask some questions."

Callum pointed to the door. "And I told you to fuck off."

One of his mates in a stained white vest said, "This is our *hoooome*." Slurring his words. More stoned than tripping, a little weed taking the edge off one day-long hangover or another.

Martin said, "I can start eviction proceedings this afternoon."

The lad swayed. "You can't, man, this is, like... our home."

"Sure it is." Martin peeked out into a hallway and wandered through.

Callum followed with the same indignant words. They arrived in what would have been the living room in a family abode.

Six or seven sleeping bags rumpled on the floor.

A leather couch with the stuffing spewing out.

A jagged hole smashed through the wall into the next house.

The stench of human decay.

A sharp vomit-jet hit the back of Martin's throat. He swallowed.

One decaying human lay on the sofa, track marks up his arm, the belt still wrapped above the elbow. Drooling. Eyes open but heavy, and a dark stain spread around his groin.

Martin said, "Is he okay?"

"Yeah," Callum said. "That's normal for Dev."

Dev?

Martin dead-eyed Callum. "Talk to me about Simon Larson."

"Don't know him."

The guy on the couch stirred. "He, like, means Si." The chap's face barely moved.

Callum said, "No, Dev. He don't."

Dev.

"Actually," Martin said, "I do mean Si."

"I mean, *he* don't know who you're asking about. Dev knows nowt. Now..." Callum took a knife out of his trouser pocket. Small blade but sharp, with a serrated edge. "You know the way out."

Callum would have to stand aside to let Martin out. And he didn't stand aside.

Martin said, "If anything happens to me, my colleagues know I'm here."

"You gonna leave?"

"Sure. Then I'll come back with a van full of smack-head-hating coppers full of adrenaline and testosterone."

Callum's bottom lip stuck out briefly, and he carefully put away the knife. With his shaggy curly hair and full lips, Callum would certainly be popular when he scrubbed up. He said, "Si ain't coming back here. We told your piggy friends everything last time."

Martin said, "You all knew him?"

"Me and Dev showed him the ropes, but we ain't heard from him for months."

"You're in the same line of work?"

"When I have to be."

Dev gingerly raised himself to a sitting position, grinned at Martin, his teeth rotten and complexion blighted with acne. He might have been even younger than Callum. He said, "Who are you?"

"DS Money," Martin replied. "Si lived here a while?"

"On and off," Callum said.

"Can I see his room?"

"Ha!" It was Dev. "His room. Good one."

"We're pretty communal," Callum said.

"Still." Martin nodded to the staircase which had no carpet.

Callum sighed but led Martin upstairs, paint flaking from the white banister. He opened one door to find drug paraphernalia scattered around a king-sized mattress on bare floorboards, on which two girls and three young men were lying. All appeared to be sleeping. One of the guys was naked, his own waste crusted brown on his buttocks and thighs and on his portion of the bed, having splattered the girl's legs next to him.

Again, Martin gagged and stepped back out. "How the hell do you live like that?"

Callum shrugged. "*We* live downstairs."

Martin tried the next door along but it was locked. "What's in here?"

Dev joined them, breathing as heavily as if he'd scaled a mountain. "We don't go in there no more."

"Why?"

Dev's turn to shrug. "It smells *really* bad."

The next room along was marginally more acceptable than the faeces-and-heroin room, but only because it was empty. Callum said, "Okay, knock yourself out."

"This was Si's room?"

"Some of the time."

"Is it where he took his clients?"

"Sometimes."

"Mostly Si used the Shack," Dev said, lighting up a cigarette. "He used it more when his girlfriend came round."

"Girlfriend?"

"Nah," Callum said. "He didn't have no girlfriend."

"He did, man." Dev waved his arms. "What was her name?"

"He preferred guys. I *know*, okay?"

"Got a name?" Martin asked.

"Dev," Dev said.

"I mean for the girlfriend."

The witness statements all said he was exclusively boy-orientated.

Dev said, "I can't remember that, man. Like an old lady name, though. I laughed, cos it sounded like he was banging a granny."

Callum clipped his friend's ear. "He was not *banging* her."

"Was he banging you?" Martin asked.

"Sometimes, yeah." Callum scoffed. "She wasn't his girlfriend."

"But you do know who Dev means."

Dev.

Dev returned Martin's stare with a frown.

"Maybe," Callum said.

Martin asked, "Was she questioned by the police?"

"Nah, course not. She pissed off just after he did. I don't know where."

"Who might know?"

Callum glared at Dev, but Dev clearly had no idea what he'd done wrong.

Martin said, "Jealous?"

"Fuck you," Callum said. "And no. We're all independent here. Like Pretty Woman."

Martin made his way back along the landing. "Somehow I can't imagine Julia Roberts bringing Richard Gere to a shit-stained mattress."

"Well aren't we all la-de-da."

Martin took the first two steps but had one more thing. "You said you're all independent here."

"Yeah," Dev said. "It's like a rule, y'know?"

"Si knew it too," Callum said. "But this girl, we all knew she was one of Tug Jones's bitches."

Another familiar name. "Tug Jones?"

"Yeah. She worked his stable out of Lille Park. We wanted Si to send her away, but he wouldn't."

"Tug Jones. He's a pimp? Is he still active?"

Dev laughed. "You'd know better'n us, Rosie."

Rosie...

Martin rushed forward and pinned Dev to the wall. "What did you call me?"

Recognition suddenly flashed over Dev's eyes too. The name Rosie had unlocked something.

Martin said, "Dev, do we know each other?"

Dev looked at Callum, a lop-sided grin forming as he shook his head. "I didn't, but now, yeah. Wow, I thought you'd died, man."

"I'm sorry, I don't—"

"Don't say you don't remember me." Lucid now, adrenaline spiking. Hard to imagine Dev had been smacked out on the couch only ten minutes earlier. "Please. Don't say that."

"Why?"

"Because you're a big part of my life, man. Promised you'd take care of me if I kept my mouth shut."

Martin had all-but forgotten why he'd come here. *I know this kid.*

Callum, meanwhile, was either an amazing actor or this was all news to him.

"Did I hurt you?" Martin asked.

"You *made* me." Dev pulled away and pointed into the shit-infested bedroom. "You made me like this."

"Like... what? A drug addict?"

"I was an apprentice at B.J. Rawlings."

"Who's that?"

"A building contractor," Callum said.

Dev picked up the fag he dropped when Martin went for him. "Dealt a bit of weed on the side, but that's it. Nothin' else. Me and some friends, all of us in shit-paying slave labour jobs, but when we got full-time jobs, with proper wages, we'd've given up the dealing. Then you came along." He was shivering. "I'd been done for burglary before, so I was on your radar, gave you good tips on people fencing stuff. *You don't remember me?*"

Burglary. Another bell went off in the distance of Martin's brain. He'd read it somewhere.

Dev said, "The warehouse break-in? Yeah? Remember now?"

Martin's mouth worked open and shut but no sound emerged.

Dev said, "You needed someone off the hook, and forced me to take it. Inside, I got involved in *this* shit." He slapped his own arm. "Then I couldn't get another job, nothing, not even free work. Now I'm with these guys because the only fuckin' thing that means anything to me is getting that shit back inside me. All because of *you*."

"You had a choice," Martin said.

"Yeah, six years for dealing or six months for the warehouse job. *That* was my choice." From spaced-out moron to an angry, bitter ex-con in minutes. "You look at me and think I'm some smackhead who rents his arse out for fifty quid a pop. You see a scumbag who pissed his own life away. Well that's too bad, because before you came along, I was on my way out of here. I could have had a job, a family, *everything you people have*."

His spittle reached Martin's face but he didn't wipe it off. He'd seen placid guys snap in a split second, and Dev might have been gearing up for it. He was a scrawny kid, and Martin was able to handle himself in The Before, but was so out of practice it left a question mark over any outcome. Plus, there was Callum to consider.

"It was you," Dev said, his breathing slowing, hands shaking worse than before. "Everything bad in my life is because of you."

Martin said, "Devon Carlisle."

Dev nodded. "You *do* remember."

"How? How did I do this?"

"One of Tug's boys," Dev said with a sniff. "Got caught like a twat, and y'know…He was more important than me."

Tug?

"Except he wasn't, was he?" Martin said. "Everyone's important."

"Unless you're trying to corner the market, and your main player needs a favour."

"What do you mean?"

"Ask Tug." Dev lit another cig. "Ask him if I'm more important when he's got a business to run. And don't pretend you're on my side. You and him know what you did. You and Tug."

"So, what, me and this Tug guy? We were partners or something? Where can I find him?"

Callum said, "Don't go messing there. He'll spark you up if you threaten him."

"Sorry, 'spark me up'?"

Callum made a gun with his finger and thumb. "Tug Jones is okay. Looks after his people. Refurbed the community centre down Saint Augustine's. No graffiti now. Nothing."

"We were partners, though?" Martin said.

Dev took a long, slow drag, exhaled high over Martin. He said, "Partners? Ha! *Partners*?" Dev pointed, the fag between two fingers. "He *owns* you like he owns Lille Park, man. He fuckin' *owns* you."

The Territory

I won't let you down, he told Cupinder Rowe. Then, on his first day, he broke into a squat without a warrant, ignored the illegal drug use, and walked away from an addict willing to pull a knife on a police officer.

You already did, she'd said.

He'd come away with valuable intel, though. There was no girlfriend in the file, no Devon Carlisle interviewed, so he offset letting her down in one way by making progress in his assigned case. When progress grew into a result he'd have some leeway. Right now he could ask discreetly about his own assault but could not allow himself to become distracted. His objective was Si.

But those things Devon Carlisle said, the assertion that he and 'Tug Jones' were partners... if you associate with criminals and you are the victim of a crime, the most obvious culprit is one of your mates.

Si's original file listed all the squat residents as male, yet this evening Martin counted three females, plus the person Dev claimed was Si's girlfriend, and whoever else was present in the knocked-through house next door.

On the edge of the city centre, Lille Park spread out as an oasis of green. Walking distance to offices and shops, it also offered access to pubs and clubs, and to late-night strip bars that sent horny drunk men out into the night having been aroused but not fulfilled. So, while it made a lovely spot to munch down a chicken Caesar wrap and sip a coffee and read a Kindle, it was also a great place to throw on a mini-skirt, hoik up a pair of boobs, and strut around waiting for some titillated patrons seeking to finish what the lap-dance started. It was a long walk from the squat, so Martin parked nearby, already flagging from his first full day on the job. He called in and left DI Rowe a message about where he'd be.

Now dusk, the girls would soon appear, and so would the men who lurked on the outskirts, 'protecting' the girls, watching everyone who entered or departed what was deemed their territory after dark. The rent-boys—*male sex workers*—turned out much later.

Martin settled onto a bench ten yards inside the park's entrance and sipped a cappuccino from a cardboard Caffè Nero cup. Over the next half-hour, high-heeled women of all ages strutted by. The older ones all propositioned him, but the younger ones carried on toward the river, where a path led between the Blue Pussycat table dancing bar and the Knock-Knock club.

Even in The Before, the park was a haven for the prettiest hookers to clean up and be home by midnight counting their cash. Unless they were in a 'stable' of course. Then a girl worked until her handler gave her permission to turn in. And that wouldn't be until the foot flow dropped.

By eight P.M., Martin resumed his role as police officer, and asked around about Si, starting with the women in their thirties and forties along the tree-lined path. He showed Si's picture and asked about young girls with old lady names. Some gave a, '*Hmm, no, sorry*', but most regarded him with a shake of the head, handing back the photo and watching the path again as if he wasn't there. Some just told him to pay them or fuck off. One said she had seen Si around but not for weeks. Maybe months. No, it was before Christmas.

At the riverside, sure enough, Martin found the women got younger and prettier. More than once he had to pry his eyes away from chests and legs. As he worked, two hooded figures floated around the tree line, watching, maintaining the same distance as he walked. He questioned three women before he stopped in his tracks and gazed out west up the River Aire.

He could see the bridge from here.

His bridge.

The only memory flashes he had experienced were of blurred lights, pain in his back, the taste and feel of water in his mouth and throat. Still nothing else came.

It would.

Probably.

In time.

He turned to find two men in hoodies in his path. Standard uniform both for regular, everyday youths wanting to be left alone, and for people with reason to hide their faces. Here, one such person was black, the other white. The black man spoke first. "What's happening?"

Martin showed his warrant card. "DS Money. I'm looking for this man." He presented the photo he'd been flashing of Si, establishing up-front that he wasn't interested in them, their boss, or any of the girls.

"Just fuck off." The white guy shoved Martin in the chest.

"Easy," Martin said, taking two steps back.

The black guy reached under his loose top and kept his hand there, hood concealing the top half of his face.

"Okay," Martin said. "I'm leaving."

Then the black man frowned. "Rosie?" He broke into a grin. "Oh my fuck. Hey, *Rosie*. What's *happening*? I heard you got *iced*."

Another friendly scumbag recognising him. And as for '*iced*', that was a slappable offence. Another American affectation street thugs had adopted, along with calling the police 'feds' and the judicial system 'the man'.

"Who the fuck is this guy?" The white guy pointed back up the path. "Fuck off."

"Nah, he's cool," said the black guy. "This is *Rosie*. The Money Man. Ain't here to cause trouble, right?"

"Right," Martin said.

The white guy frowned Martin's way.

Martin said, "Why don't you introduce us?"

The working girls had spaced themselves further apart, giving the men-folk room to talk.

"Pauly," the black guy said. "You heard about the boss man's problems with Curtis Benson's crew? Rosie and Essex Boy made 'em disappear."

Curtis Benson. Another street kid done good. Large territory, ran a network of bars and clubs that aided distribution. He was on the up in The Before, but Martin had no idea of his current status.

"Cool." The white guy remained unimpressed. A youngster paired with an older hand, earning his spurs by facing down a copper. But when the copper was an ally... "So you're one of our pets, huh?"

"He ain't no pet, Pauly."

"No," Martin said. "I'm not."

The River Aire flowed to his left having passed through the city centre under the train station. 'His' bridge crossed at the final point before the water snaked out into the suburbs and, eventually, onward to the North Sea.

The black guy cracked a wide grin. "Man, you must have some shit on your brass, lettin' you back in like that. What they got you doing?"

"Penance." Martin showed them the photo of Si again. "It's strictly day job. Nothing personal. Got to play the good boy, right?"

"Sure thing. Lemme see that." He took the photo and passed it to his buddy Pauly.

Pauly said, "What is he, one a' them batty boys?"

Batty boys. Chav nickname for homosexuals. Growing out of

date in The Before period, so either it was making a comeback or this kid was older than he looked.

"He's kinda familiar," the black guy said. "But here's the deal, Rosie. If he's selling his bum-hole in this place, him and his batty-pals won't be round til later. And right now, you're scarin' the girls *and* the punters. So, hey, how about you do us a solid and come back after midnight? No one here'll talk to you, no matter how tight you are with Tug. 'Kay?"

He put the photo away, feigned understanding. *Tug* again.

If Tug was amongst the FOI reading materials then Martin had time to nip home and check him out before coming back to chat with the lads who emerged from their nests after midnight.

He said, "Thanks, fellas. I'll come back then."

The white guy jutted his chin toward the river. "We catch you botherin' the girls again, I'll shove that ID up your arse."

"Pauly," said the black guy in a low tone.

"Fine," Pauly said. "Whatever. He should wait in the Shack."

"The Shack?" Martin said.

"Where the poofters take their marks."

The Shack. Mentioned back at the station, and at the squat. A safe place for the lads to operate out of view of the city centre flats, making it easy for the police to look the other way. A small, disused warehouse at the south end of the park, fenced off by chain-link on one side and water on the other.

Couldn't hurt to get the lay of the land.

The Shack

Wishing he had brought a torch, Martin stepped inside the Shack, hoping for... *what*, exactly? Some sort of osmosis-like transfer of information? A dilapidated old storage facility, formerly for storing goods heading to the rag trade up the rivers and canals, and latterly became a council project that never materialised, and now—like Rose Grove—owned by a property developer. The company commenced work on it a few years ago, but only got as far as digging foundations and rectangular exploration holes that opened like large graves. When the world's financial institutions imploded, the project grew too expensive to continue. Until its value increased sufficiently, the rent boys owned this land, a place to take their clients, using the office-style Portakabins the builders left behind. The tripod floodlights mounted ten feet high looked in remarkably good nick, but it was unlikely they would work now; any generator would have been stripped and emptied long ago.

The warehouse itself felt damp and humid, and the stuffiness rattled in Martin's lungs. Rats scratched nearby and a fog of urine hung in the air. In the gloom, the cabins lined up between ceiling supports, symbols daubed on the side of each, meaning the lads retained or shared the same pads whenever possible. A shame they didn't write their names so Martin could take a nosey at Si's place. The closest one was locked but he looked in the window.

Double mattress.

Unlit candles.

Massage oils lined up on a row of bricks that served as a shelf.

As he explored deeper, beyond the Portakabins, figures shifted in the shadows, sleeping bags like those in Rose Grove lined up against the walls to reduce the angle of any breeze. People slept, murmured, grumbled at the intrusion, unable or unwilling to move. Random homelessness, the next step down from a squat filled with excrement; alcoholics, drug addicts, the mentally ill, all co-habiting on stretches of cardboard. Stale booze mingled with the piss and faeces from further up. Martin turned back.

On his way past the Portakabins, a window's steel grille now seemed to have been dislodged, either newly damaged or the wind had picked up. He kicked through the debris and rubbish and pushed at the metal sheet.

It swung as if on a hinge, the fold of metal or straining screws likely to snap at any moment. The view opened onto the river, the lights of Leeds twinkling in its rolling current.

From here, Martin could again see the bridge.

Cars zipped back and forth as the city transitioned from a hub of business and retail to a buzzing village of booze and dancing, shagging and fighting. Even on a Monday, it would be busy, with uniforms out in force. Although the public's footfall was around twenty percent of a Friday or Saturday night, it didn't deter those determined to beat the frustrations of their lives into the face of someone who looked at them wrong.

For the first time, Martin wondered if he had been the victim of a random attack, if he'd told some loud-mouthed prick to shut up, or broken up a fight and been punished for it.

No one had floated that possibility, though. It didn't *appear* random, and there were no pictures or CCTV of the incident. Except...

Except, from his position in the Shack, there were clearly three CCTV masts. White poles taller than the surrounding lamp posts, black balls perched on top, high-def cameras roving all around.

The FOI file did not contain details of the investigation. He was relying on word of mouth for that, from DCS Black, and from DS Ball and DS Cleaver, who Martin hadn't seen since the hospital.

It was as Martin pulled the metal sheet back over the window that he heard a quick, clattering movement behind him. He tried to turn but a meaty hand grabbed his shoulder and pushed him into the wall. A cloth bag went over his head, a knee pressed into his spine near his shoulder blade, and a drawstring tightened around his throat. He tried to fight, kicking and scratching and bucking as hard as he could, but whoever it was dragged him to the floor and pulled him along by his neck. A second set of hands gripped his legs, and a third held him up by his coat, the pressure off his windpipe for now.

Then he was airborne.

He thumped down on his side and four sets of feet landed beside him. Someone knelt on his skull while another someone yanked his hands behind his back.

This had to be one of the foundations, but between the strangulation and the impact of dropping five feet, Martin was too winded to think straight.

He felt breath on his ear and a voice growled into it: "Okay, Rosie. Time for a chat."

Bag Nabbing

The man's voice was gruff and his breath wisped hot through the bag. "Nice idea, Rosie. Playin' them all for fuckwits."

"Thanks," Martin said.

The meaty hand that first touched him grabbed his head and rubbed his face in the dirt. Dust clagged at the back of his mouth and he needed to cough. He wrenched his head side-to-side, but once the meaty hand found purchase it was able to hold Martin still. That knee returned to his spine, close to the stab-wound this time, an additional jolt flashing out into the scar tissue.

"Smart mouth fer someone in your position." The meaty hand let go and Martin spluttered until he felt clean. "Now, you listen. Okay?"

Martin nodded. Coughed hard. His spit and breath rushed back at him.

"Good, Rosie. Good. Because we need to be sure you aren't going native for real. We need to know it's all a trick, otherwise certain people are gonna be real fuckin' nervous. And when certain people get real fuckin' nervous, other people get real fuckin' dead. You with me?"

Martin nearly told him the narrative was pretty simple, but settled for nodding again.

"Then let's start with the arse bandit you're hockin' around these parts. No fucker here is interested in him. No one. No one's gonna talk, so pack up and go home. Next, let's just be sure you're not gonna go against the things you agreed. Stay off the Bankwell unless you're invited. Is *that* clear?"

This time Martin didn't answer.

"Is that *clear*?"

Martin said, "I don't know if I can."

"Okay. Fine. Sure. No problem."

Martin's face was thrust into the dirt again. He couldn't take a breath, not even a muck-filled one.

A woman's voice said, "Let him speak, Gordo."

"No names! What the fuck is wrong with you?"

"If he's faking it, he knows exactly who we are. Let him go."

The hand on the back of Martin's head loosened, then the knee in his back disengaged, and those holding his wrists released him. With his shoulders creaking, he flailed onto his back and pushed himself into a sitting position and reached for the bag.

"Leave it on," Gordo said.

Martin complied. "Whatever your business is, I know fuck all about it. I swear. I won't make trouble. But the Bankwell Estate... I have to do my job. If I'm assigned to it, I'm assigned to it. Maybe I was involved with you before, but I'm not now. All I'm interested in is the missing kid."

Breathing came from beyond the sack.

Martin said, "He's probably gone now, nowhere near the Bankwell anymore. But anything else I come across while I'm looking, I can look the other way. I *will* look the other way."

The woman said, "You're sticking with that memory story, then?"

"Yes. I mean... it's not a story, it's—"

"Sure," Gordo said. "If you're sticking to it, see you stick to it. Especially where we're concerned." A pause, then, "Count to a hundred then take off the bag."

Martin nodded once more. His assailants made scrabbling noises as they pulled themselves out of the foundation hole, but he couldn't help himself. He said, "Dave? You there?"

One of the people stopped moving.

"You're them, aren't you?" Martin said. "The people I was in with. My bad crowd."

Feet scuffed beside him. Everyone else was motionless too, but he could tell a single person remained alongside.

Martin said, "Was it your idea? Or were you too scared to say no?"

The person breathed in deeply, then out again through his nose. In a whisper, so Martin couldn't be sure if it was Dave or not, he said, "Just don't fuck with us, Rosie. Don't turn on your friends."

Then he was gone.

Martin obeyed the instruction to count to one hundred, partly because they might have been watching for a while, but also because he needed to get his breath back and stop his hands from shaking. It was after he heard the woman that he realised he had been the victim of a bag-nabbing, a form of punishment reserved for particularly offensive criminals who evaded justice at the hands of the courts. Typically, these were rapists and granny-bashers, but more recently Islamic hate-preachers and white-trash wife-beaters had made it to the bag-nabbing list.

The identities of Martin's assailants were a toss-up between the Professional Standards Department, who had seen a conviction slip away through witnesses withdrawing their testimony, his new colleagues in MisPer who didn't want a bad egg in their box, but prime suspects were his old pals who stood to be exposed if the crimes they committed in The Before were made public.

He was about to remove the bag when the gruff voice of whoever 'Gordo' was filled the hole from above. "I don't believe you, Rosie.

No one does. So step carefully. Better still, I hear the retirement option might still be on the table. Take it, and fuck off."

His footsteps receded.

Martin pulled off the cloth sack and checked his surroundings. Yep—in a hole. He was in a hole shaped like a grave. Placed there by people who should certainly not be policemen.

From now on, solving Si Larson's disappearance was just one step. The only way Martin could redeem himself fully was to make a list of names, and ensure that all saw jail time. To do that, he needed to delve into his Dead Time, and finally work out who assaulted him, and why.

HISTORY

Skiving

It was enough for Martin to abandon work for the evening. He would try the males after midnight another day, when the pimps weren't out protecting their business. That night he dug out the FOI file and listed a number of names that stood out, along with those news stories he found via his phone in the hospital. He read until three A.M. but could not concentrate, so he slept until seven, showered, filled himself with coffee and jam-laden toast, and went through the file again. At nine A.M. he received a text message from Cupinder Rowe asking where he was. He replied that he was reviewing the file and making a list of places to visit, but she reminded him she wanted daily in-person updates. A bit of back-and-forth followed until they agreed a lunchtime appointment.

Martin was an experienced copper, so the short leash was new to him when he was so used to setting his own hours. The text exchange suggested Rowe believed him to be skiving. Actually, he *was* skiving, but for all Rowe knew he had a lead that required him to attend it at odd hours of the day. His morning reading was nothing to with Si Larson, at least not beyond getting the lay of the land and understanding the names that were hampering his progress.

Si Larson occupied a world Martin was all-too familiar with, and since Tug Jones's territory spanned the Bankwell and consumed Lille Park, Martin had every right to check him out in the course of a MisPer investigation. Even though Tug was more likely connected to Martin's past than Si's, that didn't make backgrounding him less relevant.

Plus, since he was planning on working late into the night, the tax-payer was getting the sweet end of the deal.

The files sunk in now he'd slept. He still had no idea who the OTT club were, but he now knew it consisted of Dave Essex, at least one female, a big guy called Gordo, and a silent type. Going 'Over The Top' with Martin last night could have been a panicked reaction. While he was out, with nothing to gain or trade, he was no threat. If the brass wanted something back, and Martin knew about their activities, well... say no more.

He eventually found Tug Jones in the FOI documents. When he'd first read it, he skimmed the name, seeking details, the juicy stuff, but now Tug seemed out of place. Tug Jones was Martin's off-the-books CI, the one he paid from his own pocket and contributed to his demotion. The problem now was that he couldn't go searching for Tug's file using his own log in. It would surely be flagged by PSD, and if not them, then Cupinder might find out somehow. After last night, Dave wasn't a realistic option, which left Martin with one source of intel: Rose Grove.

Working Class Hero

Martin found Fortescue Apartments on his sat-nav, a seven-minute trawl through the Bankwell Estate to a complex in the shadow of two twelve-storey tower blocks. The council had painted the balconies bright primary colours in an attempt to alleviate the gloom normally inspired by such structures, an attempt that failed partially thanks to the eighteen flats making up the duplex in which Tug Jones's girlfriend lived.

Red brick.

White paint flaking.

Graffiti abound.

Either the money for the Bankwell's paint-job ran out or they were only interested in making the place appear jolly good fun from a distance.

The information on this place came straight from Callum, Dev having taken a higher dose than usual, and thus being 'unavailable'; but he'd be 'fine after a bit more later'. Callum just wanted Martin gone as soon as possible.

The first door Martin knocked on in Fortescue Apartments was answered by a man in his sixties wearing a smart formal shirt and a cardigan, carrying himself with a military mien and speaking in a similar fashion. "Tug? What sort of a name is Tug?"

"The sort belonging to a guy who people don't like hanging round their homes. Tend to be scared of him."

"The day I'm scared of some idiot like that is the day I scuttle off to my grave. I know who you mean. Number eighteen. Always bothering that nice girl, but she won't hear of it."

Martin pretended to note something down. "You talked to her?"

"Yes, yes, briefly."

"What's her name?"

He thought for a moment. "Sorry, I don't think I ever asked. Or maybe I did. Anyway, number eighteen. She's blond this week."

Martin tramped up the stairs to the first floor and located number eighteen, a wooden door with thin, frosted glass. No music played but laughter sounded from within. The laughter stopped when Martin knocked. Footsteps. A growl that did not come from a human. Someone yelled at the non-human to shut the fuck up. More footsteps. A female form bloomed behind the glass.

"Police," Martin said.

The chain rattled and the door opened to reveal a blond woman in her mid-twenties in a blue silk robe that stopped at the top quarter of her thigh. Martin held out his warrant card so she could reach it if she wanted.

She said, "*Rosie?*"

Martin said, "Er, yeah."

"Rosie! We thought you were dead!" She shut the door, fumbled off the chain, opened up, and threw her arms around Martin. "Tug! Come quick! It's Rosie!"

Martin clumsily reciprocated the hug and attempted to see into the hall beyond:

A door to the right leading to a kitchen.

A second door to a bedroom.

A bathroom.

Cigarette smoke floated from the final doorway. A Rottweiler lumbered out, pulling hard on a rope lead attached to its collar. A thick forearm followed, and finally a buzz-cut-haired white man in

Bermuda shorts and a string vest emerged, holding tight to the rotty as it growled and scrabbled at the floor.

Tug Jones's build would have suited a middleweight boxer, a day's stubble speckled his face, and his muscles popped rather than tensed. His expression remained neutral as he approached. The dog halted and its growling ceased as it gazed at Martin with the same bewilderment as the woman. Tug let go of the lead.

"Rosie," he said in a strong Yorkshire accent. "Fuckin' 'ell, it is *you*." He frowned and cocked his head at the woman. "You gonna let him go, Caz, or do I have to cut yer arms off?"

"Sorry." Caz stepped backwards to Tug, who snaked an arm around her. "Just... surprised to see him."

"Yeah, you an' me both. You coming in or what, Rosie?"

Martin entered and took a chance in patting the dog. It pushed against his hand. No denying a connection with Tug Jones. A close one, too. Dogs like this were guard dogs, *working* dogs, and they didn't form bonds lightly.

Tug beckoned him using his whole arm. "Caz is surprised, but my boys said you paid a visit to Lille. Sorry, hun, should've mentioned it. Guess time got away from us last night." He held Caz tighter. "Looking for some batty fun, eh, Rosie?"

Martin forced a smile. "Not for personal use."

Tug laughed, as Martin had hoped.

In the living room the black man from the previous night smoked a spliff in a rocking chair, the sort an old lady might be reluctant to part with. He raised his chin in greeting. "Hey. You want some?" He offered the spliff. There were three roaches in the ashtray on the coffee table.

"On duty," Martin said, lowering himself to a large footstool.

Tug sat heavily on the couch, taking Caz with him, keeping his arm around her. "On duty? Ha! Fuck that, Rosie. Have a toke."

A toke, yeah. Fill his lungs and send his brain swimming to a fluffier plane. Martin said, "I can't. Really. I'm being watched by my boss and the PSD—"

"The fuck's the PSD?"

"The Professional Standards Department. They discipline police officers who—"

"Oh, IA, right. Why din't you say? P.S. fuckin' D. Jesus."

"IA," Martin said. "Right."

"Okay, Riccardo, put it away." Tug kept his gaze on Martin as he spoke. "You remember Riccardo? My army-boy backup."

"Army?"

"Ex," Riccardo said.

"Ex," Tug said. "Why they kick you out again?"

"Admin error."

"Cunts."

"Yeah," Riccardo said. "So, Rosie, you're back. Essex boy know you're here?"

"No," Martin said. "Me and Dave are working separately now."

Tug rubbed his stubble. "Heard you was about to get busted before you got yourself killed. Only, you didn't stay dead, eh?"

"No."

Tug removed his arm from around Caz for long enough to light himself a regular cig. "Why are you here, Rosie?"

Good question. Martin had planned to let Tug do as much talking as possible. Answer closed questions with 'yes' and 'no', try to assess how much Tug knew about his condition. Beyond that, he had no plan.

Martin replied, "I need a favour."

Tug sat forward, his round biceps bulging, allowing Caz to sit up straight for the first time. Her stare drilled into Martin; he met it briefly, kept his attention on Tug.

"A favour," Tug echoed.

"Yeah. Listen, after all that happened last year I need to keep a low profile. I'm doing my arse-licking act and trying to find someone. Arse-bandit who used to work Lille Park." Martin took out the photo and held it out to Tug. He didn't take it, just moved his eyeballs that way and back at Martin. Martin's arm grew tired, gave away a slight tremble, so he replaced the photo. "His name is Si Larson. Simon. I'm trying to get back in the boss's good books, so I need to find out what happened to him."

Tug sat back and extended his arms across the back of the couch, feigning 'relaxed'.

Riccardo stubbed out the joint and shifted to the edge of the chair.

The rotty perked up its ears.

Caz's eyes glistened and blinked.

Martin planted his feet firmly.

If he had to run he could get through the door, slam it shut to keep the dog at bay at least temporarily. He'd reach the outside door before they got out of this room, but he couldn't remember if Tug locked it.

Tug laughed once more. "You look scared, Rosie. What you gotta be scared of? We're all family."

"I've been away," Martin said. "You don't know me now. Anything could have happened."

"Like bustin' yer brain when you went swimmin'."

He knew. Of course he knew.

"Let me enlighten you, Rosie." Tug licked his lips and a facial tic kicked in, and something inside Martin told him he'd seen that tic before, and his legs flooded with tension, muscles hardening. *Adrenaline.* Tug continued calmly, though. "When you went down I was on the way up. Now I'm up. All the way up. Ain't no one else on this estate, no fucker but me. I'm good to the people who stay outta my way, and sometimes I give back. The school one of my kids goes to, got 'emselves some new computers fer Christmas. I'm the local kid who's done good."

"And the community centre," Martin said.

Riccardo held up a fist of solidarity. "Working class hero, yeah."

Tug shot him a look that made him lower the fist. "But, like, you wanna run women, you go through me. You wanna run drugs, any sorta drugs, you go through me. I hear about any independents, I don't care if it's pills or weed or smack or blow, they get a visit, they get one warning, then they get gone."

"Bold," Martin said. "We protect you well enough?"

"Never touch the crime, man. Shit, Rosie, you taught me that. Keep it out of my hands. No guns, no H, no E, no—"

"No knives?"

"Not unless I'm eatin me steak with it. Always let the young uns carry the product, reward anyone who takes a fall for ya, and only give guns to the people you trust with your life." Tug nodded at Riccardo, who shifted his weight and nodded back. "So what you selling, Rosie? Amnesia?" He extended the word, like 'amneeeesia'. "Cos if you're tellin' the truth, that means you don't know shit about me, or Essex-Boy, or any a' the shit your IA pals got on you. You won't even remember the fun you had gettin' your bitch wife in line, and you're back to bein' that stiff-arse prick I met way back when. You *that* guy, Rosie?"

Martin said, "I'm not here to give you trouble, Tug."

"No, but you did fuckin' lie to me."

"I'm sorry, Tug. I am, really—"

"No one really knows if you're lyin' about it," Tug said. "But there's two options, right? You're tellin' the truth, so you're useless to me. Maybe even tryin' to set me up. You wearin' a wire Rosie?"

"No, of course not, I—"

Tug held up a hand and Martin shut his mouth. "Or you're fakin', and you're fakin' it with me. Maybe you're workin' fer a competitor or some shit. So I got a decision to make." When he sat forward on his elbows, positioned to spring forward, both Riccardo and the dog set themselves similarly. "I let you out of here and take a chance you're just gonna go find the boy... or you don't leave."

"Spark you up," Riccardo said.

"Yeah," Tug said. "Spark you up good."

Martin said, "People know I'm here. It's my last known—"

"Bullshit, Rosie. You wouldn't take that chance. You ain't stupid. Your bosses're watchin' you. Barely got away with it last time, so you're gonna tell 'em all about us? Nah, Rosie. You're alone here."

Martin's armpits were damp, his legs screaming out to run. He said, "My sat-nav."

"Your what?" Tug said.

"My sat-nav. And my phone. They're all cloud-synced. They'll know I was here."

"Caz?" Tug's facial tic spasmed again. His fingers laced calmly together. "Why'nt you show Rosie out, hm?"

Caz nodded and stood up quickly, sweeping her arm toward the door. Martin stood and took a moment to smooth himself down and said, "If you see me around, I'm only looking for the lad. I'm not in your business."

"Thirty seconds, Caz," Tug said. "Be back in thirty seconds."

She ushered Martin down the hall and they stepped out of the unlocked front door, and she wiped tears from her cheeks. Held both his hands in hers. "Does that mean you don't remember *me* either, Rosie?"

"I'm sorry, I—"

She said, "I'm stuck with him then?"

"What? Why—"

Tug called, "That's twenty seconds you been gone, Caz."

She said, "I have to go," and nipped back inside and slammed the door.

The Loyal Wife

Martin had seen Tug's type a dozen times; a small-time hoodlum who thought he was Scarface. But that didn't mean he wasn't dangerous. A kid who worked his way out of the gutter through sheer brute force; sold more than his peers, got lucky in a fight or ambushed someone up the chain; showed the balls necessary to run a minor crew, which grew at an exponential rate as soon as his rep got traction; then one day his stomping ground is large enough to call 'territory' and he might order the beating or even killing of a rival or someone who 'disrespected' him, and suddenly he feels untouchable. To the extent that he might believe his own hype enough to put down a copper.

It's bullshit, of course. Martin put away plenty of these baby Scarface wannabes in his first couple of years as a detective inspector. Most coppers working the narcotics beat do. Work with a team, gather the evidence methodically, and once the Crown Prosecution Service believes it's enough for a conviction, a team of armed bastards knocks down the wannabe's door at four A.M. and leads him out, handcuffed in his underpants, while his neighbours watch on. One day, it would happen to Tug too. But not on Martin's watch.

Martin would not face him in a closed environment again, not without backup

All he'd accomplished this morning was confirm that he and Tug maintained some sort of relationship during his Dead Time. But Caz seemed off there, and not simply the fear of a gangsta's girlfriend. Again, Martin picked at the theory that he'd been undercover after all, using Caz as an *in*, and promising her an *out* to inform on Tug. But facts are a pain in the arse sometimes.

No record of him assigned to such work.

Nothing from his friends or colleagues.

Still, Caz was keeping secrets from Tug, and Martin was a part of them. Would he have been so dumb as to start boinking the girlfriend of a violent criminal? He wasn't thinking clearly during that time, so why not?

Even Tug knew Martin abused his own wife.

And what about Julie? If Martin was ever to reconcile his actions in the Dead Time he would have to confront what he did to her, work out *why*.

He was already ten minutes late for Cupinder's meeting, so put his foot down. The sooner he got Si Larson out of the way, the better. He planned to work the case into the night, so if he managed to dodge any questions about where he'd been today he could take a look at his own crimes against Julie, although he'd have to go through a proxy.

When he hustled into the squad room, Wadaya was the only squad member working. Cupinder Rowe's door was closed but she was visible through the glass, speaking on the phone. She clocked him and pointed to his desk. He dropped his head and obeyed, but as he passed Wadaya he paused.

Dave Essex had located Julie pretty quickly, so she probably wasn't *that* well-hidden. She must have trusted in the court order.

"Hey, Wadaya." Martin sat on the next chair along.

"What? I'm busy."

"I'm a complete bastard, right?"

"Right."

"But I don't know how much of a bastard."

"So you say."

"Yes, so I say." *Maybe this was a bad idea.* "Can you pull my wife's records? Injuries, hospital admissions, that sort of thing."

"Not without a lot of questions."

"They only flag people of interest though, people like me. They only data-mine what information has been accessed if it gets lost or misused. You control it, just let me view it. See what a monster I was."

"You think I'm going to go along with that? Not a chance."

"DS Money, you're late." Rowe was at her door. "In here, now."

"Good luck," Wadaya said to his back.

The roasting wasn't quite as bad as he expected. A rebuke that made him feel like a first year constable, but necessary for appearance's sake. She reminded him to check in each morning, but he got some leeway when he explained he had to work Lille Park late at night. He told her that this morning he'd been to see a suspected pimp who knew the park well and would help him with Si's friends.

They agreed Martin could check in by phone if he was going straight out on the job, but there needed to be some sort of face-to-face daily, even if it was at the end of shift. They also agreed— more agreement from Rowe's side than Martin's—that he wouldn't work alone in the park. She would assign someone, probably from uniform, to accompany him. When they were done, Cupinder headed for a meeting with DCS Black, and Wadaya was nowhere to be seen.

His terminal was unoccupied.

One of the IT security measures was that all personnel had to lock their machines to a screensaver that required password input to reactivate, even if stepping away for a few moments.

Wadaya had failed to lock his machine.

Martin leaned over the keyboard and accessed the domestic abuse database, did a search for Julie Money, and came up blank.

He tried the general system search and it threw out only two incidents.

'Only' two.

Two too many.

The first was a report of suspicious injury filed by Dr Solomon in early 2014 in which the patient reported slipping down the stairs, but injuries—ribs, face, arm—were consistent with being punched or struck repeatedly with an object such as a pipe. Police investigated but concluded there was no evidence to bring a prosecution.

The second entry led to PSD coming down on him for spousal abuse. Julie was examined first by an NHS doctor and then by a police forensic physician, who found evidence of scarring consistent with burns by an object similar to a cigar end; three of her fingers had been broken and badly set along with her nose; historical, unreported injuries, not treated by professionals. Ribs showed signs of older injuries, and new ones were more obvious.

A freshly-broken collar bone.

Ruptured eye socket.

Internal bruising but not bleeding.

She had endured a beating that Martin had obviously carried out—at least his former self did—and historical trauma suggested a far longer period of abuse, and they covered it up as it happened.

"Fucking monster," he said.

"Yeah," Wadaya said. "Get what you need?"

Martin stood to his full height, turned to Wadaya holding a steaming Starbucks cup. "Sorry, I couldn't resist—"

"Save it. See that?"

Martin looked at where he was pointing.

"It's a camera," Wadaya said. "If I get busted for accessing this, you're on film. Hope it helped."

Although Wadaya retained his stony face, Martin recognised the hint. And as Martin exited into the corridor, he tried to shake the sensation from his fists, the body memory, of punching a helpless woman.

Still, maybe, in Detective Constable Wadaya, he had at last recruited the first ally of his New Life.

P.S.D.

It took Martin a good ten minutes to talk his way through PSD's door, and when he got inside it was the Irish fellow with the thin moustache who escorted him. *Derek*, Helen had called him. On the way to Helen's desk, he told Martin he was actually DS Derek Laughlin. As they arrived, Helen left her chair without acknowledging him and the three convened in the DI's office, a similar one to Rowe's, only there was no sign on the door, and it was large enough for a coffee table and four padded leather chairs overlooking the car park.

Martin's assertion that he was here to offer his help in nailing some bad coppers was met with silence, so he added, "The OTT club."

Helen took a pen from her pocket, rested an A4 pad on her lap. "What of it?"

Martin said, "I was a part of it."

"Can you offer evidence of their wrong-doing?"

"No, not exactly."

"Then what good are you to us?"

Martin wondered if she sat with her scar to the light on purpose. A reminder of his deeds. He said, "Me and Dave—DC Essex—ran an off-the-books CI called Tug Jones."

"I know," Helen said. "That's the main reason you're a detective sergeant now instead of a detective inspector."

"Yes. And fully deserved." He watched their faces; both stone. "The thing is, I have been hearing things about Tug Jones.

Through the course of my current enquiry, I mean. As a consequence, I met with him today—"

"You met with Tug Jones?" Laughlin said.

"Yes. It was dumb, I know. I didn't fully understand what I was getting into, but it's becoming clearer."

"And?" Helen said.

"*And*, I think the OTT club decided the best way to keep crime figures under control was to install someone at the top of the chain. We used Tug's intel to put his rivals away in exchange for... I don't know. Stability, maybe?"

Helen tapped the pen on her chin, while Laughlin jigged his foot like a bored teen.

Martin said, "What do you think?"

"I'm not sure," Helen said. "Are you saying this definitely happened?"

"I don't know. I just don't know for sure. It looks that way. I have history with Tug, the bag-nabbing the other night proves the OTT club are worried, and—"

"Bag-nabbing?" Laughlin said.

"You were the victim?" Helen asked.

"Yes," Martin said. "But I'm fine, thanks. It was a warning rather than a punishment."

"DS Laughlin is a recent transfer from across the mountains. He's not familiar with your strange ways." She explained to Laughlin what a bag-nabbing was, then said to Martin, "Why do you think you wanted to get Tug installed? To control the drugs trade?"

"Well, yes. It would make sense. If coppers go OTT, it tends to mean they're trying to make a difference. It's wrong, but... you know what I mean. Someone beats up a suspect it's not because he wants to beat that person up. It's because they think it'll lead to a result. A lesser crime to stop a bigger one or secure a conviction. That's what I think we did. We so badly wanted the results and the kudos, we went over the top and put a bunch of troublesome people away. Installed someone we thought we could control. Maybe we were wrong on that, and yes we should be punished, but… I want to help. I'm willing to dig into this, in conjunction with my current case, because there's some cross-over… not a lot, but…" The noble speech he'd rehearsed was now full of clauses and sub-clauses, and the blank looks from Helen and Laughlin gave him pause, so he tried to get back on track. "In short, I don't have the evidence, but I believe the OTT club abused its position in law enforcement, manipulated criminal activities, and turned a blind eye to a drug dealer climbing the ladder. With my help you can put away the people who beat me up, and DOMU takes a significant scalp from the Bankwell."

"And you might even locate your misper," Helen said.

"Yes, of course. It's all tied in."

"Tied in?"

"Well, not tied in. I mean, there's cross-over. Territory, drugs, prostitution."

"And you're not trying to use your misper to worm your way back to the big time."

"No—"

Laughlin said, "Cos y'know, I may be from over the mountains in Lancashire, but here or there, informin' on yer pals ain't the best way to get ahead."

"They're not my pals."

"They were," Helen said. "You talk about the OTT club in the third person. Like you weren't there every step of the way. Like you weren't in any way responsible."

"I wasn't. At least, the *real* me wasn't. *This* me, the me sat here now. *I* didn't do any of that."

"Didn't do this either?" She indicated her scarred face.

Martin looked away. "I don't remember it."

"But I do. Those hands, there. I remember them very clearly." She slipped her pen back into her jacket, having written nothing. "You won't accept responsibility. Like a pissed-up scumbag waking up in a cell after kicking the living shit out of some bloke outside a club. Can't remember, didn't happen, don't deserve to be punished."

"That's not what I'm saying."

"So what are you hoping for with this kind offer? Jail alongside them?"

"No," Martin said. "I want to rebuild trust. I want to go undercover. I *wished* I was undercover before, at least then I'd have a reason. But send me now. Make it official."

"With your record, Martin? No way could we get insurance for that sort of op."

"Insurance? I just want to show I'm a good copper again. I promise you, Helen, my over-the-top methods are done with."

"Why do you keep saying that?"

"Saying what?"

"Over the top."

"The OTT club," Martin said. "That's the nickname people gave us isn't it?"

Laughlin chuckled. "OTT club. Yeah, that's what people called you. You and your mates kinda liked it, ya did. Like two fingers at the brass. Helen, do you wanna tell him or should I?"

Helen hadn't cracked even the beginning of a smile. "That's why I'm sceptical about their—*your*—motives for installing Tug Jones in the Bankwell. Folk called you the OTT club, sure. But it doesn't stand for Over The Top."

Martin sat back, cold suddenly.

Helen said, "OTT stands for 'On the Take'. You're a bunch of corrupt bastards, Martin. *On the take*."

OUT OF THE FOLD

Grass

Those words were the final thing Helen uttered, and Laughlin led Martin out. He told Martin that PSD were well aware of the OTT club's connection to Tug Jones, but had never been able to trace the money. It was, PSD believed, as if the OTT club were mercenary subcontractors sweeping the ground ahead of Tug's empire-building. If you could call lording over the Bankwell an 'empire'. He also told Martin to stick his intel up his arse and not come back unless it was with a signed confession or audio-visual evidence they could use in court.

Martin entered the stairwell and descended the staircase.

PSD were still hopeful of convicting him along with Dave Essex, Gordo, and whoever else was involved in his Dead Time. And if they could afford to reject intel from an inside source, it meant more evidence existed than he'd been privy to.

"Fuck," he said aloud.

The word reverberated down the booming stairwell.

"Girlfriend giving you a hard time, eh?" came the voice he'd last heard from inside a bag.

Martin said, "Gordo?"

"Wow, you heard a name and remembered it. Congrats." From wherever he was, he clapped sarcastically. "You're scaring us, Rosie."

"Who's 'us'?"

Footfalls echoed from below.

"You know," Gordo said, the footsteps rising.

Martin ascended one flight, back up to PSD's level. The door was now locked.

"Gotta face us sometime." Gordo sounded nearer. "May as well be now."

Martin examined the corners of every twist of the stairs as he climbed. No cameras here. Why would there be? Suspects were never brought this way. He said, "Fine. Why don't we grab a coffee in the canteen?"

A throaty laugh grumbled up as Martin arrived up on four. Gordo said, "I don't like coffee."

Martin tried another locked door. "Call yourself a copper?"

Again, the laugh burst up the walls like some B-movie horror villain. Martin moved more quickly, but, as he expected, he couldn't exit to five either. The stairs continued upward, and now a stiff breeze rose the hairs on Martin's neck.

"Do you get it, Rosie?" came Gordo again.

Martin crept up the next flight. A shadow stretched down the final dozen steps, reaching for him. Rounding the bend, looking up, he found Dave holding the door to the roof. As Gordo's footsteps grew louder, Martin lowered his head and rose up into daylight.

Dave stepped out behind him. Already waiting amongst the air conditioning ducts were a woman and a man, neither of whom Martin recognised.

Both white.

Slim.

Crisp suits.

The big guy, Gordo, emerged from the doorway and Dave wedged it open with a breeze block. Gordo lumbered over, a fiftyish guy with a rugby-player's build and a suit much smarter than Martin expected. He had pictured the guy in sweaty short sleeves rather than a matching pinstripe.

Gordo wafted his hand, ushering Martin toward the man and

woman in amongst the ducts. Between the towering aluminium machines, the white noise blared and the vents radiated warmth, where no one could listen in on a wire, and no radio mic would function.

Dave came up behind, placed a hand on Gordo's shoulder as the larger man said, "P.S. fuckin' D. Really? What the fuck, Rosie?"

Martin said, "No bag this time?"

"Fuck you."

"Martin," Dave said. "I'm sorry about the other night. It was a… a voting thing."

"Yeah?" Martin said. "Which side did you fall on?"

"You know which side, mate. I had to go along."

The woman said, "Fucking grass." She spat a huge gob of saliva at him, hitting his trousers.

Martin rounded on her, his voice a growl. "Fuck you, bitch."

Gordo shoved Dave aside but one word stopped him.

"Hey!" It was Dave. "Back off. Back off now!"

"He's been talking to the bad guys," the woman said.

"He doesn't know who the bad guys even *are* in this."

Gordo said, "Can't take any chances."

"But he doesn't *know*," Dave said.

"Don't worry," Martin said. "I don't care anyway. I'm out. All the way out. You, PSD, I just *don't care*. I don't care what you got up to, I don't care what I did either. It's in the past. I'm moving on. You want the truth? Yeah, I did. I talked to PSD."

"See?" Gordo said, advancing. Dave stopped him again.

"But they want all of us. They don't want any of us to get away. So no, I'm not going to be a part of what you do, but I won't grass on you either."

"You already did," the woman said.

"I tried. And failed. Right now, all I want is a fresh start."

Gordo's shoulders relaxed. "That's easier said than done, Rosie."

"Why?"

"Because of Tug Jones. Your plan isn't an option."

Dave said, "There's more to it than simply walking away."

"And you aren't walking away," the woman added.

"No," Dave said. "Just a minute."

"Vote time." The woman adjusted her mouth as if prepping more saliva. "I vote we—"

A new voice: "What's going on here?"

All turned to DC Wadaya in the doorway, a telescopic truncheon in his hand, retracted for now.

Gordo pointed to the stairwell. "Fuck off. Now. This is private."

Two more figures emerged behind him, two uniformed constables. Martin had met them before, guarding his hospital room. Both dark-skinned; Asian or Middle Eastern.

The woman whose name Martin still didn't know sighed hard. "Fucking police Taliban."

"What was that?" Wadaya said, extending the truncheon with a practiced flick of the wrist.

"You really care about this fucked up piece of shit?" Gordo said.

"No. But he's our fucked up piece of shit. And he's got work to do."

Martin shuffled away from the air-con ducts toward Wadaya and the constables. "You following me?"

"My cousin Ricky here saw DS Nicols messing with the doors and checked it out. Saw you, called me."

"Rosie," Dave called. "Gimme a chance, okay?"

Dave had been on Martin's side up there, or so it felt. Was Martin on the receiving end of a good-cop/bad-cop routine?

Dave separated himself from the others. "Martin, if you want out, that's fine. I can work it out. But two things: one, it has to be one hundred percent clean. No going back, not ever."

"I can do that," Martin said.

"Two, you won't like it. We need your word on this."

Martin glanced at Wadaya's grim expression, tried to read it and failed. "I'm out, Dave. I can take whatever it is. All I want is to leave it behind."

"Come with me."

Martin thanked Wadaya and assured the trio he was okay now. He walked down the stairs with Dave in silence, then through the station and out to his car. Dave insisted on driving, but he wouldn't say where.

Getting Out

Martin tried several times to get Dave to talk, but all he got back was the implicit notion that it wasn't over yet. The bag-nabbing was the stick, the roof was supposed to be the carrot. They'd been waiting for him, were going to invite him for a chat, but then he diverted up the stairwell to PSD, and things got fraught. Yet despite this, Dave told him, his mission here was to convince Martin to come back into the fold.

"I can't see it," Martin said.

"Keep an open mind."

Martin had grown seriously angry at the woman up there. Moreso than at Gordo. Was spitting really that much worse than a knee in the spine? Or had Martin grown into a serious misogynist during his drugs-use, ingrained it in himself so deeply that he couldn't shake it even now he was clean?

They skirted the city centre without passing through it, using the oddly horseshoe-shaped 'ring-road' to skip over to Harehills, past the parks and into the industrial area.

Martin asked, "What did Gordo mean by the break not being so easy?"

Dave concentrated on the road. "Complications. You're about to meet the biggest one."

Dave turned off the road into a cobbled street lined with empty red-brick, rumbled right to the end, and pulled into a small lot with twelve-to-fourteen storage containers of the sort transported on cargo ships. They were the only two humans around.

"Relax," Dave said. "If the guys were going to hurt you seriously they wouldn't have taken you to the roof of a police station."

"Guess you'd have brought me here first."

"Or jumped you in the park again. You're going there tonight?"

"Yes. I met a few of the guys Si lived with. Now I need a better picture of him."

"You know word's probably got around. Mothball it. They won't talk."

"They might," Martin said. "I was still getting paid while I was I hospital, so I've had no living expenses for three months."

"Three months' wages." Dave whistled. "That's a lot of cash alright."

"I can afford a few back-handers to boys in need."

"You know that's what got us in trouble before."

Martin said, "Yeah, but fuck it, right?"

"Right."

The pair smiled, Dave advancing to full-on chuckle. Martin reminded himself that Dave had led him astray, one of those facets of the Dead Time he had to leave behind, and forced the smile from his face.

Dave killed the engine and got out. Martin followed him to a blue metal container with red ones either side and another blue one on top. Its dozen-or-so cousins towered two high and formed narrow lanes. Weeds grew through cracks in the concrete, and all Martin could hear was traffic from the road a hundred yards beyond the cobbled street.

Dave unlocked the door with a chunky key and swung it open in a wide, screeching arc. They both stepped inside and Dave picked up a torch and handed a second to Martin, then closed the door behind them. The torch beams cut through the gloom to a car, its boot facing toward them.

An aged Mercedes.

Maybe fifteen years old.

A hatchback.

Silver by the look of it.

"Whose is this?" Martin asked.

"Just some guy." Dave opened the driver's side door without a key and hit the boot release. "The paperwork matches the reg and the owner is overseas."

"Not very secure," Martin said.

"If they're already into the container, what's the point in locking the car?" Dave flipped the boot.

Five rucksacks of the size a soldier would wear on exercise in the field. One each.

Martin said, "This is what I don't want to see?"

"Pick one."

"Any?"

"Whichever you like," Dave said.

Martin hefted the nearest one, clipped open the hasps. The top part inside was closed with a drawstring. Martin took the toggle between his thumb and forefinger and squeezed. Slid the toggle down. Opened the bag. He should have felt surprise at what he saw, or even shame, but he recognised the now-familiar sensation of numb inevitability.

Of course. What else would it be?

"Two hundred and fifty-thousand," Dave said.

Martin pulled the drawstring shut over the bricks of twenties and fifties. "This is from Tug?"

"And his backers," Dave said. "We put him in place, and this is ours now. We can't 'get out' as you put it. There *is* no clean break."

"I can give my share back. Assure him—"

"You don't get it, Rosie. You really don't. You can't walk away because there's nothing to walk away *from*."

"You're right," Martin said, dumping the cash back in the boot. "I don't understand."

"We're *already* out. All of us. We did as we were told. We earned our money. The mission is complete." Dave clapped Martin on both his shoulders. "It's *over*," he said. "No one can touch us, Rosie. All we have to do is lay low until we can shift this abroad. It's ours. Our retirement is a done deal."

Temptation

Martin opened the bag again and held a wad of fifty pound notes in his hand. Ten thousand pounds bound by a paper band.

He said, "This is the money they can't track."

"Correct," Dave replied. "Went through all our accounts in forensic detail. Warrants, data mining, the full Monty. But they didn't find anything because there was nothing *to* find. Once they get bored of us, all we have to do is mail it one brick at a time to a contact in Switzerland, or nip over there with a few of them on holiday, and he sets us up with untraceable numbered accounts. As long as we keep our heads, we're golden."

"Gordo doesn't look like he'll keep his head. Or the girl. What's her name?"

"Danni. Danni Holdsworth. The other guy is Nick Grayson. But that's not important. What's important is you understand something. *You* set this up."

"Me?" Martin said.

"The container, the car, the drop-off with the cash. It's all you. Now, I'm not threatening you or anything. We're friends. I want to stay that way. But you need to understand, if we go down and I'm offered a deal, you're the main man of this conspiracy."

"I'm the—"

"The brains, Rosie. You're the brains here. The ringleader. You'll fall harder than the rest of us. All you have to do is keep quiet, take the money, and forget about this stupid fuckin' conscience you've developed."

Two hundred and fifty grand apiece was plenty on top of their pensions. Jesus, if he took the retirement DCS Black had offered he'd be sitting pretty right now.

Not just an easy life, but a luxurious one.

"I don't know," Martin said.

"It's already been earned. You don't owe Tug anything. You can show your boss how hard you're searching for this bum-muncher, earn your gold stars, and still come out smelling of... heh—Roses."

Martin's smile flickered back to life. No hassle from the OTT club, no way for PSD to touch him. It was clean, and he would be clear of all of them.

But not clear in himself; he was not that person anymore, so wouldn't taking the money make a lie of that? Accepting the bribe from a known criminal...

He flashed back to Julie, to the file on Wadaya's computer. What he'd done to her was unforgivable, so why not take the cash, give it to Julie even, or pay for some surgery for Helen.

They wouldn't take it though.

It was his money, earned through a criminal enterprise.

"No." Martin stuffed the brick of fifties back inside and tied the cord. "Split it between you, but do not include me. It's all yours. I won't say anything. If I do, I'm in jail for over a decade. You have my silence. It's a simple out."

"Damn it." Dave leaned on the car. "I really hoped I could talk you round."

"Why?"

"Because Tug spoke to Gordo. If you don't come back to us, you have to go to Tug."

Martin waved his arm at the bag. "Why the hell do I have to do that?"

"Because he's nervous. If you want out for certain..." Dave lifted one rucksack from the boot. "You have to return his money.

There's no splitting it. He needs to be sure you're on the level."

"When?"

"Now, Rosie." Dave closed the boot. "We go to see Tug right now."

Snap-Happy

Every avenue Martin explored took him closer, answering questions surrounding both himself and Si Larson. Right now, though, while he should have been preparing to brief a uniformed constable about the trawl of Lille Park, his activities were all about himself, and building a future free of the grime he'd collected during his Dead Time.

Martin's Scarface-wannabe analogy was reinforced when he and Dave were shown into Tug Jones's inner sanctum, the basement room of a Bankwell pub called the Lancelot. Tug didn't own it, but the Lancelot projected a reputation as a drug-friendly hole frequented by working-class chemical aficionados. Dave explained that its rep had cooled with the authorities of late, largely thanks to the OTT club's efforts in making fourteen arrests in a six-month period. It was only seven-thirty P.M., so the punters were mainly unshaven older men sipping bitter whilst waiting for the football to kick off. Downstairs, in Tug's room, the walls were as yellow and cracked as the bar above, but some effort had been made with the furniture

A C-shaped sofa in red leather occupied one corner, two iPads on the table nearby.

A mini-bar more well-stocked than any hotel room.

A pool table with overhead lights.

A football match was about to kick off on a fifty-inch plasma.

Tug sat on the sofa in black jeans and a white vest that accentuated his physique. Two women—fit bodies, bags under their eyes—sat beside him in short skirts and low tops, one on each side, his arms snaking around them as they sipped champagne, and the pool table saw a hulking black man in an ill-fitting suit cracking balls alongside Riccardo. Both paused to eye Martin and Dave's arrival, standing motionless as the pool balls came to a rest.

The setup was a mishmash of the fantasy of all up-and-coming drug dealers, and the scuzzy reality that not everyone who sells narcotics ends up in the V.I.P. room of The Best Club in Town.

Working class hero.

"Whatchu want?" he said.

Martin presented the bag of cash. The beefcake guard took it from him, pool cue in-hand, and delivered it to Tug. On the table, the guard opened it and Tug feigned nonchalance.

He said, "Why you bringing me this?"

"Tug, he's okay," Dave said.

"Yeah? Why don't *he* explain it?"

Martin said, "I'm looking for a kid. Si Larson."

"And?"

"And, I want to do it clean. I want to do it right. I want nothing more to do with your business. This is your money back... to show you it won't cost you anything. You profit from it, in fact."

Tug tapped the two girls on the shoulder and waved toward the door. They scarpered, snatching the champagne bottle from the ice bucket. Tug closed the rucksack and tipped it off the table onto the floor and leaned back, spreading his legs. "Take a seat."

Riccardo waited, pool cue pointed at the ceiling.

Martin said, "It's okay, we—"

"Take a fucking seat."

Dave shuffled by the guard and lowered himself to the couch more than an arm's length from Tug. Martin moved to sit beside Dave, away from Tug but Tug slowly pointed at the spot beside him. Martin ended up a foot away from him, able to smell the weed and booze through his cologne.

"So you wanna wash yourself clean of bad ol' Tug."

"I want a new start," Martin said. "I promise, I won't cause trouble—"

"And you think this batty boy is your way out, eh?"

"I'm going to the park tonight to ask around. I have a lead."

"Oh?" Tug narrowed his eyes. "What's this lead then?"

"I'm not sure I should—"

Tug suddenly lurched. Martin tried to jerk away, but wasn't fast enough. The aggressive move morphed into a gesture that was more of a hug, then Tug's marijuana-breath filled Martin's ear. "I can help you."

"Help me?"

"Sure."

"Okay…"

"You just haveta keep hold of that cash. You stay happy, and I stay happy." Tug reached for the table, came back with an unlit joint, and placed it in Martin's mouth. "Get me?"

"Thought you never touched the crime."

"Personal weed-use ain't no crime I gotta worry about."

Martin said, "I can't—"

"You *will*."

Tug clicked his fingers and the guard, towering over them, flicked a lighter to life. Riccardo paced toward them.

"Take it," Tug ordered.

Still in Tug's hold, Martin leaned toward the flame. Touched the spliff to it. Sucked in the smoke. It filled his lungs. Then his brain. He exhaled and a fluffy, tingling wave swept through him.

He said, "Whoa, that's strong."

Tug grinned. "Only the best skunk for my best police-bitch."

He resumed his previous position, and Martin took another hit without being asked. The smooth ripple flowed through all his limbs.

"That's enough," Dave said.

Martin passed him the joint. "Sorry, here."

"That's not what I meant."

"Aw, now who's the stiff?" Tug said.

Dave shifted slightly, the hulking guard now looking down on him. "We're here to talk about Martin."

Tug passed one of the iPads to Martin. "Then let's talk."

Dave relieved Martin of the spliff but didn't toke. The guard grunted but Dave didn't shift, just eyeballed the larger man. Riccardo came up beside his mate and Dave stubbed out the joint on the table. The hulk-man reached for Dave, but Tug held up a hand.

"Don't matter," Tug said, tapping the iPad in Martin's hand. "This is the fun bit."

Martin unlocked it without a passcode.

Tug said, "Photos. Album 'Rosie'."

Martin tapped the icons as ordered and a series of thumbnails flipped onto the screen concertina-style. The skunk hit had made him sluggish, and he blinked to focus.

Women, mostly.

Young women in various states of undress.

"Check it out," Tug said.

Martin opened the first photo into an app that let him scroll smoothly through the album. The shots were all taken in the same location, some sort of V.I.P. room in a club, of the sort Tug would have envisioned himself owning when he really hit the big time. A lot were blurred, but the first clear one featured a blonde with pigtails, wearing a tight short dress, performing a sexy dance on a table. The next saw more people, time-stamped a few minutes after midnight. Four girls in skirts, dresses, hotpants, all in their early twenties, at least one in her late teens max. They cavorted with beer bottles, champagne and shot glasses. Then a man's arm appeared, grabbing a shot glass. More blurred images followed.

When they cleared up again, the time was two A.M. and the girls had changed or simply disrobed, as they all now wore lingerie. The camera aimed from a static position, as if on a tripod, snapping away at random.

In the next, one of the girls was topless.

Martin scrolled faster until he came across the inevitable shot of himself off to one side.

"You like?" Tug said.

Dave let his face drop into his hands.

Sure enough, Dave also showed up in the peep-show. Both he and Martin wore casual attire and touched the prancing girls on their legs and backsides. In another, both men snorted lines of white powder off the taut stomach of a naked girl with a Brazilian strip quaffed to perfection.

By three A.M. all the girls were naked. Martin had shifted nearer the camera and was in the middle of unbuttoning his trousers. Next, his pants were down and he was fully exposed, semi-erect, his thighs shaved, the inked flames fresh on his stubbly skin. Next, a blond girl bent over and took his cock in her hand. In the next, her mouth all-but concealed it, her hair slung to one side, revealing a tattoo of a robin behind her left ear.

"Jesus," Dave said.

"Yeah." Tug wasn't quite laughing but he was definitely happier than Martin had seen him to date.

The photos grew more porn-like as they went on. Martin scrolled and scrolled, forcing himself to blink.

He and Dave were soon both naked, sometimes in different shots, sometimes penetrating girls in unison in a variety of sex positions, the two fiery tongues bursting from Martin's arse visible far too often. The men's wild eyes and gormless mouths betrayed what must have been a gargantuan quantity of drugs and alcohol. Martin barely recognised himself; the joy, the unbridled glee.

By four-thirty A.M., Dave lay crashed out on one of the couches to the side, still naked, but Martin kept going strong.

Holding the iPad, he double-checked the times. If this was correct, on the same day, he'd been at this for over an hour and a half. He hadn't been capable of that for years, since he was as young as those girls he was fucking.

Then the Martin on-screen really did seem to believe he was a porn star. He posed with hands on his hips, with three girls attending his bulging penis, including the blonde with the robin tattoo. Another displayed a bumblebee at the top of her left breast. Odd that he was now drawn to the tats. Perhaps he didn't want to focus on his distended penis's purple head, misshapen as if there was too much blood flowing in.

It had never looked like that before.

After this came the finale. A hand reached in from off-frame, another tattoo prominent, this one circling the slender wrist, a daisy chain. It gripped Martin's cock while the three girls waited with their mouths open. The photographer required a dozen blurred snaps but caught the key moment as semen erupted and covered the girls, as if this really was all some staged porno shoot.

Again, Martin couldn't ever remember being this virile. Viagra must have played a part.

The next picture was a dark-haired girl of about twenty cleaning him up with a loving expression, the girl with the bumblebee tattoo. Early twenties, maybe. Then a series of comedic shots of a half-dressed Martin lining up food on Dave's sleeping body.

Then they ended.

The worst thing, though, as far as Martin was concerned, was that as he swept through them, these gross parodies of himself, he'd grown semi-aroused, and didn't dare move the iPad in case he gave it away.

"I didn't know," Dave said. "I swear."

"He didn't," Tug confirmed. "But he does now."

"The girls," Martin said. "They were all…? You know…"

"All legal. One of them barely seventeen. Well, now she is. Sixteen when this was taken."

"End of last summer," Dave said. "When we took down Marco D'Arcy."

Tug grinned. "My treat."

"But if this is out there…" Martin couldn't finish.

"You're done as a copper, yeah."

Martin said, "So what do we do?"

"Well," Tug said, "I'd hate to spark up my favourite pet copper. I prefer my pets to obey me out of love, or at least mutual benefit. Beatin' on you means you wanna escape. This cash, I gotta have you keep it. I gotta have you to remember not to fuck me over, Rosie, or this party, and your money affairs, they go public."

"I could burn it."

"Best if you keep hold of it. You never know. If you go down, it'll be useful when you get out."

"I want the photos," Martin said.

"Sure." Tug retrieved the iPad, tapped on the screen, brought up an email programme, and the folder *wooshed* out into the ether. "There you go."

"Not really what I meant," Martin said.

"Oh, you want them deleting. Sorry, ain't happenin'. But I can give you somethin' better, Rosie. Something you want real fuckin' badly."

"What?"

"I don't have nothin' to do with that batty-boy shit. I just let em get on with it cos it's more trouble to clear 'em out. But it ain't natural, y'know? But I asked some questions around the place after you left me today." He placed a firm hand on Martin's knee. "Rosie, if you take the money, stay useful to me when I need info now and again, keep lookin' the other way to my business, if you agree to that, I tell ya, these photos stay off the cloud... and I can give you Si's girlfriend."

"Okay," Martin said. "Deal."

"Edith," Tug said. "Edith Long."

PROGRESS

Dilemma

After finalising the details of his deal with Tug, Martin and Dave drank a couple of pints in the basement room, watching the match and making nice with the drug-dealing pimp. Martin and Tug shared the remainder of the spliff, but Dave declined. Outside, unable to look at him the same now he'd witnessed the undeniable evidence of their shared deviancy, Martin turned down Dave's offer of a lift, saying he would use the walk to clear the fugginess. Dave took the money away.

'*The*' money?

Dave took *Martin's* money away.

The stroll into the city centre took him an hour, in which he replayed his current predicament over and over.

First, the deal with Tug: there was no clear way out beyond murdering Tug and erasing the photos from his device and whatever cloud storage he employed.

Second, the money: earned as a direct result of his Dead Time activities. Those activities, no matter how depraved, could never be undone. And it was doing nothing but sitting there, anyway. It wasn't a threat, and keeping hold of it made a violent thug less likely hurt him or use the blackmail to destroy him forever.

Third, and most importantly, he had the best lead on Si Larson in months. Everything else was secondary for now. It was his way back in, how he would rebuild his career. Just because he was on the hook with Tug, it didn't mean he was going back to that level of corruption.

Fourth: Tug was a suspect in Martin's attempted murder. The blackmail suggested a strain in terms of their business relations, so perhaps Martin had found a way out, one that could only be blocked using lethal force, applied by Tug himself or—more likely—by ordering some foot-soldier to perform the task.

Yes, Martin had been corrupted by vice and money, but that person was a fading odour to the man he was now, an old coat that had lingered too long near a bonfire some months earlier. No escaping it, but it did not define him.

So screw it. He accepted that sliver of corruption offered in the Lancelot. He couldn't touch Tug for any crime he might commit, and even though he would have to hide from Helen Cartwright and his colleagues in MisPer, his conscience was clear.

A lot of 'buts'.

The first step to redemption was accepting he'd done bad things. Now he was using those bad things to channel into one good thing: he would give Si's parents closure, or he would return their son to them.

Strolling the streets of his home town, Martin's buzz was waning, and he knew he'd open a bottle of something when he got in, to take the edge off. Maybe a couple of paracetamol or ibuprofen.

A woman caught his eye. She paced slowly back and forth in front of a shopping centre that had closed for the night. A building site in The Before, the behemoth now gleamed in the soft halo of Leeds's night-lighting. The woman, though, was wearing a short skirt, high heels and a leather jacket, too much makeup, and displayed a nervous shake as she smoked. Martin approached and asked how she was.

"Fine," she said. "You after a bit of fun?"

"How much?"

"Much as you like."

"You know what I mean, love."

"How do I know you're not a copper?"

"I *am* a copper." He showed her his warrant card, putting it away too quickly for her to examine his name. "But it's never stopped me before."

She looked sceptical. "Yeah? Fifty."

"For everything?"

"My bum-hole is off-limits."

She absently pulled at the back of her skirt. Up close, lines streaked her face into which foundation was clumped in places, and her eyes were sunken as if the sockets were too big, although, to Martin, her breasts seemed in fine nick. There was no doubt she was a drug addict; not attractive enough for someone like Tug Jones to consider part of his stable, yet desperate enough to put herself out here for anyone who might be passing. Martin could take her off in a taxi, pick up her narcotic of choice—heroin most likely—and hit them both up before returning to his flat for a night of anonymous, furious sex.

His dick pulsed in his trousers. Tug's photos had triggered some sort of muscle memory, and suddenly Martin had no desire to take her anywhere. Pay up, pin her in the doorway, satisfy himself, then scoot off home and watch the latest episode of *The Walking Dead* with a whiskey or two.

He thought of Si, though.

He thought of Edith.

He thought of the girl in Tug's photos, the one with the Robin tattoo behind her ear. Whoever the girl with the daisy chain tattoo on her wrist might have been...

He opened his wallet and handed the woman three twenty-pound notes.

"I don't give change," she said.

"I don't want any. And I don't want to see you again tonight. Is that enough to keep you off the streets?"

"Til tomorrow, yeah."

"Then maybe tomorrow you'll change your mind."

"Yeah maybe." She stuffed the money in her bra and walked away, calling back, "After all, tomorrow is another day."

Edith?

As far as Cupinder Rowe knew, Martin was working all evening, and he didn't want to make a liar out of himself, not on top of everything else. He popped into Sheerton to see the duty sergeant and cancelled his backup constable, which was met with less enthusiasm than he expected.

"I still have to pay the bleedin' overtime."

Instead, Martin now agreed with any number of people that the park and rent boys were less valuable than the girl omitted from the original investigation. The HOLMES database returned three Edith Longs, one of whom was two years into a three-year jail sentence, a second registered as living in Scotland, and the third had a record for prostitution, drug possession, and several counts of shoplifting and being drunk and disorderly. He popped four paracetamol from the packet he bought from the petrol station, borrowed a laptop that someone from the MisPer team had left out, and drove with a fogginess for which he should probably have been arrested.

Edith's last known address was listed as Belle Isle, a short distance beyond the Bankwell and not as deprived, although that was a relative term. Belle Isle was still one of the poorest areas of the city, with a similar mix of people to the Bankwell; tough, hard-working types and a minority of scummy fuck-ups who blamed society for the absence of a mansion in their lives.

Edith's mother was one of the latter.

It was almost nine P.M., and if there had been no lights on Martin would have gone home to sleep, but since there appeared to be a fair amount of activity, he knocked on the door and asked to speak to the girl who might point him to Si Larson.

"Haven't seen her in over a year," said the woman who answered the door. "She in trouble or what?"

"No," Martin said. "We think she might have information about a missing person."

"Well, if you find her, tell her..." She thought for a long moment. "I don't care. Tell her whatever."

She started to close the door, but Martin said, "Just a couple of minutes, Mrs Long. Please."

"What for? And it's Miss."

"I'd like to know a bit about her. If that's okay."

"I'm well-fucking-busy."

Behind her, a cacophony of noise crashed out of a lively house with a number of kids. According to Edith's file, her mother was thirty-one, making her fourteen when she had Edith. Not that that automatically made her bad, of course. Only that she spent her life giving birth and raising kids on a very low income, which often resulted in what he now saw and heard behind her.

"I won't keep you long, I promise," Martin said.

She sighed with her whole body, and invited him in.

Where the squat in Rose Grove carried the air of people caring more about their next hit than their hygiene or general health, Veronica Long's residence stank of hot fat, and a girl of about ten or eleven yelled down the stairs, "My fucking stupid sister hit me!"

Her mother yelled back, "So sort it out between you!"

Veronica Long took Martin into a lounge.

Battered PVC couch.

Matching armchairs.

An entertainment centre with a cathode-ray flat-screen.

Bookcases spilling over with DVDs, computer games and even a couple of books.

A toddler—a girl—munched a chocolate bar on the floor of the lounge. Martin checked his watch: yes, it was after nine in the evening. With her mouth full, the little girl asked, "Who the fuck's this?"

She was *four* at the most

Martin sat where directed, on the edge of the couch, while Veronica took one of the chairs. She asked, "Right, what do you need to know?"

"Just—"

A series of bumps and bangs from upstairs shot Veronica off her chair and to the bottom of the stairs where she shouted at full volume, "STOP IT YOU FUCKING IDIOTS!"

Then a child started crying somewhere else in the house.

"Now look what you've done!" She stomped off up the stairs.

When Veronica failed to return after several minutes, and the chocolate-covered foul-mouthed toddler took herself out of the room, Martin ventured up the stairs. All had been quiet, but not silent. He poked his head into a bedroom where the eleven-year-old girl listened to music on headphones on her top bunk, while another girl—this one about fourteen—read a Stephen King novel on the bottom. The older girl acknowledged Martin with a, "What?"

"I'm DS Martin Money," he said. "I'm looking for your sister."

"Gonna arrest her?" She pointed to the top bunk.

"Not that one."

"Oh. Edith. No, sorry, haven't seen her. Lucky cow."

"Lucky?"

The girl placed a One Direction bookmark in her place and closed the book. "Wherever she is, she's out of this house. So she's lucky. And I'm happy for her."

"You aren't worried?"

"Why would I be? What could be worse than here?"

Veronica's voice came from down the landing, "Oi! Are you talking to Brittany without a lawyer?"

Martin offered the girl a sympathetic smile and, thinking of Rose Grove, followed the voice to a room with a double bed, a cot, and a rocking chair in which Veronica breastfed a baby, presumably a boy due to his blue, digger-covered onesie. A man lay on the bed, staring daggers at Martin as he removed a pair of headphones.

"Stan knows why you're here," Veronica said. "Okay, my statement is pretty fuckin' simple. So's his. Sometime last year, she dropped by claimin' she wanted to see this 'un when he come home from hospital," meaning the baby, "but I think she was after sympathy cos she split up with some bloke who treated her like shit. Before that it was last Christmas. Never heard from her on my birthday, or Stan's, no mother's day card, nothing. Got cards through for her sisters but not her mum. That's what she's like."

"Are you the father?" Martin asked the man on the bed.

"Nearest thing she has," Veronica answered for him.

Stan's eyes seemed to have trouble focusing. It was only now Martin detected the aroma of alcohol sitting heavy in the room, a bottle of supermarket whiskey open on the bedside table alongside a packet of cigarettes and a lighter. They'd placed the cot at the bottom of the bed.

Martin said, "How long has Stan lived here?"

"Long enough to give me two more of these buggers."

So the four-year-old and the boy she was feeding.

"He's been good to us," she said. "Works, too. Not that he lives here full time," she added quickly. "I mean, I'm a single mum, but he spends time with 'em. Don't give us enough to affect—"

"I'm not going to report you to the DSS," Martin said. Another legal compromise.

She breathed easier. "Still, I can't help you with Edith. Leave us yer card and I'll call if she turns up."

Tired and hungry, Martin scribbled his current number on an old card with out of date info, and headed for the stairs. The fourteen-year-old looked up from her book, stared at him.

Martin said, "Okay?"

"Yeah," Brittany said. "Fine. Why?"

"Thought you wanted something."

She glanced to the side, toward her mother's bedroom. "No," she said. "It's nothing." She went back to her book.

Unable to think of anything else to say, Martin trudged down the stairs. If he could think up an excuse to return, he would want a longer chat with Brittany, preferably without a responsible adult present.

The Trail

Martin arrived home around ten P.M. where he remotely logged on to the HOLMES database via the borrowed laptop, poured two fingers of scotch, and knocked back a couple of ibuprofen, which failed to alleviate the ache in his head which he supposed came about through a combination of the skunk come-down, the depression of being present in a household held together by co-dependency, and the need to make some sort of headway in either his own case or Si Larson's. No matter how much information he gleaned, every new avenue led nowhere. The offer from Tug that he would help in any way possible seemed to be exactly what the investigation needed. What investigation wouldn't benefit from a criminal guiding the police through that world? What copper didn't yearn for guaranteed co-operation from witnesses?

Such witness cooperation was all good and well, but first he had to locate a viable one.

Martin and Si actually had that in common. Both surrounded by mystery, but both denied any sort of company to protect or avenge them.

Witnesses.

Immediately before his bag-nabbing, Martin gazed upriver to the bridge, confused by the presence of CCTV masts in the vicinity of where he was stabbed, and the absence of any images.

No.

He could look into that in more detail later, maybe once he had some leeway with the brass at work. He couldn't go scouring CCTV angles and coverage when the request would have no relevance to his current case. It would need signing off by more than one senior officer, and the location would not go unnoticed. If he could get Wadaya on side more firmly, perhaps he could help.

For now, he focused on Edith Long.

He skipped the petty theft, the suspended shoplifting charges from when she was fifteen, and noted the names of her associates arrested at the same time she was taken for D&D, hoping they might connect to Rose Grove or Tug Jones. Unfortunately, nothing linked in with those people or the facts that Martin already knew. No Si Larson, no Devon Carlisle, no Tug Jones. Just a litany of arrests and cautions after being picked up at house parties, shouting abuse on the street, or fighting outside pubs in which she was too young to get served. From shortly before her sixteenth birthday to around three months shy of her seventeenth, Edith long got herself arrested eleven times for a variety of anti-social crimes, but always got away with community-based sentences. After the eighth incident in which Edith found herself sobering up in a police cell, social services assessed the family over the course of a week, concluded it was 'functional', whatever that meant, and marked for review at six months intervals. Subsequent reviews were not included.

For Edith's tenth and eleventh encounters with the law, her address was no longer the same as her mother and sisters, having bunked up with two women in their twenties. And one of them did cross-reference.

Sonia Baines. A sex worker known to frequent Lille Park, which was clearly Tug Jones's territory now, although she had not been arrested since the time during which the park was overseen by Marco D'Arcy, currently residing in HMP Wakefield. Tug inherited the park and, it seemed, Marco's 'stable' of girls, after Marco and several of his close associates were arrested in August 2014, while

Martin was confined to a desk thanks to the investigation into his domestic abuse allegations.

Marco D'Arcy.

The guy whose sentencing sparked a party and landed Martin and Dave with an iPad-based porn-shoot.

While Martin's name was not officially present for Marco's arrest, one of the other arresting officers was, indeed, Detective Constable Dave Essex.

Marco

The inmates at Her Majesty's Prison Wakefield are mainly category A and B offenders, meaning murderers, rapists, and perpetrators of violent or sexual crimes against children. The population averages 740, of which Marco D'Arcy was, feasibly, one of the least dangerous. He was technically serving several sentences relating to breaches of the Sexual Offences Act 2003, specifically section 52—*causing or inciting prostitution for gain*—and section 53—*controlling prostitution for gain*—which in everyday parlance makes him quite the entrepreneurial pimp. The prosecution also alleged he perpetrated the rape of Sonia Baines and Edith Long, both of whom failed to show up for trial along with five other alleged victims. When those charges were dropped, the judge should have discarded them and not factored them in to the sentencing, but might still have done so, subconsciously at least. Add the six assault charges, and the fact that one of the girls under his control was a few weeks shy of her sixteenth birthday, and the judge was happy to bump him in with the worst society had ever produced. Looking deeper into the case, the names of the OTT club all came up as investigating officers, all except Martin's, but he suspected he may have played a part in clearing the decks for Tug Jones to march over the newly-vacated land.

A bag of cash and several photos existed that hinted strongly that way.

With no current whereabouts on Sonia Baines, Martin had little option but to meet with Marco first thing in the morning, an interview to which Marco only agreed if Martin picked up coffee from Starbucks—a venti caramel latte no less. It took some time to convince the governor to allow the unconventional meeting, but a combination of Martin's plea that Marco may possess information on the disappearance of a seventeen-year-old girl and an eighteen-year-old boy, plus the bribe of a posh coffee of her own whilst on duty, swayed her to facilitate a private room.

Marco D'Arcy was a short, weaselling black man with bad teeth and patchy hair. He swaggered as he walked, like he hadn't a care in the world. It was actually a family room, so they were surrounded by bright wallpaper and colourful toys, plus a panic button for if things got out of hand. The governor insisted Marco remained cuffed throughout, but permitted enough slack to sip his coffee.

Martin turned on the recording app on his phone and explained to Marco that Edith Long was a person of interest for him.

"Edith." Marco rolled the name around his mouth. "What do you need to know?"

"Everything."

"I don't care what you're doing with her. Just don't hurt her."

"Hurt her? Marco, I'm trying to *find* her."

"Leave her alone, man. She's a nice kid. Done nothin' to you."

"She's gone, Marco. Might be in trouble."

He scanned the room as he drank the coffee. His frown remained full. "So you're not here to, y'know, threaten me?"

"I brought you a coffee, Marco. I'm concerned about Edith."

"She got out, didn't she? Out of the life?"

"Maybe. Or she might have got in deeper."

Marco smiled, his crooked teeth showing black in the gaps. "I hope she got out, man. I liked her. Really liked her."

"You didn't like the other girls you exploited?"

Marco licked foam from his lips. "Edith was sweet-as, man. Sweet-as."

"When did you last see her?"

"She was still working for me when your mates took me down. Shit, I wish I knew where she was. Wish she'd visit. We were good friends."

"And Sonia Baines?"

"She missing too? Good. Bitch said I raped her, got Edith to play along too, then didn't have the balls to show up at court. Wish she was still workin' Lille Park. That Tug Jones, he makes me look like employer of the fuckin' year."

Martin sipped his own coffee, feeling a tad naughty that he made Marco's a decaf. "Marco, tell me about Edith and Sonia. They were friends?"

"Friends, yeah. Sonia had this sister, went to school with Edith, that's how they met. This is good shit, man." He meant the coffee. When Martin said nothing further, he continued. "Came to work for me, like, early in the year. Needed money. She'd dropped outta school or got kicked out or some shit, but she liked to party, know what I mean? Like... *party*." He stuck out his tongue and gyrated his hips a couple of times. "She didn't like the work at first, but I got her in the right mindset. You know what that is?"

"You doped her up."

"Naw, I never do that. *Never*." He sat back, offended. "Only fucked up niggers and crack-fiends like Tug Jones do that. It's stupid, gettin' a bitch hooked on smack. One, she don't perform so well and needs, like, two hits a night to get a couple a' hundred quid in. Two, their shelf-life ain't what it should be. They stop washing, don't look after 'emselves. They get bed-sores, STDs. Takes 'em a year or less to get so far stuck in the shit, well... I can't use 'em no more."

"Because your clients won't pay as much.

"Right. I put out a premium product. Those girls work for me cos they want to. I don't put pressure on 'em or nothing."

"But you were convicted of it."

"Hey, some bitch brings me another bitch who wants work, I gotta train 'em up. Get 'em in that, you know…"

"Mindset."

"Yeah. Concentrate on the money. That's not a dick inside you—that's what I tell 'em—it's a roll of twenties. You're fucking a roll of twenty pound notes. If you get a fat sweaty piece of shit, think like you're at the gym, that the sweat's actually yours. If it's a dick in your mouth, fuck, man, it's a lolly-pop you gotta—"

"I understand, thanks. Tell me about Edith."

"Right. Yeah." He took a long pull of the coffee. "She partied. She drank. She did a bit of blow, some weed, tried the heavy stuff too but it didn't take with her. Not at first, anyway. She tried to quit the life, but… I never had to threaten her or nothing. Maybe it was all the dick she sucked or rode before we met, but she took to Lille Park so easy. She knew what she was doing. No breaking her in."

"Did you rape her too?"

Marco's fingers dug into the paper cup, probably would have crushed it if there wasn't a quarter of the drink left. "They told 'em to say it. The cops. They told Sonia and Edith to make up that shit about me. Edith was my favourite bitch, man. I fucked her over and over, whenever I could, even when she started hanging with that batty boy—"

"Si."

"Yeah, him. Think she was fucking him too, I dunno. Guess he was only gay when they was paying him. Baby might even be his, but I doubt it."

Martin sat back sharply. "Baby?"

"Oh yeah." Marco relaxed his fingers. "Didn't you know? Edith was pregnant. Why you think she was trying to get out of the life? She took it real fucking serious. Up the duff at seventeen, and no idea who the daddy is. Me, batty-boy, or her step-daddy."

A second jolt fired through Martin, one he tried to suppress so Marco D'Arcy wouldn't see the reaction. "Her step-father? He was abusing Edith? Do you know when it started?"

"Long time ago." Marco now lost a bit of that nervous energy. Licked his lips again, focused on Martin. "Sort of girl she was, she made a deal. Even after she left, she'd see him twice a week. Voluntarily."

"After she got away?"

Marco leaned back in his chair as far as the cuffs allowed. "She, well..." He finished the coffee and crushed the container, and said, "She couldn't let him start on her sisters now, could she?"

The Right Thing

Martin was late again. He watched Veronica Long's house from in his car down the road, where it appeared to contain Veronica herself and the two youngest kids. After yesterday's chewing-out about reporting in, he didn't want to let Cupinder Rowe down, but sometimes there are crimes so awful that such considerations shrink away to nothing. Right now, he did not care who stabbed him, or how much he'd hurt his friends, or what he'd done to his wife; he didn't much care about Si Larson right then either. All he cared about was the withdrawn fourteen-year-old girl he met last night, and the eleven-year-old teetering on puberty, and the toddler who knew how to use the word 'fuck' in context. He wondered if Veronica was aware of her boyfriend's tastes. If so, how did she allow that man to do what he did? Was she scared? Did she even suspect?

Martin sent Cupinder an apologetic text message to say he'd be late and that he would explain everything, then ignored her callbacks and other texts while he reviewed the names of officers he might need to speak to at the Child Safeguarding Unit. But he didn't want to bother them unnecessarily. Marco D'Arcy wasn't exactly a reliable witness.

While he was waiting he considered what could arguably be a more significant revelation: Edith was pregnant. Prior to Marco being sent down, she and Sonia Baines were able to add rape to his pimping charges, which fell through when Sonia and Edith failed to materialise at the trial.

Because of the pregnancy?

Possibly.

He made some calls to the Child Safeguarding Unit and received several promises that people would return those calls, and then he drove around for a while. He didn't even know which school Veronica Long's kids attended, so no way to head them off there. He tried the social services lines and was told to file a report with the family's case officer, but since there was no indication of abuse—sexual or otherwise—Martin would need some better evidence than a conversation with a convict to take the case officer away from her hundreds of other pressing families.

By three-thirty, Martin had stacked up a dozen missed calls from Cupinder and ignored eight texts. But he'd pinpointed the nearest school and parked at the end of the street through which he expected Brittany would walk home. He gambled correctly, watching her from a distance.

She bobbed along the pavement alongside the eleven-year-old, whose name he had since learned was Brooke. His approach was not orthodox, and nor was it even remotely how he'd been trained, but the moment he shared with Brittany in her room, that silence after she told him she was happy for her sister having got away from the house, it felt like a hint now. Coupled with the tentative moment where she looked like she really wanted to speak to Martin, it might have been hope or it might have been absolutely nothing, but he had to try here.

Forget having a female officer present.

Forget the specially trained people form the SGU.

Forget social services.

Building a case like that takes time, but with compelling evidence of an immediate threat, the usual bureaucracy could be shunted aside, and that was what Martin was aiming for here, as he leaned against his car, avoiding any sight-lines from the house.

At first, Brittany's eyes widened and she bit her lip and her eyes darted around the street, but as Martin told her he wanted to listen, and promised to believe whatever she said, those eyes filled with tears, and she buried her face in his chest and hugged him tight. That her sister, Brooke, did not run or even seem remotely confused, told Martin he had more than one witness to Brittany's ordeal.

"It's over," he said, patting her back. "It'll all be okay."

Martin wasn't surprised to find Cupinder Rowe in her office well after nine P.M. and even less surprised to see her jump up from her desk and arrow right for him. After leaving Brittany and Brooke with the Safeguarding Unit, he spent two hours in a coffee shop with the borrowed laptop where he drank three Americanos and wrote out his official report, emailed it to the children's unit's detective chief inspector, cc'd in his own boss, and headed to the pub where he necked two double whiskeys, despite craving more. A spot of weed, maybe—or something stronger.

"What the hell is wrong with you?" Cupinder said. "That is not your case!"

"It crossed over directly and I received information I had to act on."

"Have you been drinking?"

"A small one to take the edge off—"

"*Drinking?*"

"I'm not on duty. I just wanted to see if you were still here."

"First thing, Martin. First thing, we go through this in detail. Bring everything you have. A minute later than nine A.M. and I end your secondment. Clear?"

"Clear," Martin said.

Assessment

According to the clock in her office, it was actually eight-thirty A.M. when Cupinder said, "From the beginning."

"Okay." Martin tried to address DC Gurdeep Khaira and DC Carol Webster, as well as DI Rowe. "Si Larson went missing on the 19th December. He's a sex worker known to prostitute himself to men in Lille Park after midnight. Sometimes he uses the building known as The Shack…" Martin indicated the structure on a three-metre square map of Leeds that he tacked to Cupinder's office wall an hour earlier. "And sometimes he brings others here to Rose Grove, depending on occupancy and how much the client wants to spend."

"Quickie or the personal touch," Khaira said. "We know this."

"DI Rowe said from the beginning."

Webster nodded.

Martin said, "So he occupies Rose Grove with a bunch of other people. Most of them, if not all, are drug addicts in the same line of work. He had a relationship going on with Callum Jackson, who still lives at the address. However, new information came out of my visit, namely that Si Larson had a girlfriend."

"He swung both ways?" Webster asked. "Is that intel solid?"

"I think so," Martin said. "I confirmed it with a source who is active in that area—"

"Tug Jones," Cupinder said, reading from Martin's report. "Your old CI."

"Yes, but no money changed hands, officially or otherwise. He doesn't want an unsolved crime on his patch."

"*His* patch?" Khaira said. "I thought *we* were the ones who have patches."

"I'm using his own terminology, Gurdeep. If I may continue…?" With the go-ahead nod, Martin said, "Edith Long is his girlfriend, but she is also off the grid. We have people searching for her electronically right now—name changes, hospitals, GPs, credit cards—but I think she's hiding."

"Who from?" Cupinder asked.

"Perhaps her step-dad."

"Or whoever killed Si," Webster said.

"Why do you think he's dead?" Martin asked.

"Don't you?"

"I did. Before I learned about Edith."

"What?" Khaira said. "That he was into girls as well as boys? That's hardly—"

"Marco D'Arcy said she was pregnant before he went down. That was in *August*."

Webster said, "Marco D'Arcy who claims your mates set him up?"

"The very same," Martin said.

Cupinder indicated Martin's phone. "According to the recording it sounds like he was scared of you. That you were threatening Edith. He didn't realise you were trying to help her."

"We're all aware that I used to do some pretty dodgy stuff, but let's focus on the task at hand, okay? I don't know about the situation with Marco, but I do know he took great pleasure in telling me Edith was pregnant. He also confirmed she was close with Si Larson, and that her discovery of the pregnancy coincided with her trying to get out of the life she was in."

Cupinder said, "So she made a deal with her step-father to have regular sex with him, if he promised to leave her sisters alone. But she had to stop seeing him to protect her own child."

"I think so," Martin said. "Even if it meant Brittany had to face him next."

Webster waited a moment before asking, "How does that help us find Si? And why does it mean he isn't dead somewhere?"

"It's his baby," Martin replied.

"How do you know?"

"I don't. But it makes sense. Even if it isn't his *physically*, the girl he cares about is knocked up by one of two misogynistic men, or by himself. By all accounts, Si isn't a bad guy, so he'll stand by her. He'll help her."

Khaira said, "Why does that mean he's definitely alive?"

"It doesn't," Martin said. "But it gives him an incentive to actively hide."

Cupinder considered it. "To get her away from the men who hurt her, or threatened to."

"Some quick maths gives us a neat timeline. August, Edith finds herself pregnant. Possibly two or three months by then. Si sneaks around with her, calls off his relationship with Callum, hides the pregnancy, saves up enough money to run, and he's gone. By December, it's almost Christmas, and don't all couples want their new lives to start by then? Moving house, a new couch, refitted kitchen? Whatever, it's always, 'let's get it sorted by Christmas'."

All agreed with him.

"That's the best case scenario, though," Martin said.

"What are the others?" Cupinder asked.

"That he's dead. That she's dead. Let's not forget, she was a prostitute who made good money for Marco D'Arcy. When Tug Jones took over that territory, she'd have belonged to him. Si taking her away, even six or seven months pregnant, it's a problem for him. Then there's the step-dad to consider."

"And Si's ex-boyfriend," Webster said.

"Callum? Sure, add him in. Jealousy's a powerful motive."

"So three viable murder suspects," Cupinder said. "Or he's hiding out and playing daddy."

Martin didn't vocalise the fourth suspect. If Marco really did rape Edith, Sonia, and the others, they chose not to show up for trial out of fear, but if he didn't, then someone had coerced the girls into making the accusation. The arresting officer was Dave Essex, and for the first time Martin was thankful for the PSD investigations. He was desk-bound at the time, otherwise there could've been a conflict of interest here. Yet, for all Dave's shortcomings, his weakness and greed, Martin didn't believe he was a killer. It didn't mean he had anything to do with Edith's disappearance. She'd been spotted as late as December, after all. Long after the trial.

Martin said, "She'll have given birth recently, probably February or March at the latest. Look for her, even though she's not officially missing, and we should find Si too. At the very least she's another witness."

"It's the best lead we've had in this case for months." DI Rowe said this without criticism or blame, or even complimenting Martin. Just a statement of fact. "Well done everyone. I have a good feeling we might even close this one."

ALMOST THERE

9 til 5

The rest of that morning went by like a dream. Not that it started out that way. Cupinder put Webster and Khaira on the case of checking hospitals for young women giving birth using an alias, and in their presence ordered Martin to go back over the less savoury suspects to nail their movements around the time Si disappeared, in case it wasn't happily-ever-after. When the two DCs were gone, Cupinder closed the door and told Martin about the Long household.

"Brittany spoke freely about the step-father. Claims her mother knew about it, but Stan was always promising to never do it again. It happened mostly when he was drunk, apparently. Problem they now have is that Ms Long is adamant she knew nothing, and is in fact denying her fella would do that. Says Edith is a lying bitch."

"She assumes that's where we got the tip from," Martin said.

"Correct. The SGU is letting her believe that for now. The man himself, Stanley Schutt, he's been questioned under caution but not arrested. Yet. He denies it all, but Brittany has been quite specific. Social services have removed all the kids for the time being and journalists from the Sentinel are circling, looking to assign blame already."

"Scum."

"And they want to know who the hero detective is that exposed the abuse."

"Right. Hero." He tried not to smile. "Something leaked from social services?"

"I guess so. Right now, you've got the attention of a few higher-ups, including Daniel Black. You did good back there, and you're doing well with Si Larson. Keep going."

On his way out, the dream-like morning commenced when Wadaya stopped him and told him he respected what he'd done, and if he could be of assistance in the future, Martin only had to ask.

Shortly after that, he took a call from the head of the Child Safeguarding Unit to be told he could question Stan Schutt after they charged him, which would be by the end of the day providing Brittany's statement checked out medically and with the observations about Stan himself.

In the canteen, word had got around that Martin nailed a paedophile, and he received hand-shakes from people he'd never met, and a back-slap or two from guys who seemed stilted in their compliments. He guessed these were people he alienated during his Dead Time.

Then, back at his desk in MisPer, he opened an email from DS Derek Laughlin from PSD, informing him he was under investigation for a serious breach of procedure. With Rowe out of the office, Martin printed it, and stormed out without a word to those around him. Instead of barging in to PSD he headed straight for the DO-MU floor and, more specifically, DCS Black's office, and caught him as he was leaving.

"Serious breach of procedure?" Martin said, waving his prop as intended. "I *saved* those girls."

Black snatched the email. Read it. "Hm." He adjusted the paper to arm's length to take it in properly. Smiled. "Remember that chat we had some weeks ago? When you were recuperating?"

Martin said, "You wanted me gone."

"Yes, yes. Well, you've seen your record. Remember it or not, you still did what you did. We just never proved it."

"Right. So now you—"

"So we decided to monitor anything you did out of the ordinary. Such as taking a laptop home without the appropriate training course being done."

"Laptop?" Martin said. "*Training?*"

"You removed a laptop from your department without it being assigned to you, and without conducting the correct training course pertaining to security of mobile devices."

"I didn't even realise there *was* a course. Wait. Is that what this is about?"

"Security is very important, Martin."

"You're doing me over a *laptop?*"

The big man smiled. Actually, his mouth did. Not his eyes. He tore the email in half. "Not anymore, Martin. What you did with that family... it would be a poor show of us to discipline a 'hero' over something so minor. Do the training course this afternoon and you're off the hook. It's all online." He dropped the pieces in the confidential recycle bin and moved for the door.

Martin said, "So that's it? I can ignore it?"

When DCS Black responded, his face seemed trapped in shadow. "For now. Keep up the good work, find this kid, and maybe PSD will start to look elsewhere, and forget about the past. Maybe."

And with that, Martin Money floated back to his desk, and joined Khaira and Webster in checking hospitals in the region. If they failed to find Si Larson alive, it was a distinct possibility that he'd have to list Tug Jones as an official murder suspect.

The dreamy morning ended outside in the sun, lunch and coffee with Wadaya, Khaira and Webster, then he returned to complete the annoyingly simple online course before he could recommence his actual work.

Once the system gave him a reference number, he fired it to DS Laughlin.

While Khaira and Webster would return to their own cases tomorrow, leaving Martin to pick up with other forces to ask about Edith, it was still progress. So, with no follow-ups that required him to attend in person, he clocked-out on time, marking his first nine-til-five shift since returning here. He had no chance to work on his own stabbing at all, but there'd be plenty of time later. Right now, he was looking forward to getting home at a reasonable hour, ordering a takeaway, and drinking nothing but water or tea for the rest of the evening. It did not work out that way, though.

Waiting at his door was the last person in the world he expected to see.

"Julie," he said.

"Hi Martin," said his ex-wife. "I realise this might be a bit illegal, but... Cupinder called and... I had to see for myself."

He barely heard the words. Barely registered the fact that she was now in breach of her own court order. He was more concerned with her hand stroking the smooth, round bulge that now represented her stomach.

Julie

Maybe it was the talk of pregnancy around the office that did it, maybe his newfound commitment to a cause, or even his legwork on the Long family. All he knew for sure was what Julie told him next.

"It's yours, Martin." She was around seven months gone, so it fell within the time that he was physically hurting her. She crossed her legs on the couch and said, "Cupinder told me that... she believes you."

"Believes me?"

"The story you're telling. That you don't remember your... your bad side."

She talked like Martin, like his Dead Time was Mr Hyde to The Before's Dr. Jekyll.

She said, "You can't remember the day it all changed, can you? When you came home at five in the morning. Eyes like saucers. You wouldn't tell me what you'd been up to or where you'd been. I pressed you. You'd never hit me before, so even that one slap felt like the end of something. Of us, maybe."

"When was that?"

"Summer, 2013. After that you were sorry, and there wasn't a repeat for months, but I still wanted to know what happened to you that night. Whenever I broached the subject, you clammed up. Then it got worse. I can't remember exactly when. It was still cold, so winter I suppose, but it was the year after. You hit me again, but

I stood my ground this time. You made a fist. I didn't get up after that."

Martin turned away, stared out the window.

"But it wasn't you, was it? Not this you. Standing right here."

"No," Martin said. His hand tingled. "It was the other guy."

"I think it was when Helen moved to PSD that you really started to grow distant."

November 2013. Martin knew the timeline by now. He said, "Summer was when Helen and I stopped working together in SLIT."

"SLIT?"

"The Street Level Informant Trading initiative. Part of the DOMU setup. November, she joined PSD and then in April I was harassing her."

"Because I'd been talking to her," Julie said. "I really wanted to get you away from that Essex bloke and the others."

"It got so bad Alan stepped in, right?"

"You two fought over Helen's involvement with you, with her trying to help me win back my husband. My *real* husband. Because I love him, Martin. I really fucking love him."

Martin pulled away from the window, revealing the tears on his cheeks. "He loves you too, Julie. So much that it hurts. Every day. All he wants… I have to stop talking like that. All *I* want, is to prove that bastard is gone for good. But he's always here." He held up two fists. "He's always there. Even after I solve this kid's disappearance, even if I solve my own stabbing, I might uncover even more. Do you know I have a bag full of money? Illegal money?"

"You carried more cash than you used to, but… a case full?"

"And a fake passport. I hurt Helen, hurt Alan—my best friend—and I beat you rotten, while you must have been pregnant already."

"It was that night, when you punched me and I fell down the stairs. It was that night they told me I was expecting. That you, the bad you, was going to be a dad. I called Helen and she told me you were being too slippery, that the tough love thing wasn't working, you weren't taking the hint to stop with the drugs and booze. The man I married was gone forever, so I decided to leave you. Not only for my sake. Now I had other responsibilities."

Martin heard the echo of Edith Long. "You never thought about…you know…"

"I never even considered it."

Martin sat beside her, hands clasped in his lap.

Julie said, "You've helped people already, and so far nothing you've said or done contradicts your story."

"You think I couldn't make it up?"

She gave him an 'oh pu-lease' look. "When you were the other person, the bad one, you were terrible at hiding things. Drugs, a bit of money here and there. Sometimes you'd even come home stinking of sex and whiskey. I knew exactly what you'd been doing."

"Then why come here tonight?"

"Because I want to believe you. I want to believe that the man who punched me and threatened me and shagged hookers and strippers and took drugs and accepted bribes, I want to know that man is gone."

He'd smoked skunk

Accepted his money back.

Looked the other way from several crimes.

So he told her. He told her absolutely everything, from the hospital onward; the new things he'd learned about himself that were not in his file; he recounted the temptation of the prostitute, the painkillers and whiskey, his meetings with the OTT club, and his actions in getting the children removed from Veronica Long.

"It's me," he said. "I know it's all me. I did those things. I slip so easily into that person and I can't stop myself." He wiped away another tear, a failed man, crumbling, admitting his sins, his weakness. "It was all me, Julie. You were right to force me to stay away."

"But you're coming back," she said. "You did those bad things this week, but you stopped yourself. Just like the old Martin. The real Martin."

It was as if her husband had been declared dead, but now he'd been spotted alive and well.

"You should go," Martin said.

"Wait." She took his hand and placed it on her belly, near the top.

A lump prodded his hand. "Shit! Was that…?"

"Your son," Julie said as another hard nub of a mountain grew under her dress. "I don't want to be a single mum in my forties. But I have to be sure."

"I have to be sure too."

Then the second thing happened that surprised him more than anything else this week. First, she turned up on his doorstep. Now, she kissed him. She kissed the man who hurt her, threatened her, cheated on her.

"What the hell is going on?" he said, pulling away.

"What do you mean?"

"Are you…" He nearly said 'wired' but it sounded so Hollywood.

"You think I'd be taping this?"

"I don't know, I…" A few days ago he thought Dave had spiked his drink.

She stood up. Fiddled with the top button on her dress. "Want to check?"

"There's no need. I'm sorry. I—"

He swallowed back the words as Julie kept unbuttoning her dress. She slipped it off her shoulders, leaving her in a sturdy maternity bra, large black panties, and sheer tights that came up over the lower half of her beach ball-shaped stomach. He took her all in, returning to that tiny, slightly upturned nose of hers set amongst a scattering of freckles.

She said, "It's not exactly lingerie, but then I didn't expect to be undressing for you tonight."

Martin sensed his groin react immediately. "You can do that. Still? Like this?"

"You never slept with a fat chick?" She unhooked her bra and let her swollen breasts sway. "Be gentle with these."

Martin leaned forward slowly, and kissed her far more tenderly than she'd kissed him. They progressed to the bedroom, where she undressed him, and finished undressing herself. He kissed her all over, taking in everything about her—her shape, her taut skin, her smell—and spent time to ensure she came even before he entered her. When she stroked his legs the tattoos felt raised somehow, more sensitive, but with the lights off he could hide them from her. The angle she insisted upon was strange, with her leg slung to one side, almost doggie-style yet they remained face-to-face. He said "I love you" so many times that when it was over he was actually ashamed of letting his emotions spill with such freedom.

She whispered, "I love you too," and they fell asleep tangled in each other's limbs.

In the morning, he awoke alone and, for a long while, wondered if it had been real. The smell in the room let him know it was, and the note on the kitchen counter confirmed it:

> *I wonder if I made a mistake last night. I'm sorry if I got your hopes up. I woke in your arms and all I could think about was that you __did__ do those things, and you were unrepentant at the time. That said, you seem genuinely sorry now, and if Cupinder thinks you are a good man again, perhaps I can accept you too.*

In time.

Last night was wonderful, but it was definitely too soon. I need to see that you can keep going on this track, and perhaps when you finally come back up fully, we can work on that. For now, go do your job. If Cupinder tells me you've stayed the course, I'll be in touch when Jonathan is born. Maybe you can see him.

Find the boy and girl, Martin. I know you can do it.

Julie.

Martin should have been sad, but he wasn't. He was confused and… something else. He read the note again twice, and sure enough, that something else he was feeling didn't change.

He was suddenly very, very scared.

Coming Back Up

It wasn't the brush-off that confused or frightened him, nor the demand that he continue to prove himself worthy of seeing his son; that was all perfectly reasonable. More reasonable, in fact, than the woman he hurt so badly turning up and sleeping with him. That in itself was confusing enough.

The confusing thing, the *scary* part, was one phrase that the note contained. One phrase that was so out of place he had to read it again, then again, and another three times. In everyday speech it could have been glossed over, but in the context of the note, it had *one* meaning only.

...when you finally come back up fully...

He couldn't shake that from his mind. Everyone he'd spoken to since he woke up on New Year's Eve, everyone he asked, all the paperwork he scoured for the past three months... all of it denied the thing he'd hoped so badly for.

...come back up...

When you are married to a copper, you learn the lingo, the police-speak. You learn that those mouthy young boys who yell obscenities at tutting old people and steal from shops and throw stones at passing cars, you learn they're called 'scrotes'; you know the bosses are called 'the brass'; you learn new terms for describing people like 'IC1 male' means 'white guy'. And, if your husband has a special assignment, you might learn more clandestine terminology. Slang terminology, but it is, nonetheless, undeniable.

When an undercover officer loses contact with his handler, he 'goes dark'; when an undercover officer finds himself more aligned with the people he's spying on, such as an environmental direct-action group, he has 'gone native'; but when the assignment is over and he returns to his family and his colleagues, often tainted but still on the right side, he 'comes back up'.

...when you finally come back up fully, we can work on that...

Why would Julie believe Martin was going to 'come back up' from somewhere, unless he'd been infiltrating some group?

Or was he reading too much into it?

His close relationship with Tug Jones

The desperation of DCS Black to pension him off.

Helen Cartwright suddenly dissolving their partnership.

Dissolving their partnership shortly before he started treating Julie like shit.

If he accepted an assignment she didn't approve of, one that went terribly wrong, that resulted in him hospitalising his wife, getting addicted to drugs, and finally being stabbed almost to death on a freezing cold night... the West Yorkshire Police would be looking at a huge lawsuit. And expunging the data from their servers... that would mean criminal charges.

If he wasn't reading too much into Julie's note, of course. Which he was sure he wasn't. The context was clear.

She thought he was undercover. The only reason she would believe that would be if he told her, and if Helen didn't deny it when they talked.

Helen knew...

Could she have known? And sided with the superintendent?

Is that why I hurt Helen? Because she risked blowing my cover with Tug?

DCS Black was Martin's boss at the time, and as soon as Martin woke up there was talk of retirement, of getting him out. The FOI request landed quickly, so they wouldn't have had time to wipe it from their servers. The data had already been eliminated, unless—

Unless it was never official. If the red tape and insurance for the op couldn't be justified, if DCS Black sanctioned an unofficial assignment, placing Martin with Tug and his gang, using Dave Essex as a way in...

"Jesus," Martin said out loud. "I'm sending Daniel Black to prison."

But before he could even begin formulating a plan, his phone made a loud ping—a text message. From a phone number he didn't recognise.

Edith is here. Come quick. Dev.

LOSING FOCUS

Sighting

The squat on Rose Grove was marginally cleaner that it had been on Martin's previous visit. Marginally. The kitchen carried the scent of bleach, but Dev couldn't peel himself from the couch in the living room. Callum insisted Martin go through, seemed to know how it made him feel, and that caused Callum to smile. Martin's gag reflex didn't kick in this time, probably due to the less-pungent atmosphere, but it was far from pleasant. Dev lay on the sofa with a dumb smile on his face, while three sleeping bags stirred in the corners of the dim, hazy room. Two now had the luxury of fold-out cots. By the fireplace, a Tupperware tub sat with the lid beside it, filled with surgically-wrapped syringes.

"Love what you've done with the place," Martin said.

Dev raised his head from the sofa's cushion. "Oh, hey. Yeah, the cleaning, that was her."

"Who?"

"Edith."

Martin came into the room fully. "She was here? Handing out needles?"

"She brought some sheets too, antibiotics, those bed things."

"Does that happen a lot?"

"Every couple a' months," Callum said, entering behind. "Her and them church folk. She doesn't come by much, but she did today."

"Why?"

"Heard her old mate was here."

"*Si?*" Martin said, rapidly scanning the other sleeping bags.

"No, don't be daft," Callum said. "Raquel. Hey, *Raquel!*"

One of the sleeping bags released an arm that waved and a groggy voice said, "Fuck off."

Callum strode over and shook her gently. "You want the coppers all over here or what? Just talk to him."

She turned over and moved the lank hair from her face and, with help from Callum, she sat up. Her low-cut top sparkled with sequins and a push-up bra gave her tiny breasts a sort-of normal appearance; she looked like she'd been working the street, so there'd be a short skirt under that sleeping bag. A recent hit washed serenely over her face, now mixed with annoyance at being disturbed. Her eyes were as dark and hollow as the others he'd met here, but there was an attractiveness to her. She wasn't quite as filthy, lacking the ingrained muck under her nails.

"Do I know you?" Martin asked.

She said, "I doubt it."

Martin crouched before her, taking in her face. Someone from the Dead Time perhaps? It wouldn't surprise him, but then he'd never had so much as an inkling when he ran into people from that phase of his life. Not Tug, not Dave, not the OTT club. He got nothing. Now suddenly he knew someone? No. He must have come across her either in The Before or since he woke up. He tried to separate this waif from the images he'd seen, the women he'd met.

He said, "Oh my God. Sonia?"

"Yup," she said, locating a pack of cigarettes. "Guess you do know me."

"Wait," Callum said. "You told us your name's Raquel."

"I did?" Sonia gazed around, as if surprised by where she was. "I tell guys that. Sorry."

"Sonia," Martin said. "You know Edith? Edith Long?"

She lit a fag and blew smoke into the air. Sat back on her bed with a wicked eye to Callum, who watched. She reached for some water and drank. At least it *looked* like water. She splashed some more in her face, trying to wake up, avoiding the cigarette.

"Sonia," Martin said, "Please, if you know where Edith is, I need to see her."

She sat forward, cig dangling from her lips, and focused again. "Oh, fuck. Not you!"

Then she bolted. So much quicker than a smack-addict should be able, but in sufficient quantity adrenaline is as powerful as cocaine. She slipped at the door, ran the wrong way, then clattered up the stairs on hands and knees. Martin easily caught up with her on the landing, beside the locked door into which no one ventured. She kicked and yelled, dragged them both to the bare floorboards, but Martin finally subdued her without hurting her, his arms circling hers, pinning them to her sides like a giant cuddle. When Callum arrived, they were horizontal, but his presence calmed her.

He said, "You okay down there?"

"Great," Martin said. He asked Sonia, "You going to help me? I swear I just want to know she's okay, and see if she can help find someone I'm looking for."

Callum nodded. He didn't come across as high or hung-over for a change.

"Here," Sonia said.

Martin relaxed his hold on her. "What do you mean 'here'?"

She said, "This room."

"The one you don't go in because it smells so bad?"

"Yeah. Let me go."

Martin released her fully and Callum crouched beside them both.

Callum said, "I didn't know about it."

Martin propped himself against the wall, sitting on unthinkable things on that rare bit of carpet. "About what?"

"The room."

Sonia said, "It's hers. It was."

"We asked Si to take her out of here, but he insisted she have her own room," Callum said. "He stayed with her sometimes, but he stayed with me too. Until he stopped staying with me."

"You lied," Martin said.

Callum gave a shrug that said he didn't care. "She ruined everything. Sexy little bitch. We didn't know she was pregnant until after."

"You didn't notice?"

"It was winter. We ain't got any heat. She was always wrapped in layers."

Martin lightly touched the door. "What went on in the room?"

"She kicked it," Sonia said. "The habit. Si helped, but he couldn't quit. He cut back, like, just enough to keep going."

Smack addicts mostly take the drug in order to push away the outside world, to hide in a cocoon of oblivion. But when they want to quit they will start by cutting down, taking it only when the body threatens to rip a hole in time and space if they don't. It's the switch from being a willing participant to being held hostage.

Martin said, "What is in this room?"

"You really don't want to know," Callum said.

While plenty of missing persons investigations end with a body, at least they had confirmation Edith was alive, and had been able to leave before Martin got here. That left Si. Which would make this a murder inquiry.

"Open it," Martin said.

Callum took a key from his trouser pocket. Sonia backed away, refusing to even look at the door. As Callum fiddled with the lock, he said, "I lied for a reason. No one was supposed to mention Edith, not ever. We promised Si no one would find her. No one would know where she went."

The key turned with a clunk.

"That's why you gave Dev that look," Martin said. "Because he was betraying a promise to your ex-boyfriend."

"A promise to a brother." Callum made a fist around the doorknob. "We're all in this together. Whether it's together-together, or just in the life, we're all part of one family. We look out for each other, even when we're pissed off. The only thing you never do is steal."

"But Edith stole Si from you, didn't she?"

"Not like that," Callum said. "You sure you want me to open this? Because when I do, I'm heading over there."

Martin said, "Open it."

Callum kicked away the cloths and newspaper that had been stuffed in the crack at the bottom and a waft of something rotten rose up like disturbed insects. He said, "Last chance."

Martin held his hand over his nose and mouth, and nodded.

Callum opened the door and, as promised, shifted down the hallway. Martin stepped inside.

The Room

The box-room was bare except for a deflated airbed on the surprisingly thick carpet. Martin had attended enough scenes containing dead bodies to know the stench that filled the room was decomposing human matter, but could not see any obvious sign of a body. He stepped inside, holding his breath. Within a second, a hundreds of black, chunky flies coating the window erupted into a thick, buzzing cloud, and pelted him with tiny, hard bodies as they swarmed for the doorway. He spat several from his mouth, and ducked, then crouch-walked out and pulled the door shut, but not before hundreds of those flies zipped out and all around the house in a panicked exodus, the individual bodies clicking as they hit some new solid object.

"What the fuck, man?" Callum said. "You let those fuckers out?"

Martin staggered towards him, his lungs bursting free. "I didn't know about the flies! You didn't tell me!"

"Oh yeah. Sorry."

"What is that place?" Martin said. "Did someone die in there?"

"Die?"

"It was Si, wasn't it?"

"No, man. Look, she—"

"She was here," Martin said, jabbering now. "She and Si, they started as friends, but she was shagging him and the baby might be his, so ... so she's here and—"

"Hey, calm down." It was Sonia, her eyes heavy after the adrenaline come-down.

"No, not calm. I can't be calm." Martin pulled at his own hair, clawing at the flies tangled in there. He went back and faced the door. "Si brought her here. Pregnant. Due in... anytime December to March. She... No, Si disappears in December, but she..." Martin looked sternly at the pair. "She was still here when Si stopped coming round. Wasn't she?"

"Yes," Callum said. "She was furious with him for ducking out. She didn't have anywhere else to go."

"So she must have..." He couldn't finish the sentence. The notion of her going to a hospital where her stepfather might have tracked her down, or where the authorities could have taken her baby away... a baby she already loved so much before it was born that she was willing to sacrifice her sister in order to save it... no way would she have risked anyone getting their hands on her, or her child.

"She gave birth in there, man, yeah." It was Dev Carlisle, having crawled up the stairs. "Hey," he said to Callum. "Do you know, there's, like, a ton of flies downstairs?"

No one could look at the door except Martin. He had to see. Had to know what happened.

"She had nowhere else," Sonia said, echoing Martin's thinking. "She had to..."

Martin opened the door and strode in. The remaining swarm of pellet-like flies battered him as they fled into the house, and he ignored the screams and shouts from the trio outside. He had to really thump the window to open it, cracking the wooden frame in the process. In seconds, the room contained only a scattering of flies, clear enough for Martin to focus on that deflated airbed.

It took up half the tiny room.

No other furniture.

The formerly-blue object, and everything around it, splattered with brown stains.

Maggots ingrained in the carpet in wide globs.

Martin had to hang his head out the window to take a breath, but when he returned and dared to crouch close to the airbed, a small lump became apparent under the cloth.

He lunged for the window again, vomit rising quickly. He gulped it back, returned to the room, and yelled, "You fucking animals!"

Dev appeared at the door, hand to his nose and mouth. "Hey, we, like, can't afford to clean and stuff, man."

Martin had to see for himself. Had to see what had driven Edith underground. If she was still around here when Si went missing, then she was actually another dead end.

But there was no way anyone could leave this alone, not now.

Lacking the rubber gloves of an evidence kit, he used the cuff of his jacket to nip the corner of the airbed. He would have taken a breath if he could, but in the absence of clean air, he peeled the cloth back. It came away with a tearing sound, the dried blood having formed a seal. And there, on the surprisingly-thick carpet, a pile of stained rags crawled with maggots.

Withdrawing a pen, he reached with the tip of it, a pen no one would ever use for writing ever again, least of all him.

"That's so gross," Dev said.

Martin's lungs burned, demanding air, but he poked the rags and let the maggots drop, until the pile unravelled to reveal a mound of rotting flesh. A generic substance, with a greenish tint, a porous surface where the flies had laid their eggs, but—

"It's not a baby," Martin said, turning to Dev.

Dev pulled a face. "Of course it's not a baby, man. That would be, like, so fuckin' cruel."

Sonia showed up at the doorway, hand over her mouth and nose, and said, "It's her placenta. The man came and took the baby, but he left that mess."

"Man?" Martin said. "What man?"

Knows a Guy

So once again, Martin made up a feasible lie to Cupinder Rowe about why he wouldn't be at the morning briefing, and, once again, found himself in the company of Tug Jones. The Rose Grove crowd insisted Tug had nothing to do with taking the baby, and sure as shit didn't deliver it and leave Edith's detritus splattered all over. They told him again that Tug was a good guy, but emphasised Martin shouldn't cross him, shouldn't interfere with his business, or accuse him of having anything to do with some baby-thief. They needn't have bothered with such a strong defence of their working class hero. Martin didn't suspect Tug was directly responsible. However, little happened in this corner of the city of which Tug was unaware, making him the one informant who could help Martin locate the correct person.

Allowing them all to do some speed, Martin's questioning of the trio revealed that, after Si stopped coming round in early December, and the police ceased their inquiries, Edith came back out of hiding. None of the three knew where she'd been, but she took up her old room, reminding Callum of his promise to Si to look after her and keep her safe. *And* to keep her secretly hidden. She somehow did not touch heroin again, instead holed up in her room, reading.

"Like, books, or something," Dev told Martin when pressed on the subject.

Newcomers to the squat, and the occasional trouble-making gate crasher, all expressed curiosity about the locked room, but the core residents kept them out, ejecting many of them from the house altogether if they got too close. Edith would nip out frequently, taking whatever pooled money didn't go on drugs, and buy groceries for the house at the One-Stop Shop a ten minute walk from the squat. It did her good to get out, she said, and once a month she would catch a bus—"like, somewhere, man, I don't know"—and return with batches of clean needles and dressings for injuries sustained who-knew-where, and even antibiotics when some permanent resident needed them. No one ever asked where she got this stuff from, but there were plenty of charities around the city providing those services, and it chimed well with the fact she'd been here recently doing the same thing.

Except she no longer lived here. And no one seemed sure exactly when the birth took place, narrowing it down to between last week and about a month ago.

Only when Edith had been yelling for a couple of hours did anyone motivate themselves to investigate, and when they did they found an almighty mess in her room, and the crown of a baby's head pushing from inside her vagina. She was holding a phone that she was unable to use, but between Callum, Dev and someone called Knobby, they worked out it held a single number. They dialled it, and within ten minutes, a fat guy showed up with two fat women and shooed everyone out of the room.

Later, the fat guy carried a screaming bundle of pink limbs out of the house, followed shortly after by the women.

"So glad," Dev said. "It was, like, so loud."

"You missed a bit," Sonia told him.

"I didn't."

"When they guy came back."

"Yeah," Callum said. "He came back. This guy who took the baby, this fat dude with long hair and a bushy moustache, he came in while we were all wondering if we should check on Edith, and he shows us this shotgun and tells us to keep quiet. If the bitch dies, he says, *we* gotta get rid of the body."

Dev said, "Like, so totally unfair, man."

Edith was in bad shape, but with a pile of stuff the fat women left behind—ointments, painkillers, some massive nappy-type things. When she stopped crying, and with Sonia's help, she started taking care of herself and, slowly, she got better.

"Then one day she was gone," Sonia said.

"When?" Martin asked, but the junkies' time-frame references were inadequate.

From the rate of decay in her room, the prevalence of flies and maggots, she must have given birth four-to-six weeks earlier, although proper forensics would be needed to determine that. Martin left the squat knowing only that Edith was no longer in possession of the child she had been so desperate to raise properly, with Si Larson if earlier information was to be believed, and that the one person she was known to have contacted outside of the squat on Rose Grove, was Tug fucking Jones.

"See, you gotta understand," Tug said, "when I gave you her name, I didn't expect you to go pokin' around in business that don't concern you."

"You must have known I'd learn about the baby," Martin said.

"I thought maybe you would. If you gave a shit enough. I saw you enjoyin' that blunt the other night. Figured you'd be fucking whores and doing blow every night by now."

"Not even close." Martin looked to Caz, the woman whose flat they were again meeting in, as she sat to one side in a wispy robe, hair falling around her face, watching Tug. Never looked at Martin. He said, "But now I do know, I need a name. She couldn't have arranged this herself, and Marco is inside, so that leaves her current employer. You."

"Yeah." Tug stroked the Rottweiler and it nuzzled his hand. "But since I don't offer no maternity leave, I had to make other arrangements."

"You took her baby."

"Nah, man. She agreed to it. She knew she couldn't stay off the smack that long, not long enough to raise a kid, so yeah, I put her in touch with someone."

"I'm gonna need that name."

Caz made an audible sound like she'd been prodded.

Tug said, "Why don't you go make me a sandwich or something?"

Caz got up without a word and managed to glance once through her hair at Martin before she was gone.

Tug continued, "One thing you gotta know, Rosie. That's these people are a lot bigger than me. Reason I get to run things here is cos they *let* me. Even you and Essex boy and that Bulldog motherfucker, you wouldn't get a sniff. I run the girls, but if one of theirs comes to me for work, I gotta tell them about it."

"One of their girls?"

"They bring 'em in, see? From all over. So if some Vietnamese or Russian chicken-bitch wants work, it's probably a runaway. Pays off her debt for gettin' here, but, see, they don't like letting go a' their assets. Bringin' in hookers and strippers and shit like that, it's small bacon. You get yourself a fresh baby, and… poof. That's more money than a whole park full a' bitches can make in a week."

Martin let him talk. No point in debating morality. And interrupting would make this even longer.

Tug said, "They're mean, Rosie. They ain't gonna talk to five-oh. At least, the guy I know won't. He's got a secret, it'll cost him too much to loosen them lips."

"How much?"

"How much'll it cost him? Shit, I don't know. Bringin' in hookers for Curtis Benson and his euro-crim partners, it's a good sideline, but he gets, I heard, a hundred grand for a new baby. Ten percent finder's fee for me, thank you very much. He takes care of the papers and all that, and some dry-womb couple in suburbia heaven thinks they're getting a foreign kid from some orphanage. But if it's local, he got less overheads, right? You with me?"

"Give me a name. I swear it won't come back on you."

"He won't give nothin' up, Rosie. There's too much cash at stake. One family loses out... he's finished in this game."

"Tug, if you don't give me a name, I'm going to throw everything at this. All the departments will get involved—child protection, smuggling, kidnapping. Maybe I'll even invite MI5 or six along, see if these bastards interest them. And we'll have press crawling all over too. I know you don't want that. They'll be all over your boys, and the—*bitches*—who make your money for you."

"You really wanna go down this road, Rosie?"

"Yeah. And don't you think for a moment I'm scared of losing my job if it means shutting these guys down. The brass are all ready to forgive all the messed-up shit I did with you and Dave, all because I nailed one paedo yesterday. Even PSD are backing off. I'm on the up, Tug, and like you said—those guys are bigger than you, so what's it to us if we squeeze you?"

"Fuck you, talking to me like this in my own place."

Caz came back in. "It's my place, actually."

"Fuck you."

"No, fuck you, Tug." Caz pulled her hair back to reveal a bruise down one side of her face. "You know what they did was wrong. You know those bastards need stopping. If Rosie can do it with no blow-back on you, what's the harm?"

Tug was on his feet, and both he and the rotty glared at Caz.

Martin said, "Let me be clear, Tug. All I want is this one guy. One name. If you don't give it up, that's when I have to go scorched-earth around here."

Without taking his eyes off Caz, he said, "You ain't gonna go sparkin' him up are ya? I know you're good with a shooter 'n all that."

"No," Martin said. "I won't be... *sparking* anyone up."

"Fine," Tug said. "Name's Hardcastle."

"First name?"

"Don't know." Tug still glared at Caz as she delivered his sandwich on a delicate white plate with a flowery design.

Caz, her hair once more draped around her face, said, "He came here more than once to talk with Edith. Drives a BMW. Reg is BABE MAN69. Like he's a stud, but it's really an inside joke."

Martin said, "Tug, don't hurt her."

Tug snapped his attention to Martin. "Time to go."

"Tug—"

"Time to go."

Tug patted the dog in a way that made it growl. Or maybe it was the tone in his voice. Either way, Martin could do nothing about what might or might not happen after he left.

So he did. Just like that.

And, rather than believe he may have brought more pain to a woman who wanted to help him, he called in for a PNC check on BABE MAN69.

Martin's Money

Martin's last encounter with Dave Essex ended awkwardly, and it was more the orgy photos that made him hesitate than their shared wrong-doing. But the hesitation was momentary. He placed the call and insisted they meet. Dave said Gordo had been asking about him again since the Long family arrest but seemed less antsy about the whole thing. It was Dave's turn to be hesitant when Martin told him where to meet.

Since coming out of hospital and vowing to solve his own stabbing, Martin had allowed himself to get sidetracked by the layers upon layers unravelling as he investigated Si Larson, and he hadn't even visited the bridge on which he got stabbed. Now he waited on the pavement, the side over which he was sure he must have fallen, his attention drawn to the four CCTV masts visible from where he stood, small black balls at the top of each pole boasting a 360-degree vantage, from here all the way up several roads into, and out of, the city centre.

The first looked down from across the street on the corner of a road that led to expensive bars and a former church, a busy roundabout at its base.

The second observed from the other side of the bridge, heading out of town, a view that took in a snaking series of routes toward the M1 motorway, the M621, and the ring road, plus the bridge itself.

A third kept watch about a quarter of a mile north, the other side of a railway line that covered the bus station and a trio of new high-rise apartments.

The fourth was a bit of a reach, all the way into the centre, at the heart of the bars and clubs, but had a clear line of sight which might have spotted something, but only if the operator was following someone specifically.

The range on these things, even back in Martin's Before period, was good enough to pick out a face a half-mile away—*if* it were aimed properly. But in a general sweep, the faces would blur. Without focusing on an individual, when a chance crossing of the lens occurred, those images were always poor and grainy.

"Martin," Dave said, arriving on foot as Martin had.

Martin pointed at the masts. "The guys investigating my stabbing said there was no CCTV evidence. That strike you as odd at all?"

Dave tracked in a circle, following Martin's finger. "Yeah. Odd, that. Probably pointing the wrong way."

"Why do you suppose that is? Even if they didn't film the actual event they should at least have footage of me walking here. There's no parking for hundreds of yards, and my car was at home. So I walked from Glendale station or caught a cab from somewhere else."

"Is that why you brought me here?"

"No, but I'll get to that. Come on, you said you were my only friend. After what we've done together…"

Dave shoved his hands in his pockets and looked out at the river. "We're all in the dark as much as you. We said at the time we'd find who did it and kill them. No one fucks with the OTT club like that. Even though you were drifting at the time, the drugs were responsible for that. But you were one of us."

"I was drifting? What do you mean?"

"Less focused on the cases, not doing your job. PSD were looking at you a lot more, but the rest of us had kept clean. We needed distance, so we all agreed to cool the, er, extra-curricular stuff. Me and you, we kept up our partnership, but I was covering for you. Stuff you wouldn't even tell me about. So that night…" He mimed a stabbing. "I had no idea where the hell you were."

"Since I got involved in the Si Larson case, even though I have zero connection to the kid, I know people he knew, it's all part of that same world. The sex, the drugs, everything surrounds Tug Jones. Could he have had anything to do with it? My stabbing?"

"You were valuable to him. We all were. We were on a break, but we'd go back once the heat died. If he sensed danger, he might have. But then why help you with the Si Larson business?"

Martin leaned on the stone wall. The swollen waters flowed a couple of feet higher than usual. He said, "Phone records, CCTV, vehicle logs, witnesses. All of them gone. Then I'm pushed to leave, retire. When I demand to stay there's a token investigation. Even my closest friend, my partner in crime, he doesn't have the first clue what happened, and the list of suspects is as long as my list of acquaintances. What's that all say to you, Dave?"

"Says you're unlikely find who did it."

"Take a bigger step back. Stop thinking like a reasonable copper for a moment. If you read those facts one by one in a report or newspaper, what does it point to?"

"I don't follow."

"Objectively. Come on. List, observe, conclude. One, a police officer is stabbed. Two, no witnesses, on *Christmas Eve*. Three, no CCTV footage of any aspect of that night, despite three—possibly four—masts in the vicinity. Four, nothing but a token gesture of an investigation. Five, the people in charge want the victim to leave things alone, offer a bribe to keep him compliant. What does it add up to?"

Dave joined him, looked into the deep river, flowing fast beneath them. He said, "Objectively, it sounds like a bastard of a cover-up."

They stayed like that for a time, the water in which Martin almost drowned drawing them deeper, holding their attention until neither could tell how long they lingered.

Martin said, "I need cash."

"How much?"

"All of it. I mean all of *mine*. Today."

Dave shook his head. "Gordo will kill you if you start spending that amount."

"I'm not buying a Ferrari, Dave."

"Even that amount of cash won't uncover whatever was done to you, Rosie."

"No, but it'll peel another layer back in my other cases."

"Cases?"

"Yeah," Martin said. "Edith's own disappearance might have less to do with Si than I thought."

A Guy

When Martin explained the money would be used to bribe a criminal and not in any traceable way, Dave acquiesced, and within half an hour Martin was driving with a boot full of cash to the address supplied by Clarence Hardcastle's PNC check. He pulled up in a wide country lane a hundred yards from the gated property, one of four spaced a couple of acres apart, red-brick new-builds with black, wrought-iron railings, all apart from Hardcastle's, which was a barn-conversion transformed into a structure more glass than barn. Martin used the zoom on a police-issue DSLR camera to give it the once-over.

Set against wide, flat farmland, the house glared in the sunlight, and the manicured lawn stretched out back right up to a ploughed field. Through the ten-foot windows, children played—three by one count, all below school age—and a smartly-dressed woman with a thin waist and heavy chest busied herself on a cream couch with headphones and an iPad.

After an hour or so, Martin's back ached and his buttocks needed shifting every few minutes to prevent them from numbing. When he was ready to stretch and make a circuit of the car, he made one more sweep of the house and a fat man appeared in a suit, carrying two of the kids down the stairs, one under each arm. The third clung to his back, drawing a grin from the fat man akin to a dog with a Frisbee.

Martin's phone pinged and Cupinder's name popped up with yet another text demanding an exact time for their morning meeting.

He checked the clock. Coming up to midday. This guy wasn't going anywhere, but Martin placed the phone back in his pocket without answering. He'd already met with Tug, got this name, but there was always a chance Tug could call this chap up and say a cop had been tipped off.

Dunno who, mate, just what I heard.

Martin left his car beside the hedgerow with enough room for a tractor or lorry to pass, and walked to the front gate and pressed intercom. His call was answered with the gruff "Hello" of someone not expecting company.

"Police," Martin said. "Please open the gate."

A pause, then the five-foot railings slid smoothly aside. Martin tramped over the gravel to the front door, noting the BMW in the drive with the reg BABE MAN69 next to a Range Rover larger than his first student bedsit. Registration: HONEY 69.

The door opened to the fat man in the suit, his long hair wet-looking and curly. "Yes? Is there a problem?"

"May I come in?"

The man said, "Is it my mum? Is she okay?"

"As far as I know, sir."

"Really? Just tell me now. Has she fallen?"

Martin regulated his speech into policeman-ese. "I know nothing about your mother, sir. If she'd been in an accident it would likely be uniform delivering the bad news. I'm CID." He showed his warrant card. "Missing persons. I believe you may have encountered someone we are looking for. Now. May I come in please?"

The man—Hardcastle—led Martin into a well-appointed kitchen, a huge centre island with pans hanging over. They sat at a breakfast bar on high stools and Hardcastle clasped his hands and frowned.

"So, Detective-Sergeant Money," he said. "What can I do to help?"

"Edith Long," Martin said.

"Nope. I don't know that name."

Martin showed the photo from her police file on his phone. "This is her."

Hardcastle's bottom lip popped out in the universal body language of innocence. Shook his head without taking his eyes off the photo. "Nope, still not ringing any bells."

"You might remember her from Rose Grove, where she gave birth before her baby was removed and she was left with some ointment." Modulate the language, passive tone and words—'baby *was* removed' not '*you* removed her baby'; 'she *was* left' not '*you* left her'. He added, "No one could've been sure if she'd live or die."

"Someone took her baby?" Hardcastle said. "How bloody awful. But I'm sorry I don't know anything about her."

Martin put his phone away. "What line of work are you in?"

"Heating." Hardcastle opened his wallet, presented Martin with a card: '*Hardcastle Heating*' embossed in sleek 80s-sci-fi writing, plus his contact details. "Been supplying industry for five years now. Heh. Paid for all this."

Two of the kids sounded like they were fighting in some back room. Probably their play room. Hardcastle watched Martin.

"Sir," Martin said. "We have received information that—"

"Who's 'we'?"

"We. The police."

"Oh, right." Hardcastle pushed away from the nook and dropped off his chair, and peeked around the corner into the living room where Martin had seen the small-waisted, heavy-breasted woman on the couch with the ear-buds in. Satisfied they had privacy, the fat man returned with a lean-back swagger. "Don't they usually send two of you?"

"Sir?"

"You should have a partner or something, shouldn't you?"

"Not always, sir."

The swagger extended his legs, produced a lop-sided smile. He was practically dancing. "You bastards always have two when you wanna ask questions. I wasn't always a legitimate businessman. I did my time as a chancer. I did my time fending off questions from the filth. Usually from two filth."

"Budget cuts," Martin said.

"Nah." Pointing now. Smug. "If you had anything on me, there'd be two of you. Cos that thing you're hinting at that I did with that hooker, took her baby or whatever, it's a big deal. No way would you interrogate alone."

"This isn't an interrogation, sir." At some point Martin had found his feet and backed halfway toward the door.

"I know it isn't."

"It's routine."

"You're lying."

A child wailed for daddy somewhere.

Martin said, "You know Edith Long. You were there. You took her baby and placed it with another family. Where's the baby, Mr Hardcastle? Here or abroad? Where's Edith?"

Hardcastle's face had frozen in that squinty-eyed smirk. Now he snorted and turned his back. "Get out."

Martin untucked his shirt and selected one of several packs of money from his waistband, then pulled his jacket over to hide the rest. He tossed it onto the counter top.

"That's ten grand," he said. "Tell me what I need to know, and I'll get you another forty. Right here, right now."

Hardcastle picked up the wad and riffled the notes. "What kind of copper are you?"

"One with enough cash to loosen your confidentiality bollocks."

"For a pissy fifty-K? Are you kidding me?"

The woman came in then, and came across the pair of men deep in conversation, one of them—her husband—fondling a handful of the type of cash that normal people don't possess. She still had her ear-buds in, a tinny pop tune warbling into the air. She took in both men before shrugging, opening the fridge, and taking a can of beer back to the living room.

"So," Martin said. "Edith, and the name of the new family."

"Five hundred," Hardcastle said. "You want me to grass, you make it worth my while."

"I can get you a hundred now, the rest later."

Hardcastle waved the ten-K at Martin. "Hundred gets you Edith. The other four, that's for me breaking my silence."

"You're a saint."

Martin unpacked his waist band while Hardcastle said, "You know, Detective Sergeant, there aren't many coppers who carry that sort of cash. Not many coppers willing to pay a business-owner for information. Even fewer who give a shit about some slag who got herself knocked up and don't know the daddy."

"Be quiet," Martin said, "unless you're dishing out info."

"That place she gave birth, what a shit hole. I've helped a lot of girls, but man, that baby is better away from her. Way, way better."

"Just the location," Martin said, then added, "Sir."

"I do these babies a favour. I'm like Santa Claus. I give them a better life. I give other couples a chance for happiness. You can't know what it's like for these people. I'm not a bad man. I'm a businessman. My business is happiness."

"I'm not sure how happy Edith Long is right now."

"One of the dropouts of the world. Can't save everyone. Especially some smack-head slag who'd turn the kid into another chav."

The hundred-grand stacked on the counter, Hardcastle ignored the child yelling for daddy, ignored a different child crying for mummy, and a third managed to scream at the others to shut their dirty mouth.

Hardcastle said, "She found me through Tug Jones, scummy dealer on the Bankwell—"

"I know him," Martin said. "He can't help. Try again."

Hardcastle scooped up the ten bricks of money. "Oh dear. That's all I got. See ya."

Martin waited for the laugh, the punchline to the joke, but none came. As Hardcastle took his grin and his money toward the hall, Martin was about to say something more, something like 'come on, you can do better than that' or give a chuckle and say, 'alright, you've had your fun,' but it would have no effect on a man like this. He was as focused as any smack-head, unwavering in his pursuit. Arrest a heroin addict when he's jonesing for a hit, and he will say anything to get away; he'll scream you're hurting him, threaten, bite, spit in your mouth. He will not give up. It's the sole thing that matters.

To Hardcastle, money was what mattered. He didn't even argue when Martin proposed the transaction. He would do as little as possible for the maximum reward. Even though Martin had lied about the rest of the cash, he was still filled with a rush, that same sense of unfairness that surged through him when DCS Black tried to retire him.

"Wait," Martin said. "Okay, so you can't tell me where Edith is. You know where the couple are?"

"Yeah, I do home delivery."

"Right. Well, I have the rest in my car."

"Let me stash this."

"Bring it. I have a good bag that'll fit the lot. Better than risking the kids finding it."

With the arguing kids drowned out by whatever process was whirring inside him, Hardcastle chose a carrier bag from a draw full of them and stuffed the money in there. Martin walked with him outside, over the gravel and to his car, where he popped the boot and opened the rucksack with the remaining hundred and fifty thousand.

Hardcastle said, "That ain't four hundred."

"No," Martin said, and punched him in the kidney.

The man arched his back and Martin hit him again—same place. Then he snatched the carrier bag of cash and replaced it in his rucksack, and while Hardcastle was still stunned, he grabbed the tyre iron and cracked it into the man's knee. As Hardcastle toppled to one side, Martin helped him into the boot and closed the lid.

Muddy

He didn't drive far, just a mile or so. The shouting and thumping rocked the car too much to risk anywhere metropolitan, anywhere an observant bobby might hit his lights and demand to see inside, so Martin pulled into a rutted field with a decrepit gate, killed the engine, and waded through the mud to remove Hardcastle from the boot. The usual scrote expletives and threats emanated forth, but Martin adopted the heavy-eyed 'bored' expression he'd seen so many times used by psychos and wannabe badass children, looking down upon the child-smuggling piece of crap as he lay cradling his knee on the soggy ground.

Now, as well as the tyre iron, Martin held a can of pepper spray, standard issue for constables, although detectives are allowed to carry it too. He said, "Where'd you deliver the baby?"

Hardcastle tried to sit up but his hands sunk into the mud. "Fuck you, I'm suing your fucking arse."

"Okay. Have it your way."

Martin's foot sunk into the mud too, as he stepped forward and brought the iron down on Hardcastle's other knee. A howl burst from him, and Martin paused to check all four corners of the field. Nothing. No one. He retreated to the gate to double-check the road held no walkers, and came back to Hardcastle.

"Give me names. An address. You don't know where Edith is? Fine, I'll take whatever piece of shit you sold her kid to."

Hardcastle moaned. He said, "It's not fair. It was a legitimate transaction. She got her cut."

"How much?"

"Ten K."

"Out of?"

His gaze trained on the mud. "Hundred grand." He looked back up at Martin. "But I got overheads! I got staff, I got a mortgage. What's she got, huh? What good is she to society? Look at me. Look at my family. All good people, man. We *contribute*."

Martin sprayed the bastard and his fingers tingled with excitement as it turned the man's eyes red even before his own mud-caked hands reached them. More howling. Laying there, in the dirt, sinking. Hardcastle would be pulling the muck out of his pockets for weeks. If he didn't chuck it away.

Martin said, "Names."

Hardcastle shook his head.

Martin dug his hands into the ground and flipped Hardcastle onto his face, hooked both arms behind his back, and cuffed them.

Years ago, he and Julie were burdened with several molehills in their garden, an animal tunnelling and kicking up the mounds. Martin wanted to dig the mole out and hit it with a spade, but Julie insisted on a 'humane' trap, which Martin bought at a garden centre. It took three tries, lifting the sod over the rodent's tunnels and placing the tube in the run armed with dog food, hoping for a bite. Martin discovered the culprit one morning lying in the tube, dead, its snout mangled and bloody. When Martin researched the product further, he learned that moles need to eat every four to five hours. If it entered the tube early evening and could not escape, it would have been driven mad with hunger and tried to batter its way out. Through either starvation or brain damage, Martin's nemesis had died quite horribly. And while he never told Julie the truth about the mole's death, there were many nights, even weeks later, where Martin did not sleep so well, thinking about the poor little creature.

But today, even as he ground Hardcastle's face into the sodden field with his knee, he knew tonight he would face no such troubles.

Ten seconds the first time, then let the man breathe.

Martin said, "A name."

No response, so back the face went, into the mud, and this time he held it there until Hardcastle started choking, and only then did he lift it up to allow the spitting and coughing.

"Levine," came the coughed word. "Levine, on Sparrow Road."

Hardcastle hung his head, lolling over his shirt collar, Martin holding him from behind.

Hardcastle said, "I don't remember the number. I swear."

"Okay," Martin said. "Now Edith."

"I told you, I don't know—"

Again the knee, again the back of the neck, again the impotent thrashing and mewling. When he yanked Hardcastle's face up again, this time he was coughing and sobbing both at once, a weird hacking, blubbering sound, punctuated with snot.

Once the coughing ended, he said, "I don't know! I swear. Jesus, you're better equipped to find her. Probably working some fuckin' charity!"

"Charity?" Martin said. "Shit."

"Please, leave me alone."

"Shit," Martin said again. "I've been so dumb."

He uncuffed Hardcastle and waded back toward his car.

"Hey," Hardcastle called, and when Martin turned to him he asked, "How about my money?"

"Yeah," Martin said. "Cos that's really happening."

And Martin left him there, sat on his arse in the wet filth.

Police Work

Edith associated herself with homeless charities before she gave birth, and she'd continued bringing clean needles and condoms to her old friends afterwards, so what the hell was Martin doing bribing and torturing an odious piece of shit in a field when good, old-fashioned legwork would reap the same information? To be frank, it was a strange sort of epiphany. He'd been so engrossed in this sub-human world of drugs and abuse and corruption that he'd already forgotten what proper police work was about. Okay, he now possessed the location of an illegally-purchased baby, but—again—that could have been achieved through other means.

His goal since waking up on New Year's Day was always two-fold:

1) Find who tried to kill him.
2) Get his life back on track.

His focus on the first part faded as the Si Larson case took on new dimensions, stalling due to more important issues, as the original investigation had done, stacking up questions to be answered later. The second part, though, slipped further away with each lie he told Cupinder, each bribe he took, each joint he smoked. Each and every time he looked the other way while scrotes and coppers broke the law.

No more.

All day, Martin mooched around homeless shelters, churches, even the local remand centre, and his good, solid police work paid off by seven in the evening. By now he'd switched off his phone and was considering buying a pay-as-you-go that no one at work could trace, but that was the action of someone with secrets, with things to hide. A bad person.

He located Edith serving meals at a shelter on the outskirts of Kirkstall, a suburb south-west of the city. Close enough to the Bankwell for her to help out from time-to-time, but not so near as to tempt her to visit socially, which was always the problem with drugs. It was like when Martin had grown aroused as his body remembered the orgy on Tug's iPad, and his extremities all pleaded with him for *just one more hit* of heroin, but he had an advantage not many addicts possess: he kicked it early. He also didn't have a direct memory of the lifestyle. The cold turkey was like the worst dose of man-flu ever inflicted upon a person, so, for him, that was the only hell of it. Real addicts, those who spend five or even ten years shooting up twice a day, they can be clean for two, three, four years, but one chance encounter with a buddy from that period, it can lead to *one more for old time's sake*, and within a month, they've lost their new job, their boyfriend or girlfriend has left them, and they're under threat of eviction. The worst part? They won't give a shit about it, as long as that sweet, sweet honey flows into their veins.

People. That's what Edith needed to be away from. She wasn't hiding from the police; she was hiding from the things that made her an addict. Her step-dad, the party lifestyle, the friends she simply couldn't let down. And now she worked here.

Clean brown hair, long and shiny.

A blue roll-neck sweater, smart jeans, and leather boots.

Tired eyes, but a genuine smile.

She ladled a couple of fists of mashed potato onto a middle-aged man's plate beside his sausages. The heavily-tattooed lady next to her operated the gravy-station.

Martin had made himself unkempt but he wasn't quite full-on

tramp. He stayed off to the side, where the other men—mostly men; two women—ate in silence. Some were streaked with a substance, black and unimaginably smelly, while others appeared quite clean, perhaps showered and wearing donated clothes, and more than a few wore tracksuits and hats with flaps and rotten trainers, their teeth more gaps than enamel. Young and old, maybe twenty in total.

Edith laughed with the clientele as she worked. People who used her name, and she replied using theirs. Over the next hour she hugged four of them as they said hi. She even admonished two of the smellier patrons for being off their heads and directed them to a corner where they could gather themselves before a feed. She continued until nine P.M.

Martin followed her on foot, but she did not react when she looked back over her shoulder and saw him a couple of hundred yards away. He slowed when she did that. Not markedly, but enough to make like he was not matching her pace-for-pace. When she arrived at a five-bedroomed house ten minutes from the church, she used her key without checking all around.

Martin popped into her eye line, two metres away, and she yelped in shock.

"Fuck," she said.

She tried to close the door, but Martin was faster. He pushed his way inside and held his hands up, palms out.

Open body language.

Non-threatening.

She made a fist, door key poking through two fingers.

He said, "It's okay. My name is Martin Money. I'm a detective insp— I'm a detective sergeant with the missing persons division of West Yorkshire Police. I need to talk to you about some things."

She dropped her bag behind her, kicked it away from Martin. He showed her his warrant card.

"I'm not here for trouble. I won't create any for you. I only need to—"

"Talk, yeah, you said."

"So, can I come in?"

"What do you think?" She held up the key.

He said, "I had your step-father arrested. Your sisters are safe."

Her fist loosened.

He said, "I know where your baby is, Edith. With your help I can put the bastards away, those people who took it. I'm sure you weren't in your right mind when you agreed to it."

Her jaw opened, gaped for a second. "Didn't have no choice. No choice."

"I know. It's difficult. But please, trust me. You don't have to do anything you don't want to—"

"I heard that before."

"I mean it."

"So, you're... really here to help me?"

"And maybe you can help me too. I'm looking for someone who might be in danger."

"How'd you get me step-dad?" The fist lowered but the key stuck out, her weight on her back foot.

Martin told her about the arrest, about her sister revealing all, touched on the physical evidence but not the science. Just bullet points. He promised to fill in the detail later.

She said, "Brittany was always braver than me. I thought they wouldn't believe me. Some slag who shagged whoever she fancied."

"We believe you. The courts will believe you."

"That what you need help with? I'm a witness?"

"Simon Larson has been reported missing. Si. You were friends."

She backed away slowly, collected her bag. The key moved to her fingers and she found a door marked "2", and unlocked it. Stepped inside, leaving the door open. Martin followed her into a bedsit that smelled of lemon detergent.

A fold out couch, still folded-out, bedding rumpled.

A TV/DVD player combo unit, switched off.

Kitchenette, virtually clear of clutter; just a draining board with a single breakfast bowl and a spoon and a Wonder Woman mug.

Old wallpaper, peeling in one corner.

Edith selected a second mug from a cupboard at head height, a Superman one, and turned Wonder Woman over. Flicked on the kettle. Dropped a teabag in each cup. Her fingers trembled when they let go.

"Thanks," he said.

"So how comes you're looking for Si?" she asked over the boiling kettle.

"His parents reported him missing in December. We made little progress, but we've had some new information, new witnesses."

"Yeah? Who?" She swept her hair to the side, over one shoulder.

"Well, you for starters. Now I've found you."

She folder her arms, jammed her hands under her armpits, like they were cold. "I'm called Edith Short now. Like it?"

The kettle clicked as it boiled.

She took her hands back and poured the water and mashed the bags.

She said, "I last saw him the same time as Callum and that lot. December. Heard he might be in Manchester."

Martin showed her his phone and was about to press record when she asked him not to. Not yet, anyway. He took out his notebook. "Old school it is, then." He scribbled the Manchester rumour. "Where did you hear this?"

"About."

"I promised I won't make trouble."

The soggy teabags dropped in a shiny bin and she opened the fridge for the milk. "I know what those promises mean." She poured then returned the milk to the fridge. "Fuck all."

"I will get you the support you need. I'll put the people in jail, the ones who took your baby. I'll help you get it back, if you want to."

"What sort of a cow do you think I am? I couldn't raise a baby myself, could I? It was the best option for us all."

"I'm sure you considered it fully, Edith. But tell me about how you got in touch with them." He needed to work the connection without involving Tug, needed her to speak loosely about Hardcastle, about the phone. "How far gone were you when you—"

"I don't wanna talk about that part of me life. I made a decision, and I regret it every fuckin' day, and every fuckin' day I see the people I work with, and I know it was the right decision too. If you can help me, fine, let's do it, but right now, it's not something I can talk about. Okay?"

"Tell me about Si then. Without giving me any names you're not comfortable with."

She smiled, curled her hair around one finger. Swept it to the other side. Dropped two spoons of sugar in the Superman cup and stirred. She handed it to Martin and said, "He was nice, a right gent. Wanted to take care of us, me and the baby. I don't know what happened to him."

"Why did he want to look after the baby?"

She slurped her drink. "None of the other potential dads was interested. Except one, of course, but as you know, he vanished too."

"As I know? What do you mean?"

"You know." She swept her hair back again, smile faltering over her cup.

He sipped the tea. Stalling. And yet…

And yet, as soon as the tea hit the back of his throat, he froze.

"Perfect," he said.

"Yeah," she said. "Kinda like me."

"I didn't tell you how I take my tea."

She frowned. She froze too. Turned. She said, "Oh my God. Please. I can't do this, not like this."

"Do what?" Martin said. "Talk to me."

Her back to him, her shoulders jerked up and down. A sob.

Martin said, "Edith, listen—"

"Fuck off. Just…"

She cried now, the tears audible. Her hand swept her hair again. Her long brown hair, up and to the side.

And a small tattoo visible behind her ear.

Martin placed his tea on the counter and looked more closely.

A robin.

The photos on Tug's iPad.

The orgy.

A blond girl bent over … his erect penis in her hand … her mouth around it… her hair to one side … a tattoo behind her left ear…

…*a tattoo of a robin.*

His knees literally buckled. He said, "Oh no."

Edith's tear-streaked face parted her hair. "What is it?"

"The robin." He fixed his eyes on hers. "You were there."

"Where?"

"The club. When I— when me and Dave."

"Yeah," she said. "Course you were. Why else would you be here?"

"No, Edith. I'm here as a police officer. I didn't know—"

"Didn't know what?"

"You," Martin said, running his hands through his own hair now. "I mean, I thought I didn't know you."

"You *forgot* me?"

"Yes, I did. But not like that. I don't mean—"

"All the things I did for you! All the sordid shit you made me do, *with* you, with *other girls*, other *guys*. I thought you *loved* me, Martin! You said you fucking *loved* me!"

Loved

Martin said, "Loved you…"

"Yeah, you cheating, two-timing bastard." Edith clunked her tea on the counter and smacked Martin with her fists. No key, thankfully. Started imitating him. "*I'll leave my wife, Edith, I promise. I love you Edith. Are you sure the baby's mine, Edith? We'll be a family, Edith. I love you so much.*"

Love.

Baby.

Family.

She said, "And I believed you! Every time you let me down, I believed you."

"The baby."

"I stopped using the pill, especially for you." She wasn't hitting him anymore.

Her hands cupped his face.

Clasped either side.

Eyes boring into his.

Spittle on her lips.

"Now you're here," she said. "And I thought you were here for me, that you'd come back. I loved you so fucking much—"

"You were seventeen."

"Eighteen now. We can leave. Take that cash, and go. Paris, New York, LA. Anywhere." Her firm breasts pressed against him. "Please remember what we had, babe. Please." She kissed him.

He grew hard straight away. His hands on her hips. His fingers found the smooth skin between her waist and her tee-shirt. A roll of pregnancy fat, no celebrity trainer to work it off in the intervening weeks, but still. So smooth. He let her kiss him deeper, with tongues.

He didn't initiate anything.

It wasn't wrong.

"No," he said, and pushed her gently away. "I can't be the father."

"There's no one else, Martin."

"Your step-dad."

"I were gone from there."

"Marco."

"He was inside when I came off the pill."

Martin blinked. "No, I did the maths. I—"

"I stopped fucking him when you told me to. Last time was in June. Then you told me to go along with whatever your mate Essex said. So I did. Me and Sonia. Told them he raped us, but... fuck, I couldn't. I know it made you mad, but—"

"But then I disappeared too."

"Yeah," she said. "Where'd you go? I knew there was a good reason. There had to be."

"I got hurt. It affected my memory. I'm so sorry."

"I knew you wouldn't abandon me."

It wasn't like it was with Julie. She had been reticent, exploring him, desperate for the man he once was to return, the man from The Before, but Edith, she'd fallen for the man he became. The man from the Dead Time.

Yet, the new him was a professional, a good man. He could not sleep with this girl. Couldn't lead her on. He would not take advantage of this broken, fragile thing.

She said, "We'll take our baby back. We'll be a family."

"My wife..."

"You were gonna leave her. You said so."

"After three months? Four?"

"No, of course not. You're a good person, Martin. You wouldn't jack your marriage in for some fling with a silly little girl. You *saved* me, Martin. As soon as you promised to leave her, I never touched another bloke. Except, y'know, for money. Or when you asked me to."

"How long?"

She said, "We were together over a year, Martin. Hell, a year and a half now." That smile melted into something so fluid. Her eyes so damp, so wide. "It was love, Martin. Just because I was barely seventeen, it didn't matter."

Christ. Still a schoolgirl. Seventeen.

She said, "You took my virginity, Martin."

"Me?"

"Well, I don't count that pervy fuck living with us. He broke me seal, but you, you were the first man who ever proper made love to me. You even bought me this tattoo. It was so romantic. You even told the guy we were *married*. I know I screwed around when I was high or whatever, but that baby you put in me... it got me clean. Got me sober. I ain't touched nothing since then. When I got better, after that fucker took her away... I used the money for the rent here, went to work. I'm good now. And with you..."

He moved her arms from around him. Held her hands tight in his. Spoke slowly. "I can't, Edith. You and I... we can't."

Tears streaked down her face.

He said, "I'm investigating the disappearance of Si Larson. I can help you get your life back on track, but I can't be a part of it."

She tried to pull away, but he wouldn't let her.

Firm, but gentle.

He said, "I need you to testify about the baby. I need you to tell me everything about Si, about your relationship with him. I need to know where he is."

"You should have died."

"What did you say?"

"I wish you'd *died* in your accident."

"It wasn't an accident."

"Whatever," she said. "You *promised* to come back for me. Even before the accident, you *said* you'd come back."

"Before the accident? Come back? Where did I go?"

"How would I know? You never said nothing about that stuff. I knew something weren't right though. Don't you remember *anything*? Couple of weeks before Christmas?"

He shook his head.

"You was acting all weird, told me to hide until it was all over."

"Until what was all over?"

"I don't *know*. You wouldn't fuckin' *tell* me. So I went to the only friends I had, the druggies I was trying to get away from. Si promised to help, but his boyfriend didn't want no part of it."

"Callum."

"Yeah, shaggy haired twat. So Si left him, made out like he was fucking me, like he'd switched sides, but he weren't. Hid the baby until he went and fucked off as well."

"Why did he go?"

"Don't know that either! Heard him arguing with Callum and that Dev divvy, and some other bloke. They all wanted rid of me, but Si said he'd get me protection. Then that fat bastard showed up. Si went missing a bit later, and I couldn't get hold of you. Stuck on your secret mission or something."

"What were you hiding from?"

"I DON'T KNOW!" She pulled away, knocking over her tea. She hissed at that, and grabbed a cloth and dabbed at the mess. "You told me to hide where the cops wouldn't find me. Until you finished something, some big thing you had at work. Then you'd take me away and we'd be together. As a family."

He grabbed a tea towel and helped wipe up the spill.

Coming back up fully...

He said, "When you talk to the police, you can't mention that the baby is mine, okay?"

"Fuck you."

"I'll give you money. A lot of it."

"Do I look like I need your money? I got me own place. I got a job. I don't just serve up food to smack heads. I'm a fundraiser. Two months, I'll be in a nice one bedroom flat. I'm earning now. Less than two months after having your baby, I got a job and a life, and I'm a good fuckin' person. You left me with *nothin'*, and I started again. With nothing. I'm a good person and I'm good at me job and I don't fucking need you anymore."

"Edith—"

"I said I don't need you anymore. If you don't want me, and don't want our baby, that's fine. I made up me mind ages ago. I'm okay like this. I like me like this. It's the happiest I've ever been, and that includes when I was with you."

Martin reached for her. "Edith—"

She pulled away. "Go, Martin." She threw both towels in the sink and turned her back on him, and wept. "Just go."

The robin on the back of her neck, like Sonia's bumblebee, forced Martin to look at himself sideways yet again. And at Edith. Virtually still a child, certainly a vulnerable young woman, a girl with perfect breasts and a figure to match, even so soon after childbirth. Thin pale hands, full lips. He brushed her smooth arm.

She tensed.

He stroked his fingers up her arm, to her shoulders and then her back. His erection pressed against his trousers and his breathing deepened.

She said, "Martin..."

He said, "I'm sorry."

He rushed for the door, the touch of her still filling his fingers, some old instinctive memory filling his nose and mouth with the taste of her. He fumbled the Yale lock open, listening to the girl crying behind him, but he didn't look back. If he did, he would never leave this bedsit.

He ran out into the street, gasping for fresh air. Gasping for time. Time to think this through. To make sense of what he'd learned. To make sense of himself.

TRYING HARD

Sorting Out

"Thanks, mate," Martin said as he lifted a pint of four-quid lager from a beer mat featuring a picture of a stoned beaver.

"No problem." Dave Essex raised his own glass in toast. "Glad you called. *Mate*."

A couple of hours earlier, when his cold shower failed to oust Edith from his fantasy world, Martin masturbated furiously and came in seconds, repeating over and over what a complete cunting bastard he was for the things he did to that girl. Then he called Dave. He picked this place, Mojo's, for its dark nooks, good independent ale, and its loud music. Both men shouted to hold a basic conversation, and both men wore suits that cost under two hundred quid apiece, and looked it. Others here wore leather. They wore jeans and tight tee-shirts over firm bodies, men and women, toned as magazine models. Some wore loose floaty garments to hide their flab but still exuded fabulousness. Everyone was under thirty. Except these two men in a booth near the fire exit.

Martin said, "I need you to be honest."

"Always."

"Those girls from Tug's club. They were under eighteen."

"I don't know," Dave said to his beer. "We didn't ask. It was a heavy night."

"Listen, something's happened. Something pretty big."

"Okay. I swear,. I won't tell anyone, not even Gordo."

"I... I got one of them pregnant. One of the girls. Edith. Edith Long."

Now Dave suddenly found the green fire exit sign more interesting than his beer. "Yeah," he said. "You were never sure whose genes were growing inside her."

"So you *knew*?" Martin said, fist clenching automatically. "You *fucking* bastard. You could've told me the night Tug gave me her name. Could've *warned* me."

"Could have. Might have been dangerous in your current frame of mind."

"When Tug mentioned her I was asking in connection with my current case. Why didn't you say something?"

"To be honest..." Dave shrugged. "I figured he was fucking with you. Winding you up. I didn't really think she was anything to do with your misper. You'd learn about her and he'd laugh his tits off. Oh, and he probably wants her back working for him. You find her, he gets his piece of crumpet back."

"Cunts."

"No, Rosie. We're your *friends*. I didn't have a clue she was connected to Si Larson for real. That's nuts."

Nuts. It was *insane*. The connections, the coincidences, the undeniable truths.

Martin said, "Did I like her?"

Dave laughed. Drank some more. Gulped it, really. "Yeah. You were in love. Like any middle-aged guy with a substance abuse problem and a young shag-pony."

"Think I wasn't serious?"

"With a *child*? Fuck, Martin, she was a honey. Of legal age but still a child. You'd say anything to keep on her good side, and she was gullible enough to believe it. All that shit you had happening with Julie, this girl, she was an outlet. For all your frustration. All your problems. She was a release valve. Nothing more."

And yet she'd seemed so certain. So sure of Martin's intentions. And when he touched her, she fired pure electricity into him.

He said, "She still knew Si. *The kid I'm investigating.* Now. Months later. How can that be?"

Dave scanned the room. A hard-bodied woman in a white tee-shirt and a sleeve of flower tattoos stared back at him until he returned to his beer. His own fist formed tightly beside his glass.

"Men like us," he said. "Past our peak sexually, looks-wise, we don't often get opportunities like we had in that room. We go home to our average wives and girlfriends, and eat our average food, bought with our average salaries. We go on average dates, and we get average divorces, and hook up with someone five years younger instead of fifteen or twenty. Then, you know what happens? We start the average bullshit all over again. What are we supposed to do when we get the chance to be more than average?"

A group of four girls with cocktails muscled through the main crowd and gathered together, late teens at the most, and tried each other's drinks and expressed regret over their own.

Dave said, "We take that chance, Martin. You and I. And the others. Our friends. We grabbed the chance to earn more, to *be* more. To fuck beautiful women, to get *blow-jobs* again, like when we were young. We tried the drugs we avoided all our average lives because we both learned to *just say no,* and we found out those lives were a *lie.* Because you know what? Drugs *are* cool after all. Drugs are *fun.* They give us money, girls, and power."

"Power," Martin said.

"Yes, *power.*" Dave's eyes bulged at the word. "We could march into anywhere, any hole in the city, and put any dealer we wanted in prison. Anyone. We carved out a place for ourselves, a place that was surrounded by our average fucking lives, but there, in the eye of the average storm, we were *special.*"

"So special we didn't have to follow the rules anymore."

"Spot on, Rosie. That money you spent today, I hope it went on somethin' worthwhile."

The money.

The money still in Martin's car boot.

They finished their drinks in the din that surrounded them, that pounded through them. Dave got another round in, this time with tequila on the side. Martin downed his with the salt and lime provided. Dave followed suit, shook his head and gave a, "Whoa, that's good."

Martin said, "Si goes missing on the nineteenth of December. I last saw Edith earlier that month. She made friends with Si, shacks up with him. I want her hidden for some reason. Then I get stabbed shortly after Si goes missing. I have to declare a possible conflict to DI Rowe."

"What conflict?" Dave said. "That you knew a girl who knew a smack-head poof who went missing?"

"I might have information about it. I might even be implicated."

"Don't be soft." Dave had a habit of starting his drinks quickly, then slowing down, and this was no exception. He was nearly halfway done. "You might have encountered him in passing, but—"

"What if it has something to do with my stabbing? What if by some huge cosmic coincidence, all this relates back to the same thing? What if I was trying to protect Edith? For real, I mean. Things were bad at home, so I was going to live with her, start a family."

Dave laughed.

Martin said, "For a second, assume it's true."

"It can't be."

"Why?"

"Work out the timeline, Martin. List, observe, conclude. Right?"

"Okay," Martin said. "The list."

"In order."

"I meet Edith somehow."

"An arrest, summer 2013. Some weed den we took down."

"Okay. I start seeing her."

"Fucking her," Dave said. "You start *fucking* her. And for the record, Rosie, *she* seduces *you*. We both know she wants a copper inside her so she can get away next time she's arrested."

And she did. A lot of arrests. Few convictions. A couple of community sentences that she probably never completed due to her having a copper willing and able to screw the system as well as her.

Martin said, "I tell her I love her, that I'll leave my wife. My marriage is deteriorating anyway. Why?"

"Not sure," Dave said. "We were both into the coke and weed, started saving a bit of that money, if you know what I mean."

"As my marriage gets worse, so do I. Or the other way round. Julie wants nothing to do with me, but I want to keep her, even though I have Edith."

"Who's shagging every other bloke in her life as well. So it's not exactly true love."

"Still, I get her to leave home, take her away from the stepfather. I stop her sleeping with her pimp somehow."

Dave's grin flashed, a comedian winding up a punchline. "You wanna know how?"

"I want to know," Martin said.

"You hurt him. We hurt him."

"We?"

"Us, your friends. Me, Gordo. The OTT club. Pepper spray, batons, the works. Did over his goons, his pussy wagon. Fucked him up pretty good. Told him he could keep on running his girls as long as we felt he was useful, so he handed us names from a neighbouring territory, and you, Rosie, all casual like, you threw it in at the end he had to stop fucking Edith and Sonia. They worked the park when they wanted, but they were free of him. We made eight arrests, Tug expanded a bit more, and you got that young pussy all to yourself."

Martin's stomach growled so he poured more beer into it. "And when Tug wanted to move into prostitution…"

"We facilitated it."

The chubby cocktail girls had moved on without Martin noticing, replaced by young men and women in nice shirts and trousers, dresses and high heels; a couples night.

Dave said, "Timeline, come on."

"I got her to myself just as things were at their worst. I had the PSD investigation, the assault on Julie, and I was desk-bound. When we put Marco away, me and you, we celebrated."

"The whole club celebrated. Danni and Nick get horny when they're drunk so they go off to fuck at her place, as usual. Gordo likes his ladies plus-sized and private, so after a call to his usual agency he's off to a suite at the Hilton. But Tug, man. He's a great host. Coke and champagne. Brandy and vodka. All the girls we can handle. Your Edith, she's happy for you, all the money you—"

"So I can take her away from all this," Martin said.

Dave tapped his nose. "Spot on again."

"She joins us. Takes part in the… the…"

"Orgy, Rosie. You can say it."

"She takes part, but doesn't realise it's being filmed. Does she know Si by now?"

"Don't know. Doesn't matter." Dave took short sips now. Two in quick succession. "What matters is, she was part of it, part of your past. I tried to hide her from you now because you get all irrational about her. This love bollocks. Even in the orgy you wouldn't let anyone else touch her, not even me. Okay for other people, girls, to suck you off and fuck you, but not Edith. You were obsessed, Rosie. Obsessed with, I dunno, saving her or something."

"So when Julie left me—"

"You insisted she was yours. Only yours."

The pint and a half sat in Martin's stomach, the absence of food making it swill around. The tequila still burned his throat. He said, "I was a monster."

"You were a bit fucked up, Rosie, but you were loyal. Your big positive. Loyalty. To us, to the project, even Edith in a weird way."

"The project," Martin said. "Tug."

"Focusing the trade. Controlling the violence. A bit of money on the side as compensation for our *risk*. Yeah. The project."

There were other things to ask, but the words tasted bitter, and too large. They lodged fast in his mouth. "Dave," he said, struggling. His stomach rumbled. A sharp digging, like a trapped nerve, bit into the back of his neck. One hand actually shook. He said, "Did we ever... go undercover? I mean like a major op. Something that set me off... something that made me into... *him?*"

Dave gulped back the remnants of his drink. "I don't know what you mean. I liked *him*. We all did. *Him* was a lot more fun and a lot more fucking grateful than *you*." He positioned himself to leave the booth. "No, Rosie. The most undercover work we did was posing as buyers so we could nail Tug's competition. There was no undercover op. You became *him* all by yourself. Time you faced that."

When he left for good, Martin pushed the pint away. He swayed out into the night, his back aching, his legs tired, in need of a massage, in need of the stretches Illyana showed him. In need of rest. At home, he did not stretch, did not work. He undressed, fell into his bed, and slept.

Tomorrow would be the most difficult conversation of his life.

Cupinder Again

List, observe, conclude.

It had rarely, if ever let Martin down. Crosswords or murder or drugs deals. It all worked. So the next day, when Cupinder dismissed his theory, it took a physical effort to keep from sweeping the papers off her desk and scratching out this particular list in the varnish with the letter opener. He hadn't even bothered with a suit, instead turning up in a burgundy pullover and jeans and trainers. If what he said here today was true, he'd be on suspension later. If what he alleged was untrue, he'd definitely be on suspension later. If no one believed him, he'd quit.

"Give it to me again," she said.

"For the last time. Fine." He stepped back from the brink of destroying her desk and ticked off his list on his fingers. "I start out as a good copper, partnered with an even better one in Helen."

Cupinder said, "Okay."

"She and I, we argue about something. I don't know what, and she won't go into detail. She said it's personal, to do with how I treated Julie. But I checked. Helen and I split before Julie reported me. Before she and Helen talked. It was something else."

Cupinder mimicked his thumb indicating #1. "So, you split with your partner."

"Under circumstances she won't talk about."

"Okay."

"Then, I get involved with this OTT club. Dave Essex, Gordo, that lot. They come on board the Drugs and Offender Management

Unit. DOMU? Great results wherever they've been and Detective Chief Superintendent Black is glad to have them. Looking at the paperwork, the stats, we get results straight away. The SLIT initiative is shelved and we're out there making arrests left, right and centre."

"Going well." She popped up her first finger. #2.

"Now, though, I'm personally going downhill. I'm horrible to Julie, and Helen gets involved. I fight with her husband, my best friend. I have an affair with a girl... a *person* I've arrested and got to know socially. I'm friends with this club who take bribes and beat on suspects."

"Whilst still getting positive results."

"Yes, but how? How do we get those results? If Dave is lying to me, and I think he is, I could have been deep cover."

"Not that deep," Cupinder said. "You were around the station plenty. I saw you."

"I still have to report in. I'd have to, due to the insurance, wouldn't I?"

"Sure. Red tape, admin, insurance."

He nodded, happy she was taking it in. "Then it gets really bad. I'm in so deep, I've almost gone native. The operation is all-but over. One more piece to fit. Tug Jones."

"They'd have pulled you out."

"Not if I was close to ending the drugs trade on the Bankwell. Not if I was close to the people supplying Tug. Because that's how the drugs chain works. Growers sell to smugglers, smugglers sell to transport, transport sell to street pushers. Then the people above them. If we localise the supply, arrow it into one single point, we narrow the options. We focus the investigation."

She raised a third finger. "The benefit of having you in that deep, posing as a dirty copper, it reaps big rewards."

"Exactly. Maybe me and Dave were pretending to be bent to get close to Tug. Or maybe that was the plan from DCS Black all along—isolate the supply by banging up all but one dealer."

"Then where's the evidence for this?"

"I don't know. It's all been destroyed. Removed from the servers."

He paused for breath. Sipped from the water he'd brought with him.

She said, "They would never manage it. Trace the supply back to the transport group. It's not enough benefit to risk this."

"But what if the transport guys lead us to the smugglers? We can't stop them growing it, but we can block their entry points, take their couriers down through European arrest warrants. It's a huge coup if we pull it off."

She shook her head. "They still have no reason to cover this up. They'd have brought you back up if they saw you were deteriorating like that."

"But the note from Julie."

She raised #4. "A vague statement that could mean anything. She's not a police officer."

"The other statement, too, from my CI."

"The one you were sleeping with."

Martin waved that away. "She said I was working on something serious and I couldn't be contacted."

She raised #5. "But no specifics about what. Martin, there's no motive here."

He said, "Money, sex, and power."

She lowered her hand now. Frowned. "Martin, do you have more to tell me?"

Of course he did. So much. She would not accept his theory based on the snippets of circumstantial evidence alone.

He said, "There's more, sure. But it all points to me being a bad person. Worse than I feared. It's full-on corruption, Cupinder."

"Just tell me."

This was always the plan. Get her on the hook, chip away at her doubt, then confess all. And now he talked for a long time. Cupinder granted him his wish and said nothing until he was finished. The blinds were open and the office was full. About halfway through his summary of his first week back at work, she tightened her lips and sat up markedly straighter. But he continued to the end, omitting nothing, including the skunk-smoking, including the harassment of the smack-heads in Rose Grove, including Julie's pregnancy, including him beating the guy in the field, and including the news that he had more than likely fathered a baby with a seventeen-year-old, drug-addicted abuse victim. And a whole lot more. When he finished, Cupinder stood up behind her desk.

She said, "I should suspend you."

"I know."

"I need to make a statement to PSD."

He said, "I will come clean, but I think I'm close here. Whoever stabbed me was working either for Tug Jones or the person above him in the drugs chain, or one of the OTT club did it. Probably under Tug's orders, but still. Si Larson was friends with Edith, who was a good earner for Tug, seriously hot stuff, so if Si was going to help her escape the life, that gives Tug a motive to get rid of Si. Or Callum gets rid of him out of jealousy, or the fat man Hardcastle does him. Whoever did it, there's motivation to kill him, and me, all relating to Edith."

"Your girlfriend, Martin."

"Yes."

"Which gives you motive too."

"No. Not really. She wouldn't have left me."

"Oh?" She sat slowly. Adjusted her chair. "Not too big-headed."

"So come on, all that. No wonder they wouldn't pull me out. I had so much info, so many contacts. They'd keep me there until I got to the bigwigs, and then wash me out."

"Martin," she said. "I have to urge you to *stop*. The risk-reward situation is ridiculous. And the theory you've concocted, it's like the moon landings. Too many people would have to be involved in this cover up, and there is no way for every person in that chain to keep the secret."

Martin had never been one to accept wild or complex conclusions simply because they sort-of fit. Human beings crave patterns, they need logic, even if they have to take illogical steps to get there. The simple answer to the World Trade Centre towers falling on 9/11 is that a bunch of fanatical Muslim terrorists attacked their sworn enemy in the most effective way they could imagine; the wild answer, but one that fits the human need for order, is that the American government was searching for an excuse to invade Iraq so *allowed* the attack to occur or even conspired with the perpetrators, an idea that soothes the unpalatable notion that America is vulnerable. That it's an inside job means their security didn't fail; the conspiracy theorists are more comfortable with the notion of corruption than of vulnerability.

The trouble is, in Martin's case, the simplest explanation is that he was tempted by a lifestyle that bestowed upon him plentiful sex and money and power, and ultimately destroyed him. The complex one made it *not-his-fault*, and this is the version he clung on to, even in the face of its legion questions.

He asked suddenly, "Who assigned me to Si Larson?"

Cupinder's reaction was odd: a comic-like double-take that would have been more at home in a Bugs Bunny cartoon than a police station. "What?" Another frown, this time with an added lip-curl, a scrote's 'sarcastic' face when saying, *Yeah? Prove it;* a guilty husband, accused of cheating, insisting, *Your friend was mistaken, she didn't see me. Of course it wasn't me.*

That was Cupinder's lip-curl. She said, "That's ridiculous."

"It isn't," Martin said. "Where did the order originate? Even with your clout and workload here, you're a DI, not even a DCI. You'd need Black's sign-off, and he was so desperate to get rid of me he was prepared to let me sue the Force."

"Martin, you can't think I'd be a part of something like that." The lip-curl faded into eyes hitting the floor.

"I don't know how deep, but you're ambitious. You'd go to bat for me, but you'd accept whatever conditions they set. You'd take an order like that, even if you didn't know the background."

She paced, counting on her fingers. Mouth working silently.

Martin said, "Come on, Cupinder, think. If someone ordered you to put me on Si Larson, and now I've uncovered all these amazing coincidences, all linking *me* to someone who knew Si. Dev Carlisle, I arrested him months ago, and he ends up in a smack-den with Si. Tug Jones controls the territory where Si sold himself, he controls the park where the Shack is located. The Shack, where I was bagnabbed by the OTT club. Then there's the club itself, deeply involved with Tug, along with myself. Edith Long, I get pointed to her by Tug himself, and she turns out to be a massive part of my life too—the biggest, really—and Dave Essex hid her from me. Finally, it just so happens that she, *the girl having my child*, she and Si were best mates? A couple for all intents and purposes. Platonic, but still."

Martin watched Cupinder's reaction: motionless, hands placed together, a casual 'honest' gesture betrayed by her stiff posture.

He said, "And go wider. My social life revolved around Tug's narcotics, Tug's strippers and hookers, that district he pretty much owned—the Bankwell itself and his expansion into Lille Park in the city centre. Go stand in the Shack and you can literally *see* the bridge I got stabbed on. This whole thing circles back round on itself. It starts with me getting in deep with a corrupt police unit, and it ends with a corrupt police unit, and their criminal friends, pushing me in the direction they want me to go."

Cupinder nodded. "Back into the life."

"Back to Edith. Back to the drugs. Back to the bribes and corruption." Martin stood stock-still with her in the middle of the office, the walls a long way away, the office full of coppers another world beyond.

He said, "Cupinder, I'm being manipulated into becoming the man from my Dead Time again. They can't afford to allow the Martin Money from The Before to come back. They need me corrupted. They need me out of control. So whoever killed me before can do so again."

"You think whoever tried to kill you also did away with Si Larson?"

"No," Martin said. "I think the person who tried to kill me was given a damn good reason to kill me. I think they threatened that person's best friend, the thing he cared more about than anything else. I think I'm being pushed toward that person, in the hope I'll find him and hurt him. Or if I'm on the drugs again, I might even kill him. At the very least they'll have an excuse to lock me up."

Cupinder and Martin had barely moved. A sideways glance to the window would have found almost the whole MisPer team with their pens down, watching the office, watching the body language shift and shimmy, from aggression to incredulity, to calmness personified.

Cupinder said, "So this all means—"

"Yep," Martin said. "I think, because he thought I would hurt Edith... I think Si Larson was the one who stabbed me."

Red Tape

For Martin, undercover ops had rarely imposed upon his career path, and Cupinder even less. His first had been as a uniformed bobby, posing as a john in a vice sting. In an area renowned for prostitution, he would pull up in his car, and wait for some lady to come and proposition him. His job was to appear nervous and inexperienced, which wasn't difficult on either count. Not at first anyway. Each take-down was smoother than the one before, and soon Martin's skittish eyes and lip-biting became acting, and on the sixth prospective arrest of the night, after the young woman with the fur boa and skirt that barely covered her underwear listed her menu and prices, a moment of clarity descended upon him. He woke up suddenly, stirred from the mundane dream of a carefully rehearsed script, and asked the young woman what he'd have to do to book her and a couple of friends for a euphemistic 'party'. She directed him to a skinny Asian man with quaffed hair and a basketball jersey, smoking Camel cigarettes in a Ford Focus a couple of hundred yards down the road. In turn, that man made a call and within fifteen minutes, another Asian lad in a basketball t-shirt arrived in a BMW. The new arrival offered him four women who'd 'do anything' for up to four hours, plus an ounce of coke—if he was into that sort of thing—all for the bargain basement price of a grand. The team descended on the two Asian men, plus the original woman with the sex-menu, and Martin was disciplined by his boss.

They disciplined him because he fucked with the insurance guys.

In those days, individual West Yorkshire Police units sorted their own insurance, going to a central accounting department who required multiple forms completing whenever an operation of this type kicked off, and there were always specific conditions and parameters attached. In the case of Martin's inaugural undercover experience his key parameter was to remain in the car, drive the illegal sex-worker a couple of streets away, where the arrest would be made. He was only allowed out of the car if remaining inside placed safety at risk. Another condition was the specificity that the op was to root out those women overtly advertising sexual services in exchange for money, contrary to section blah blah blah, etc. Because Martin then went after a bigger fish, had he been hurt or worse, he would have invalidated the insurance, and probably raised the West Yorkshire Police's premium the following year. In the end, he received nothing more than a letter of reprimand that disappeared from his record after twelve months, and a big, fat, unofficial pat on the back from Detective Chief Superintendent Daniel Black.

Since then, a number of government reforms hit, including more and more subcontracting of police services to private sector firms. Now, DCS Black's forays into insuring officers for 'special operations outside of their substantive remit' (their phrase) was completed using an underwriter called Safe People Insurance Inc, a sub-division of one of the bigger corporations, but run separately to the riskier arm to serve as a financial firewall.

"So what's your point?" Cupinder asked after Martin explained all this.

Martin said, "That they can delete all manner of information from the police servers..."

"But not those," Wadaya said, "of a third party vendor."

Cupinder had invited Wadaya in at Martin's request. Of all the people Martin had encountered since waking up, Wadaya was the one who had presented the least bullshit, who had never tried to hide anything from him, and who had shown a sharpness of mind, and a willingness to look at things afresh. He was now privy to Martin's theory about him being undercover, but was spared the gory details of his sexual and narcotic exploits.

"Right," Martin said. "But how do we access the records?"

Intakes of breath all round.

Wadaya said, "We make a claim."

Simple explanations have layers. Examine them deeply enough and you'll find a level of complexity that belies its outward shell. Martin once read a book that claimed Osama bin Laden didn't truly see America as a direct enemy until he grew outraged at the Saudi royal family. Bin Laden was already an extremist, a bigot and misogynist, part of the interior's secret police who brutally enforced the religious leaders' bastardisation of the Koran, and he performed his duty because he believed wholeheartedly in this violent and oppressive interpretation. So when he observed the royals—Muslims leading a Muslim nation—fornicating with whores, drinking, and basically behaving in a way contrary to beliefs as rock-solid as his need for oxygen, he yearned for a way to overthrow them. Discovering they were propped up by America, that country quickly became his enemy. There were far more details in the book, far more complexities that took in him fighting Russia in Afghanistan, training with the CIA, and his repeated failed attempts to attack America before 9/11. But it essentially boiled down to a fanatic trying to defeat an enemy by destroying that enemy's backers. Like taking down a building by blowing up the foundations.

So 9/11 wasn't simply perpetrated by terrorists who 'hate freedom' or 'fanatics threatened by democracy' or whatever sound bites get trotted out. The road to bin Laden's hatred—and therefore his followers' hatred—was long, and complex. A simple explanation with a winding series of incidents, culminating in one vile act of mass murder.

On the flip-side, a convoluted theory, such as the one Martin had been clinging to with ever-increasing desperation, could be undone with one simple form. An email reply with the cheery note to 'Please complete the attached in full and return quoting reference..." Also attached was the .doc claim form, and a .pdf attachment outlining the conditions and parameters of a 'level 3' assignment, commenced in June 2013, concluded 31st December 2014.

The day Martin woke up from his Dead Time.

Helen Again

It was as if Detective Sergeant Helen Cartwright intentionally sat in the sunlight so it reflected off her scars. She stared at the car park from the DI office with the missing sign, while Cupinder spoke to Derek Laughlin and Martin tried not to look too smug. Omitting anything Martin learned this week that PSD could use to start a case against him, Cupinder outlined the fact that Martin was insured for an undercover assignment, but no record of that assignment existed on the West Yorkshire Police servers. Laughlin listened, made notes. Checked the printed level 3 document.

"No details on here," he said.

"No," Martin said. "It's a confidentiality thing. We wouldn't give them specifics on the op, but they have different levels of insurance depending on the risk. The highest is level five, which puts people into organisations over several years. Terror groups, the mob, that sort of thing. Level one is like my old vice stings. Level three is usually posing as drugs buys in areas that the police control and monitor. So I should have been under full surveillance."

Laughlin swiped his hand over his face. "But you weren't under full surveillance."

Cupinder added, "The police files have been wiped, so it came from a high level. You have to open a file on Daniel Black and his DCI in DOMU. They'd have knowledge of Detective Sergeant Money's activities, and would have approved the op. We need to root out exactly who orchestrated the cover up."

Helen didn't avert her gaze from the view outside. The sun, the cars, the lawn being mowed.

Laughlin said, "We'll need to look into this some more. But you know, DS Money, that Detective Chief Superintendent Black, he's had your corner this week. He strongly suggested we drop the inquiry into your unauthorised use of a laptop."

"One of ours?" Cupinder said.

Martin swallowed the sarcastic comment that almost jumped out of his mouth. He said, "I've done the course."

"And," Laughlin added, "we don't believe we can proceed with those allegations from before your assault on Christmas Eve."

"That makes sense," Martin said, "I'd expect Black to be in my corner. The closer I get to Si, either he gets to expose more of the things I did, stuff PSD don't know about, or I put away the person who stabbed me and we all carry on as before."

Helen let out a sigh and glanced briefly at the other three.

Cupinder asked, "Is something you want to add, DS Cartwright?"

"No," Helen said. "Carry on."

Cupinder said, "You don't have to be a part of this."

"She's right," Martin said. "But I wanted you here. I wanted you to be a part of this. You more than anyone."

"Why?" Helen asked.

"Because I hurt you more than most. Only Julie came off worse, and if this pans out... I might even repair things with her."

When she faced him, the eye on the scarred side of her face shed a tear. "Let's run this down, then. You think you and I argued over our respective career paths. Yes, you're right, but it's not quite that simple. You didn't want me joining PSD. I don't know about any top secret undercover DOMU assignment. That's on you. But let's say this happened, that Daniel Black set you on this path, that Dave Essex and Gordo and the other On The Takers pushed you into drugs and assault and God knows what else. Let's say that's true." She pointed at her face. "*This* is still on you." Pointed at him. "What you did to Julie, *that's* on you. No matter how daft she is thinking you've changed, that... that *animal* is still inside you. How long until it comes out again, Martin? How long til you disfigure some stripper who doesn't want to go home with you, or if some other woman you're seeing, if it's Julie or whoever, what if they piss you off and you end up punching them or kicking them so hard they—"

"DS Cartright," said Laughlin. "It's probably best if you take a breather. We can review how much participation you really want shortly. Everyone happy with a comfort break?"

Martin and Cupinder nodded agreement, while Helen wiped her eyes and returned to staring at the car park.

As they were leaving and Laughlin issued directions to the coffee machine on this level, Helen said, "Martin."

Martin turned to her.

Out of earshot of the others, she said, "The roof."

He made his excuses to Cupinder and, for the second time that week, made his way to the top floor and out into the fresh air. At least this time it was voluntary. He was alone less than two minutes before Helen joined him.

She lit a fag. "You'll have a tough time proving he was responsible."

"It'll be a major thing," Martin said. "You should come in on it. Regardless of your hatred of me. Senior officer caught covering up the mental torture of a subordinate. It's pretty interesting. And career-wise? Phew."

"Is this all you have? The insurance document?"

"It's all *we* have, Cupinder and I. But I'm doing this right, Helen. I need PSD on side if we're going to get him. You have the authority to investigate the insurance company's back-records, see who signed off on it. I don't have that. No one I can trust has that. Once you get it, you trace it back to the authoriser. It *will* come out."

"And Daniel Black goes to jail."

Martin allowed himself a laugh for the first time in... well, it had been a while. He let out a, "Ha!" and held out his arms as if welcoming the sun. "I must be the one policeman in the country who's thankful for the tangle of red tape we have to wade through. It's what's gonna exonerate me."

Helen inhaled, the cigarette's tip flaring for three, four, five seconds, and exhaled as she said, "I need to ask you to drop this."

Martin dropped his arms by his side. "I'm sorry, what?"

"I need you to drop it," Helen said. "Or it'll end badly."

"You can't be serious. I know I hurt a lot of people before, but I came to you because I thought you of all people would be willing to fight."

"Last time I fought, I got this." She pointed her cig at her face.

"For fuck's sake, Helen, is that going to be your excuse for *everything*?" He worked his jaw, the stiffness in his neck returning once again, and breathing, breathing. "What the hell? You were happy to dump me from the force because of domestic violence. To do me for running an off-the-books CI. You'll get me in trouble for a dust-up with your hubby. Heck, your guys were ready to discipline me over a missed *training course*. Helen, I've been screwed over by some corrupt *scumbag*, who gets me stabbed almost to death, and then covers the whole thing up. This guy, he knew I was on the edge. He knew I was fucking my life up, but he kept me in. He kept a fellow human being in the worst state of his life, and all to earn brownie points. Do you really think someone like that should be a police officer? Someone who puts ambition above human life? Well?"

He found his fists clenched. He'd closed the gap between himself and Helen, and her cigarette was mostly ash as she cringed before him.

He said, "I'm sorry."

He relaxed his fists and turned his back. Walked away, gave her space.

He said, "I can't do this anymore. I'm close to the person who stabbed me, and I'm close to the person responsible for putting me in that position, and—"

"It was me." Her voice was small. No louder than a squeak.

"Pardon?" Martin said.

"It was me." Stronger this time. A cough to clear her throat. She stubbed out the fag. Held herself tall, stiff. Scar facing him. "*It was me*, Martin. You weren't undercover at DCS Black's behest. You were working for *me*."

Coming Clean

"About two years ago," Helen said, "you and I started fucking. I don't even remember how we ended up doing it. We weren't even drunk. It was the end of a tough night, a death, someone innocent as usual, and we both knew without speaking it would happen. Pulled into Roundhay Park, found a dark spot and started doing it like teenagers in the back of the car.

"It became a semi-regular thing. We never talked about it when we were working, and we still did double dates, you and Julie, me and Alan, but it became kind-of formal. Hotels, our houses when we were sure we wouldn't be caught, crime-scene apartments. Yeah, crime scenes. Once SOCO had processed it of course. The first time, we were investigating a stabbing, not fatal, but the husband was still in critical and the wife confessed, and when we saw the bedroom hadn't been touched, we gave each other this look, and... well, it was good.

"And of course, we got closer while Julie and Alan got further away from us. We went on dates, which wasn't a problem, cos, y'know, we were always going for a 'quick one after work', only now the 'quick one' was often something else.

"We fell in love, Martin. Like, properly. The clincher was when we booked a week away, just the two of us. Heck, we even announced this bloody annoying training week to Alan and Julie at a dinner party. We moaned about it, and the pair of them joked about us maybe getting too drunk and getting it together. Oh, how we laughed. Listed the other's disgusting habits.

"Probably over-egged it a bit, to be honest. That's the night Julie first got suspicious.

"Anyway, we traipse off to Cornwall. We pretend like we're a proper couple. The sex is obvious, but the other things too. We try to learn to surf, and I kick your arse at it by the way, and we go on fishing trips and to candlelit restaurants, all paid for in cash that we've been stashing bit by bit so no one could let slip a credit card statement or debit card receipt.

"On, I think, the second to last day, we agree. Our marriages are stale. We're going to leave, and shack up together. We'll have to declare it at work and we won't be partners, but that's okay. We *understand* one another, we *get* the life the other leads. It's perfect.

"So, being coppers, we plan it to a tee. As soon as we're back in Leeds, we sort out a small two-bedroom terraced. It's furnished, but we buy a new mattress, and I fork out for a telly on the credit card because by then, it wouldn't matter. By the time the statement comes, I'll be gone.

"Once it's all ready, we agree to tell them simultaneously. Get home early, pack, load up our cars, then when Alan and Julie walk in, we have the talk, then drive over to our new love nest and try not to feel too bad about the people crying back home.

"So I tell him. He's angry, but more at you than me. Three months. He's angry at that too. He goes back over the fun we all had, the jokes, and he yells at me about the humiliation. How he feels like a mug and he's going to kill you, Martin. I make him promise not to. Promise not to, and he gets the house, he gets the easy divorce. I won't fight him on any reasonable thing. But if he goes for you, I'll make sure I play the mental anguish card, tell the court how controlling he was.

"I threatened him, Martin, threatened to make you my knight in shining armour, trying to help me through it, but in the process we got too close. That was my story Martin. I promised Alan I'd paint a picture of him to show he was a complete bastard, when, really, all he was, was a bit boring.

"I cried too. On that drive to the house, to *our* house, but I knew you'd offer me the comfort you'd given me throughout. I knew you'd be my rock.

"But you weren't there. I waited. It got dark. I watched the new telly bought on my credit card. It was a Saturday, so I sat through Match of the fucking Day. Then the lower league football show. And you know what happened, Martin? My phone let out that loud chirrup sound.

"I didn't even have to read it. I knew what it would say. But I read it anyway.

"It said, 'I'm sorry. Julie wants to work through it. Good luck with Alan.'

"Good luck with Alan, Martin. After midnight. Eight *hours* after you *knew* I'd left him. Left him for *you*.

"So yeah, we split as partners. I went to the place I thought would piss you off the most: the Professional Standards Department.

"It got out, of course. And when it did, I made sure people knew what a twat you'd been. It all came to a head in the car park, that argument you read about. You knew you'd let me down, you said. Insisted on doing something, *anything* to make it up to me.

"So I said fine. Get me intel on the OTT club.

"They were vague rumours then, of course. And I didn't expect your guilt to run that deeply. But two things happened quickly. First, you befriended Dave Essex. Told him the DOMU unit needed the style of policing him and his boss Gordo were inflicting, and then brought them on board with Daniel Black. He was nervous, but you persuaded him.

"Second, Julie fucked Alan.

"She told you about it, all tearful. You came to me to talk about it, and I didn't care. I wanted to know how far you'd go with the OTT club, and you said all the way. So I sorted the undercover op. You'd report on their corrupt activities, and would be allowed to accept bribes to maintain your cover, but to report the amounts each time. If you had to take drugs or administer beatings, or any of the other things we wanted them for, you'd be pulled out.

"But you didn't mention any of that to me. I didn't know. Not until Julie finally swallowed her pride and begged my forgiveness. She said you'd forgiven her dalliance with Alan, but still. You hit her about something else. More than once. I actually found myself feeling sorry for her.

"I knew you were taking drugs, too, but you insisted it was low quantities. I suspected you were lying, and I saw where you were heading. But I didn't have to do anything. Just pull you out once you made an official report. If you didn't make it official, and it got out, I might get a mild reprimand, but screw it.

"You'd fucked my life over, Martin, so bollocks if I was going to help you save yours.

"I didn't find out about Edith until you'd been screwing her a few months. I tried to help Julie, too. I felt bad about that, really I did. But we had so much intel on the OTT club that, even when I tried to stop you, I couldn't get you out. I couldn't. My first big op, and I was going to nail the most notorious police corruption of this type since the Birmingham Six.

"Then you go and beat up my ex-husband.

"Then you go and get photographed with Tug Jones.

"Then you go and push your pregnant wife down the fucking stairs, and we have to treat you the same as any psycho copper.

"Sure, I can cover up your blood tests. Smooth over the worst of your behaviour. But some of it, I can't. You end up on someone else's hook, and I can't reel you in without exposing the operation to the OTT club.

"So you've already been demoted because of the Devon Carlisle business, the Tug Jones CI thing, but shoving your wife down the stairs, having her beg me to help her? She was scared to death of you now, so I got her to safety.

"But still, you stayed out there, Martin. I begged you to come back up, but you insisted on staying. In a moment of real clarity, a week where you tried to kick the habit that Essex and the others had you into, you came and threatened me. Told me you'd see me suffer if I pulled you out. You'd be in a lot more trouble if you didn't stay down, you said. You'd need protecting if you came back up. From the OTT club. From Tug Jones. Julie was gone, you had nothing.

"You promised you'd come back up clean.

"But you couldn't. You'd gone too far. I'd lost control of you. I saw what you did to Julie and I knew there was no coming back from that. I'd had my head down so long, that I didn't know an iota of station gossip. When DCS Black called my DI in and told her you were off the rails, basically said we *had* to make a case against, you, well...

"I destroyed everything, Martin. Me and a tech guy. My DI didn't know who my agent was, and nor did Derek. No one knew, except me. You were my CI. And I persuaded that tech guy to help me wipe the servers, and all I had to do was pull his bank and phone records and persuade him the obvious tax-dodging software project would get him jailed.

"When it was done, I told you to leave. Do whatever you wanted. Take your chances. I knew you'd stashed far more cash than the ten grand you signed for, and we had circumstantial evidence on all of you for hundreds of thousands. I told you to accept it without a fuss.

"But I wasn't being completely selfish. I saw I'd gone too far, and I told Julie about the undercover work. Not the detail, just that you were so deep you couldn't even tell her. I said I'd only recently learned about it, but that it explained a lot. And she seemed hopeful at that. I gave her *hope*.

"But now you were officially free of me, you threw yourself into it. *Revelling*. Proving how much you really fucking loved it all. You used me as an excuse, went on a massive bender. For weeks. Back into the drugs and booze and hookers. Then we had the fight that scarred me forever.

"You backed into your little crime club, and I couldn't risk a deeper investigation. So it went away. You signed the divorce papers and everything got sorted quickly—the house sale, your new flat, everything.

"But you got steadily worse. Rumour was you were enjoying yourself even more. You lived in strip bars, even put the OTT club's noses out. Even *they* distanced themselves from you, splitting themselves up voluntarily, taking it easy, knuckling down. But not you.

"My colleagues built a good case. A heck of a good case.

"We were about to move on you. Then you got stabbed, and everyone wanted it to go away quietly."

DRUGS AND ART

Champagne!

Martin did not return to PSD. He didn't call Cupinder. He drove to the Bankwell with his bag full of money, found one of Tug's young street pushers, and purchased enough cocaine for a week. Then he called Dave and told him to come to the Pink Palace ASAP. By the time Dave showed up, Martin was on his third beer and fourth shot of tequila.

"Martin?" Dave said over the throbbing music.

"Yep!" Martin slid a shot over to him.

Despite the name, the Pink Palace was largely lit in blue.

A wide expanse of padded armchairs and low tables.

A scattering of booths and mirrors.

A stage, on which a young woman swung her breasts freely, dancing to some rap bollocks.

Then there was the bar, behind which women in lingerie served drinks to the clientele: a mix of working men and chavs, a stag night and a sprinkling of students.

Martin occupied his barstool and balanced precariously upon it.

"I don't care!" he said as Dave knocked back the liquor. "I don't care who stabbed me. I don't care where Si Larson is. I don't give one single fuck anymore. I'm a scumbag, so tonight I stop pretending. This is me, Dave. Let's party!"

"Listen, Martin—"

"Who's Martin? Call me Rosie, man! Call me Rosie."

"Rosie, are you sure? I mean—"

"It was me, Dave. It was all me. I was an arsehole before I started on the drugs. They made me worse, but it was still me. Enjoying the life, enjoying being so free I stopped giving a shit about everyone else, and you know what? It sounds like that was the happiest time of my average fucking life!"

Dave cracked a smile. "You serious, Rosie?"

Martin thrust both fists into the air and yelled at the barmaid, "Champagne!"

Nearby, a young woman in a bikini shouted, "Woo hoo!" and put her arm around Martin. "You wanting a private dance?"

Martin said, "You bet!"

She held his hand and pulled him away, but Dave stopped her. He said, "How about you send me that young blond thing over?"

In a small back room with a curtain, Martin sat on a firm sofa while the woman danced for him. She stripped and rubbed herself on his semi-hard cock, making him hard all the way. The rules in these places state no touching, but there are always exceptions. This girl wasn't one of them, though, and when Martin brushed his fingers over her skin for the third time, she snatched her things off the floor and strode out. Ten seconds later, two gorillas manhandled him from the booth and dragged him through the club. He tried yelling about who he was, and who the fuck did they think they were fucking with, but the bigger of the two helped him through a fire exit with a punch to the kidney.

Dave met him out front. "This way," he said, and once Martin got his breath back, they hit a bar five minutes' walk away.

It was full of students and student drinking games, one of which meant Dave caught up to Martin alcohol-wise. They did a line each in the loos, and progressed on to a hushed cocktail bar full of theatre-going types, from which a tuxedoed security guy asked them to leave after 'complaints'.

Next was a neon tribute to 60s and 70s cheesy music. Martin

danced with two beers in his hand, bought rounds for a hen night, tried to kiss the hen's maid of honour, and threw his bottle to the floor when she turned him down.

Dave hustled him out onto the street, where Martin yelled to the sky, "I WANT PUSSY!"

"There's one place left," Dave said.

The Real Martin Money

The doorman at the Blue Pussycat didn't charge them admission, just gave a professional smile, and said, "Welcome back, gents," and held the door for them.

Martin broke into a huge grin at the cavernous table dancing bar. He ordered two bottles of champagne and six glasses, and occupied a section of sofa beneath a mirrored wall large enough for him and Dave and four dancers: one in silver, one in red, one in black, and one in white. Each was stunning, as usual.

And young.

As usual.

"They're all new," Dave said helpfully.

The champagne drained away. Dances were had. Whenever a girl took Martin or Dave aside for some private time, one of the security guys spoke to her, and her smile would fade momentarily, before resuming, and allowing all the touching the men wanted. The one in silver accepted an extra fifty from Martin, in exchange for allowing him to lick her nipples. He said he wanted to fuck her.

"I don't do *that*," she replied. "But I can get you a girl who will. Just give me a line of the good stuff."

He accepted, and nipped out to tell Dave what was happening, but Dave was ready to leave, one of the girls escorting him out, and he said, "I've pulled," and the girl of around twenty-two smiled coyly. Dave mouthed, "Expensive."

It is rare to find a stripper in the UK who doubles as a prostitute, but if you know the right place, flash enough money around, they will find you. The same way Maisy found Martin. "M and M," she said, taking his hand. "Cool."

She had red hair like Martin, a shapely rear and what looked like amazing tits. Sanskrit tattoos adorned the small of her back, a line above one breast, and vertically down her right leg.

In another back room, three times the size of the dance booths, a familiar couch greeted them.

A bar in one corner, curling like a single parenthesis.

Low tables set with liquor and beer.

More mirrors surrounding the space.

Bulbs flashed red, blue, white, in time with the thumping music.

Maisy danced in the light, as professional and lithe as anyone he'd met that night, but more slowly. She removed as many of Martin's clothes as she did her own. Once both were naked, she slid her mouth over his penis and went to town. Martin got her to pause before it was too late, and offered the last of his coke. Her lips parted, teeth glowing blue, and she cut the powder expertly using a razor she produced from God-knew-where. Martin rolled a twenty and let her snort the first of four lines. He took the second line, and as soon as his brain exploded in white, he blinked hard and focused, downed a shot of something green that tasted of aniseed, and pulled Maisy toward him.

Those nonsense movies, the ones where the hooker insists 'no kissing', Martin always dismissed those, got thrown out of the fictive moment; kissing is the least gross thing a woman will do for money. It's risky, but few fatal diseases pass between humans that way. So he kissed her on the lips. She kissed him back. Tongues, too. She grabbed his cock and squeezed the base to make him last longer. She slipped a condom over him and lowered herself onto it. So plentifully-lubed, he barely felt it at first. She had to move in a specific way to give him real pleasure, as much side-to-side as up-and-down, but they soon found the rhythm he needed.

He moved very little. He couldn't, not on that couch.

That familiar couch.

The couch, in a semi-circle.

Where, to his left, his friend, his only friend, Dave Essex, once lay comatose after several hours of drugs and booze and sex.

To his right, the mirrored wall.

On top of him, a tattooed woman faking pleasure.

Giving him true pleasure.

Music, all around.

Lights, blurring his vision.

The mirror, to his right.

The angle.

The perfect angle for a camera.

For photos.

Tug *fucking* Jones.

This was his club. This was *the* club. *The* back room where *the* orgy happened. There could have been a camera there, right now. More happy snapping.

And Martin smiled. Gazed up at Maisy and groped her perfect breasts.

"Oh yeah," she said, taking his hands and encouraging them to squeeze a tad harder so the Sanskrit ink distorted. "Right there"

A surge built in his groin, but the technique was all wrong. The woman was in control here and he needed to know what was next. He grabbed her buttocks and adjusted her technique to suit him.

She said, "I like that, baby, oh yeah."

He mugged a face for the camera, a gurning comedy 'come face', but he didn't come.

Maisy said, "Tell me what you want next, baby."

He did not reply with words, but slowed her down, dismounted her, then eased her around, bent her over the couch, and entered her from behind.

"Mmmm," she said. "Right there."

And he thrusted and thrusted. More posing for the camera, giggling away. They'd look great on Tug's iPad. No money shot today, though.

Heh-heh. Money shot.

He just got that.

The Martin Money cum-shot.

Not today.

The build-up within him was almost too much, the drugs and booze holding it in place for longer than usual, and when it finally rose up and burst, Martin let out a groan so loud the people out in the club might have heard it over the music.

He sat on the couch, sweating. Grinning. His nakedness flaccid and pathetic. Posing.

"Oh baby," Maisy said, kissing his cheek. "I don't usually get off like that. Thank you so much."

Martin kissed her some more, and hugged her tight. She gave him a loving smile and he returned it. He lay down, gently manoeuvred her beside him. He lay her on his chest, their legs tangled together. His heart beat so fast that Maisy's head rocked minutely, but as they lay there, the rocking slowed. Without the coke in their systems they might have slept.

Martin continued to eye the point where the camera must have been hidden. Where it could have been that night too. Where it probably was.

Tonight was the night he'd been yearning to remember, ever since he learned of his moral downfall.

Tonight, he experienced what that other Martin experienced, the one from his Dead Time. What that man loved so much.

Tonight, he learned why it was that the Martin from The Before did not want to come back up.

Tonight, he discovered what it was to be more than average.

Lying here with Maisy, full of drugs and alcohol, and stinking of lovely, pungent sex, this was the version of himself he was born to be. Not the married man with the nice wife and box sets of Breaking Bad. But glowing peacefully in the arms of a woman who liked to paint her body in Sanskrit.

This. This was him. *This* was Martin Money.

Tattoos and Photos

The photos. He scrolled through the photos.

Martin had left the club at five A.M. and walked home. It took him an hour, and the sun split over the horizon between the low buildings of Chapel Allerton. The Moroccan cafe had just opened and he bought a strong double espresso and a sausage sandwich before continuing to his flat. The coffee helped focus his brain on things like putting one foot before the other, his shoes now as heavy as bricks. His fingers didn't work so well either, fumbling his keys at the door.

No Julie waiting for him this time. No Cupinder. No Dave.

Cupinder.

Inside, he dug out his phone, but the battery was dead. He plugged it in and drank water while listening to the bongs and pings of text messages and emails firing into the device.

He lay on his bed for thirty minutes, the room spinning, his head hollowing out inside itself, before he sat up and accessed his phone. He set up the email address Tug Jones gave him and downloaded the zip file containing the orgy photos from his Dead Time.

Photos, of his true self.

He selected shots featuring people he'd met, people he now recognised as human beings rather than pixels of a forgotten past.

Zoomed in.

Zoomed out.

Sonia.

Dave.

The red-haired girl from last night.

Edith. The robin on her neck. The glimpse of a quarter of her face.

A girl he still didn't recognise from any of his investigations, but then why would he?

The hand, grasping his shaft as he came in the porn-alike still. A daisy chain around the wrist.

Martin's own flame-legs.

He quickly Google-Imaged 'daisy chain tattoo' and found a ton of them. He tried 'daisy chain robin tattoo' and narrowed the search to tens of millions. He added '.co.uk' to bring it down even further, but the suffix might not be right in the modern world of .net, .uk, .co, .plumber or whatever. He changed it to 'UK' and added 'Leeds' and 'cheap' and 'quality'.

The first few that came up were local joints, reputable premises that did good work, but even though they claimed they were 'cheap' they clearly were not.

Not cheap enough for people who spend most of their money on drugs.

Drugs.

Tattoos.

Cheap.

There was something there, something Martin recalled from earlier, a case mentioned in passing but still caused something to rise in him, a sadness that he had not understood at the time. The detectives who took his statement in the hospital, the ones who complained how much of a come-down this case was after they helped catch a serial killer, their names were... what? Cleaver and Ball, that's right. That case of theirs, the previous year. As part of the investigation they stumbled across a vigilante of some sort, who used a tattoo artist to track down the killer who abducted his daughter, a tattoo artist who was also involved in the drugs trade. A tattoo artist named Doyle.

Martin found a news story on the local BBC site that featured the demise of the proprietor of Doyle's Emporium, a front for a marijuana business that had, of course, shut down. The files were still in the archives at Sheerton, pending a possible inquiry into events that followed.

Doyle's website was still active, an oversight on the part of the investigators, or maybe not. It would involve a lot of warrants being served to internet service providers, which costs money and time, and since the site would be of no relevance to the wider investigation, it would not rank highly in their priorities.

An extensive online catalogue featured all the appropriate images, along with the typical ink designs: the robin was there, Chinese symbols, Sanskrit, skulls, dragons, flowers, flames in a variety of shapes, although no one had modelled the idiotic joke adorning Martin's skin; whole sleeves featured, someone's back as a canvas, amusing use of belly buttons; and, of course, a daisy chain.

Martin searched his flat but the only alcohol in stock was beer, and that wouldn't do the job. So he took a taxi to where he parked last night, removed the ticket and dropped it on the floor, then got in his car and drove to the Bankwell, where he procured another baggie of cocaine and a second with speed. He did a little speed straightaway, and every sound, movement and obstacle bloomed crystal clear, making his driving safer and his eyes wider.

At Sheerton, he parked and rushed through reception with his face down, and weaved through the corridors toward Archives. In the same clothes as yesterday, his hair a mess, and tasting the cocktail of liquor and champagne in his throat, he wound a circuitous route, avoiding MisPer, avoiding the canteen, avoiding PSD, and when he arrived he went through a brief check of his ID, a grunt from the duty officer, and was left alone with the file on Doyle's Emporium.

The ledger.

The customer records.

Doyle needed to list his sales for tax purposes. Enough to cover his inking costs and rent, plus however much the drugs cost the customer. Not 'cheap' but enough to attract the crowd of which Martin was an active part.

He couldn't remember exactly how much coke was in his system right now, and his heart already yammered far faster and harder than it should, but his vision blurred as he read, unable to see straight with his head thumping. He snorted a quick, short line. His eyes watered as a tiny clump lodged in the top of his nasal cavity, not cut finely enough. He snorted hard and it shot through the right way, and he used the blast to keep himself going.

Customers.

Fake names, surely.

A long shot, surely.

But not those using credit cards.

Not Dave Essex.

Not Martin Money.

Martin Money's name, his card number, his details. He paid for a tattoo, several in fact, but there was only that one patch of stupidity on his own body. An expensive inking at the best of times.

He made several visits, several purchases. The ledger, each time, said, 'Subject: male', then, 'Martin Money, visit 2 of 4'. The large flames must have required several visits, several purchases of other goods, too.

The ledger said the tattoo Dave paid for was a bumblebee. It said, 'Subject: female'. Adding, 'Name: Vicki Essex'.

Martin paid for a Robin. Subject: *female*. Name: *Edith Money*.

Then, days later, a daisy chain.

THREE YEARS DEAD

Martin paid for a daisy chain.
Subject: male.
Name: Simon Money

.

EVERYBODY LIES

Ramifications

The confirmation wasn't like a sledgehammer. It was more like a warm river flowing over him, around him, through him.

Si, Edith.

Martin, Edith.

Martin, Si.

Dave… whoever Vicki was. Sonia, perhaps?

One big, happy family.

It proved his own connection to Si. It proved that Cupinder's order to assign Martin to Si's disappearance was part of a wider conspiracy. Yes, the C-word. That's what it was. A *conspiracy*. One that implicated more than just Martin in the operation to give control of the Bankwell and beyond to Tug Jones.

No one could ever believe it was an almighty coincidence.

Which left questions about why.

Why was Martin stabbed?

Where was Si?

Did Martin do something to Si, or did Si do something to him?

Did Si wield the knife?

If so, why did Si drop out of the world at least a week before the attempt on Martin's life?

And, considering that gap between Si's last sighting and Martin's dip into the River Aire, *why* was there a gap?

If the two mysteries—Where was Si? And who stabbed Martin?—were wholeheartedly connected, wouldn't Si have done a runner shortly *after* the assault?

Could that have been his alibi? Go dark, make like he was gone? Death is the perfect alibi.

More questions: why could they find absolutely no CCTV footage? One of the four masts *must* have seen something on Christmas Eve.

Conspiracy.

The trail of cameras that saw Si Larson on that final night of his, the 19th, it must have seen something out of the ordinary. Where could he go without coverage?

Conspiracy.

The shack, perhaps. That trail, the path through the park. But there were cameras covering the front and rear gates, and all along the street. Someone would have spotted him, wouldn't they?

Conspiracy.

Of course, cameras are only clear when you can identify a specific subject, so yeah, perhaps it was simply that they couldn't see him.

A hole in the theory.

What night to look for, though? When might he have been spotted again?

A definite, physical connection between Martin and Si. That would seal it. That would tell Martin, and whoever else would listen, that there was more to this than Helen covering up her involvement in an undercover op that went wrong. It would say that Tug Jones was manipulating someone high up in the West Yorkshire Police, someone who learned of Helen's op and would be able to use it if any of this came back to shit on him.

Forget Edith.

Forget Tug.

Forget Dave and the OTT club.

Strip all that away, and you got connection after connection between Si Larson and Martin Money, and one—*probably* one—plan to have them both wiped from existence, either physically or professionally. Martin wasn't a single victim. Si wasn't a single victim. They were one. Both victims of the same antagonist. Connect the victims, find the answer.

And that was how simple it would be.

Martin tidied the files away, calmly did some more speed, and called the one person who he knew could not be a part of it, the one person who had remained open and accepting when he might be wrong. That person would prove it all in one afternoon.

CCTV

Wadaya said no at first. On the other end of the phone, he lowered his voice and added, "Rowe is worried about you. She was angry yesterday but now she's worried. Thinking about opening a MisPer case of your own."

"I'll explain everything," Martin assured him. "I need you to check some footage. I can narrow the dates down for you, but you're the expert at this."

"Just come back. I can't lie for you."

"Can't lie for me? Then why are you whispering?"

"Because…" He made a noise, a cross between mumbling and shifting himself to another part of the office. Then, "You've done stuff you should be punished for, but I don't want to let someone else get away with it either. The evidence you've presented is pretty solid. Not court-of-law, but solid enough for me. There's more at work here."

In a way, Wadaya talked himself into it. They met in the video archives, where Martin scanned the four terminals housed between their closed off privacy screens rather than a single one in a private office. Still, the room was empty but for the two of them, so they could talk freely.

"The 20th of December," Martin said.

Wadaya manned the keyboard and wiggled the mouse to activate the screen, and signed in. "You have something new to pinpoint? A unique identifier?"

"No," Martin said. "I have a location."

"Okay, then. Where?"

"The Blue Pussycat."

Wadaya clicked and typed, clicked and typed. The CCTV images from every police-funded camera fed into a central server, accessible to anyone with sufficient clearance and a valid reason to look. The data protection act was strict in that regard. Si Larson, though, was an open case, giving both men authority to view anything that might lead to a breakthrough.

The street camera aimed down from a mast twenty feet in the air, but the hi-def technology would pick up most faces. The problem with these cameras, as Wadaya explained once again, was that if you are not sure what you are looking for, it doesn't jump out at you. If you have a reference point, though, if you can focus on that one thing, that one aspect of the scene, when you find it, you can zero in and take what you need.

Martin said, "Another reason they should have some footage on the night I was killed."

"Stabbed," Wadaya corrected.

"Well, I did technically die for a short while."

"You said you could narrow this down."

Martin issued instructions, and watched as the lens pointed at the position in question, the sole licenced premises in the vicinity, and a known trouble spot. The easiest method was to scroll through at 8x speed and slow it down each time someone new showed their face, starting at eight P.M. on Saturday the 20th December.

The day *after* anyone saw Si Larson alive.

The Blue Pussycat operated ten minutes' walk from where Si plied his trade in Lille Park, but it was far enough away to drop out of the circle of likely locations. It was also a strip club that employed exclusively female performers, so with Si being gay it would not have been considered a location he might frequent. Unless you knew, for a fact, that a regular customer of that club had a direct connection to Si, and added in the rather compelling evidence that someone, somewhere, had managed to cover up this connection for the past three months.

The first people of interest showed up around ten P.M.

Martin Money and Dave Essex, drunk and happy, kicked through a slushy evening, wrapped up in wool coats. Once they slunk inside the club, Wadaya sped up the footage. An hour or so later, a man with a large Rottweiler strutted into shot, and Martin got Wadaya to stop it and check. The man's back was to the camera, but it was clearly Tug Jones.

"You sure?" Wadaya asked, logging the movement and time on a CCTV evidence report.

Martin nodded, fixed on the screen. "Who else would be allowed in a club like that with a dog?"

They watched the tape as the hours flowed by. They did not exit, even after midnight. Looked like they were bedded in. After what Martin got up to the previous night, he didn't need a camera inside to know what was happening. Si Larson did not, at any point, arrive at the club.

But, at two-thirty A.M., he did stumble out. And he was not alone.

That river flowed through Martin again, warm and strong.

Wadaya's mouth opened minutely.

Si and Martin, on the screen, laughing. Martin had his arm around Si like they'd been buddies for years. They shared a joke. Zooming in, the faces pixelated only slightly. Then Martin kissed Si on the lips, and Si responded the same way. They stood still, held hands for two seconds, and Si departed, walking off the bottom of the screen.

The on-screen Martin stood around, though. He took something from his pocket, what looked like a hand-rolled cigarette, and lit it.

As he took a drag, his expression suggested supreme pleasure. Five minutes of this, of pacing, of smoking, checking his watch, making phone calls that ended with him stabbing at the phone with his finger, Dave and Tug joined him. Both kept glancing over their shoulders and turning round.

In the room, Martin said, "They're worried about something."

Wadaya kept watching. "Yeah."

On screen, fingers pointed. Jaws jutted. Arms flew. Not one of the trio looked happy, with Martin the least happy of all. He shook his head a lot while the other two spoke.

"Denying something," Wadaya said.

Martin nodded. "Or disagreeing."

Back to the screen, and Martin pointed off the bottom of the monitor. As he watched the silent exchange, his fingered played through his hair, hands gripping his skull like a claw. Finally, Dave placed an arm around Martin's shoulders, spoke into his ear. Slowly, Martin nodded. His shoulders slumped and he nodded some more.

"He's agreeing," Martin said.

"That's you," Wadaya reminded him. "You're speaking in the third person."

"I have no memory of that."

"Does it matter?"

"Fine," Martin said. "That's me, agreeing with them. Whatever *we* were arguing about, they've sold it to me."

That was the last this video saw of them. Wadaya checked the surrounding masts for the minutes after Martin, Dave and Tug walked off the bottom of the screen, locating them five minutes later at the entrance to Lille Park, Martin arguing with them again. He appeared to be trying to prevent Tug from getting into the park, stood in his way. The dog barked and lunged for him. Tug held onto it, gesticulating wildly at Martin, but this camera was in autopan mode, moving side-to-side, from the river over the park and out to the road, then returned again. By the time it swept back from the river, the three men had vanished.

And just like that, Si Larson was no longer a suspect in the stabbing of Martin Money.

"Want me to check the south end?" Wadaya said.

"Why don't you do that," Martin said. "I need to go somewhere."

Wadaya placed a hand on Martin's arm to stop him leaving. "You need to report this to Cupinder. It's a direct conflict of interest."

"I need the truth. I'll get it now, tonight. I promise. We can't get it through official channels, you know that."

Wadaya held on to him, observed the screen, the slow pan of the camera.

Martin said, "Come on. You've trusted me this far. You said it yourself, there's more going on here. A lot more."

Still, Wadaya monitored the screen, the park inching across.

"Please," Martin said. "I could have stopped it, I know I could. Whatever happened to Si next, I could have stopped it, but I need to know exactly what it is."

"They want to pin it on you," Wadaya said.

"I know."

"They'll do whatever they have to. If it means saving their own arses, they'll do anything."

"I know that too."

"I can't help you anymore."

Wadaya let go of him. He stood up slowly, feeling the wound in his back for the first time in a while. His energy was dropping.

Martin said, "Thanks."

"What for?"

"Believing me."

Wadaya handed Martin a phone. A Samsung S5, an Android device. "It's my personal phone. Just in case."

Martin scrolled through his own phone for the numbers he would need, and exited the room, dialling on Wadaya's loaner. The first voice he heard belonged to Tug Jones.

"I Remember"

"Time to stop fucking me around, Tug," Martin said, his voice echoing off the gents walls.

Tug laughed. Fakely. "You got this all wrong, Rosie-boy. You don't tell me that shit. Ever."

"I remember."

Silence on the other end.

Martin said, "I remember."

A snort. "I heard you."

"So let's sort this out. Now."

"It's a busy night. Tomorrow."

"Now," Martin said. "I'm heading there."

"Where?"

"You know where." Martin hung up and ducked into a cubicle and called Dave. No answer. He called again, but again got no answer. While he chopped two lines of coke on the toilet seat, he sent a text saying, 'It's Rosie. I got a new phone', and Dave called back within seconds. Martin said, "I remember."

Dave said, "Bollocks do you remember."

"Last night," Martin said, "knocked loose a few brain cells. I was fried this morning, but then I started getting these flashes. Soon, it was like I was dreaming. All these things. All the good times."

Dave breathed heavily into the phone. "What do you want?"

Martin snorted a line and said, "My stash."

"We can't."

"I'm running," Martin said. "You should too. They're close and they're going to do us all. Bring my passports, my ID, all the gear from the warehouse. I have my money still."

"Where?"

"To where we last saw Si Larson."

Martin hung up and swept the loose cocaine into the baggie and pocketed it, left the cubicle, and checked his nose in one of the mirrors. His nose was fine, but red lines spidered through his eyes, purple smudges beneath, his pupils dilated. His hair curled into a mass of ginger wool, splayed randomly atop his pale football of a head. He was pretty sure he smelled bad. He added more speed to his coke-infused body and exited strongly into a corridor that warped a tad more with each step.

Step one, right foot: tilt to the left.

Step two, left foot: tilt to the right.

He used the wall for support.

A female police constable and her PCSO asked if he was okay. He couldn't make his voice work. The constable told the support officer to contact a first aider while she called an ambulance.

Martin said, "No. I'm fine."

"You're not," the PC said. "You need to sit dow—"

"I'M FINE!" And Martin pushed himself away, spun the wrong way and righted himself. When he did, when he found his vision, the PCSO had her baton out, and the constable fumbled for her pepper spray. Martin said, "No, don't do it."

They hesitated long enough for him to shoulder the constable out of the way, sending her flying, while the PCSO caught herself between pursuing and checking on a fallen comrade.

Martin ran hard.

Left foot: right tilt.

Right foot: left tilt.

He crashed out into the car park. The drizzle and chill wind helped clear his head enough for him to find his car. He crawled in behind the wheel and started it up, clipped a black-and-white as he reversed, and managed to get it going forward. On the steps, the female PC spoke into her radio.

Out on the road, Martin kept the car steady, hands gripping the wheel.

Must drive straight.

Must drive straight.

Must drive straight, or they'll catch you.

A McDonald's signalled that he hadn't eaten for at least twenty-four hours, but McDonalds always made his stomach yearn for a cup of tea straight after, so he carried on until he spotted a Pizza Hut.

He had to wait longer, but he ordered the full meaty one and some wedges and a 1.5ltr Pepsi Max, then ate the food so quickly he barely remembered what it looked like. He drank half the Pepsi, which quenched a thirst that surfaced after gobbling down the pizza, and when he returned to his car he moved like a predator. One who knew his hunting ground, who knew his prey, who knew the items he needed to purchase next.

And knew that he would emerge later tonight with a carcass to mount on his wall.

Confrontation

Women dotted Lille Park, their heels high and skirts short. Daughters, sisters, probably a few mothers. Some of the more shivery outliers propositioned Martin once again, though most avoided him; his fast pace, his clenching-unclenching fists, twitching side-to-side. Two guys he'd never seen before loitered in hoodies by a tree overlooking the Shack, their bodies turning, always facing Martin, cigarettes in hand, the tips glowing orange like eyes in the night.

The Shack.

It had to be. After following Si into the park, that must have been where they confronted him. The presence of the black man on the front door, the one from Tug's apartment—Riccardo? Yeah, that was it—told Martin he'd gambled correctly.

Left foot: all steady now.

Right foot: all steady now.

A dull buzz occupied the space behind Martin's forehead, but other than that, it was all super-steady all the way down the gentle slope to the boarded up former-warehouse.

Riccardo adjusted his stance, straightening his spine, shoulders pulled back, hands folded in front of him, lips tight together: basically a bouncer to the world's seediest club. When Martin reached him, he gestured with his palms up. Martin held his arms in a crucifixion pose, and Riccardo patted him down. He patted him down the way actors pat down other actors on TV—badly.

The search omitted the backs of Martin's knees and his trouser cuffs.

Riccardo rose to his full height and stood so close to Martin their noses almost touched. He said, "This is gonna be painful for you."

"We'll see," Martin said.

Riccardo held the door and Martin stepped inside.

It was quieter than when he last explored this gloomy space. No shuffles, no ill-perceived whispers far away; just the river running beyond the walls. Not a soul inside, except for himself, Dave Essex, and Tug Jones. And his muscular dog. If that had a soul.

Dave loitered several feet away from Tug, pacing in a tight circle, while Tug remained motionless, leaning against Si's Portakabin.

Martin restricted his pace. Couldn't risk a stumble. Couldn't show weakness.

He fancied a cup of tea.

Shake it off, Martin. Concentrate.

Still fifteen feet away, Martin called, "Is this where it happened, Tug?" His voice came back off the walls, bounced around the empty space. "Is this where he died?"

Tug clapped slowly, the rope dog lead wrapped around one hand.

"Stop that," Martin said, closer now.

Tug did not stop. He slapped his palms harder, his arms forming a wider arc. His mouth turned down in a terrible Robert De Niro impression. His dog growled.

Nearer, Martin said, "Fine. Just tell me, is he here, or did you put him in the river?"

The clapping stopped.

Dave Essex scuffed his shoes in the dirt.

Tug said, "Who you talkin' about?"

Martin halted, like Dave, around six feet from Tug. He said, "Stop pretending, Tug. I know."

"Really? What do you know?"

"We followed Si here. I argued with you. Then he was gone."

Tug glanced at Si, then his dog. Scratched the mutt's head. "You remember fuck all, don't you, Rosie?"

"I know you killed Si. I don't know why. Some sort of misguided bullshit. Like he was hiding Edith and wouldn't tell you where she was."

Smiling, scratching the dog's neck, Tug said, "I never heard of no Edith. Or Si. What you talkin' about?"

Dave sighed loudly. "Come on, Tug. We all went through so much. Let's tell him the truth. He deserves it."

"And who," Tug said, "the fuck... are you?"

Dave frowned. "Huh? What? Tug—"

"As far as I know, you're some arsehole Rosie here brought along."

"I'm with *you*, Tug. You know that. You got my loyalty."

Martin said, "I know we were all here that night. What was it? Torture gone wrong? Did you lose your temper? Did I? Was it me, Tug? Did I do it?"

Tug brought his hand back to his side. The dog moaned and lay on the floor. Tug said, "You really think I would say something like that out loud near a copper who's probably wearing a wire?"

"I'm not bugged." Martin lifted up his top. "Riccardo frisked me."

Badly.

Tug said, "I know you aren't wired, Rosie." He thumped three times on the Portakabin and stood aside.

The door opened and Gordo filled the space. He sauntered down the two steps, followed by Danni and Nick.

All in flak jackets.

No police markings.

Leather gloves.

Dark wool hats on their heads, rolled up.

Not hats—balaclavas ready to roll down should the need arise.

Gordo's arm levered upwards, raising a double-barrelled shotgun—sawn off close to the stock, leaving six inches of metal, the ends sanded smooth.

Martin said, "You once told me, Tug, that you should only trust someone with a gun if you trust that someone with your life. You trust Gordo?"

"Yeah," Tug said. "I got the same shit on him I got on you. I die, it goes public, y'feel me?"

Martin said, "Never touch the crime, eh, Tug?"

"You're not bugged, Rosie," Tug said, inserting fingers into his ears. "*He* is, though."

Dave had long enough to open his mouth and raise a hand as he shook his head, 'no'. Gordo pulled one trigger. A barrel exploded, ripping through every unprotected eardrum in the place. Namely Martin's and Tug's dog.

When a person knows they've been shot, they fall over. When they do not, they carry on. Stories abound about ricochets going unnoticed for hours, or if a bullet goes astray on the street someone might think a bee stung them on the back or neck, not realising the extent of the injury until they acknowledged the blood.

It had happened so quickly for Dave. The gun was in front of him, held by his friend, his comrade, and then the front of his coat imploded, a wound the size of a fist pluming red mist from around his sternum, most likely taking a hefty chunk of stomach with it. He would have known about gunshot wounds, though. It was probably why he stayed upright for the few seconds he managed. Teetering. Working it all out. Hands wavering over the damaged tissue, but too afraid to touch, needing to know, not wanting to know. His face blanched and he dropped to his knees.

Martin dashed over, threw himself to the ground to hold the man who'd concealed so many secrets from him, so many crimes. All because—he said—he was Martin's friend.

His only friend.

Dave's gaze creaked slowly toward Martin. His mouth worked, blood spitting. No sound. Then his body went limp, and Martin let it fall sideways into the dust.

For Them

Martin sat on his arse, legs out front, arms supporting himself behind. Breathing.

Danni finished checking Dave over and said, "No recording devices this time, boss."

"Yeah?" Tug said. "But he defo recorded me before?"

"I wasn't talking to you," Danni said. "Gordo, he wasn't recording." She held up his phone.

Gordo turned his gun toward Martin. "Yeah, well, he took that other MP3 to Professional Standards, so fuck him. Right, get him in the hole, and I'll deal with grass number two."

"So I *was* trying to come back up," Martin said.

Tug chuckled as he ambled alongside Gordo, that boxer's mien present in both, though Gordo would still look more at home on a rugby pitch. Both strong, both willing to use their bulk.

Fighters.

Tug said, "You really forgot everything, eh, Rosie? All the good shit, all the bad. Still don't know what went down here."

"I can work it out."

"Yeah?"

Gordo raised the gun again, Martin struggling to get comfortable in his position on the floor.

Tug placed his hand on the shotgun. "Aw, come on, Gordo, let's see how close he got."

"I don't take fuckin' orders from a jumped up chav," Gordo said, and the dog growled. "That mutt gets one inch closer, I'll put a hole in it."

Tug yanked the choke collar and the Rotty fell silent.

Danni and Nick lifted Dave's corpse and carried it toward one of the foundation holes—the one they bag-nabbed Martin in a few nights ago. It had been less than a week.

Really? That short a time?

Martin said, "Si hid Edith on my say-so. I didn't want her to be part of your world anymore."

Gordo cocked the hammer on the second barrel.

Martin pulled up his knees, hugged them, the image of a cold child. "But because I told him to hide her where I wouldn't find her, he refused to give her up, didn't he? And him and me... me and Edith..."

Tug glanced at Gordo, got the nod to proceed and said, "Yeah, you wanted to be like one big happy family, three of you and the sprog. Some new-age thing, I dunno. It was disgusting. Un-fuckin'-natural. Went on about how society or some shit told us what families were and you were all, like, fuck that shit, man. You was gonna live how you wanted."

"So you killed Si trying to get to Edith. Did I help?" Martin watched Gordo step closer through tear-filled eyes. "Was it you?"

Gordo said, "Me?"

"Who stabbed me."

"Oh, that." Gordo steadied the gun. Right hand.

"I guess I was going to blow it all," Martin said. "Me and Dave. I was already undercover for PSD, but you knew that, right?"

"Right," Gordo said. "Corrupted Dave. Turned him into a fuckin' grass like you."

"We were going to expose it all, weren't we? Get clean, but Si and Edith were in too much danger. I couldn't come back up. I needed to protect them."

Gordo sniffed. "You think that's what happened, huh?"

Tug boomed out a laugh and clapped again. "You are so fuckin' cool, Rosie. I always said, didn't I? Always so fuckin' cool."

"Step back," Gordo said, levelling the gun.

In the background, Danni and Nick rolled Dave into a foundation hole. He made a *whumpf* as he landed.

Martin spoke as quietly as he could. "Si's in there isn't he?"

Gordo cocked an ear. "Pardon?"

Whispering, Martin said, "I helped bury him."

"Speak up, fuckwit."

Martin dug his fingers into his trouser cuff. "You figured killing me would keep Dave in line, and it did."

"Jesus. These fucking earplugs." Gordo held the gun by the barrel and used his free hand to reach under the rolled-up balaclava.

Hand on the barrel.

Pointed away.

Between Martin's fingers... a syringe.

A final chance.

Martin pushed off with his bent legs, power coursing through them, propelling him up, forward, too quickly for Gordo to react. Martin slapped the gun aside and plunged the syringe into Gordo's neck and depressed the plunger.

He would have preferred a knife, but couldn't find one that he'd be able to smuggle in here in his trouser cuff. But filling the needle with a heroin and cocaine concoction, ten times stronger than what Dave wanted to inject into Martin in the hospital, made it as lethal as any blade.

Gordo convulsed straight away, the narcotic drilling directly into his brain.

Martin's moment of power dipped, though. The world spun sideways. He crashed to the floor, too dizzy to stand. A moment—he needed one moment to right himself.

Tug entered his eye line, hand out, dog leading him.

Reaching for the shotgun.

Martin reached too, had to reach it, or he was dead.

Tug let go of the rope.

Scrabbling. Growling. Jaws clamped around Martin's right arm.

Yelling.

Threats.

Orders.

Martin was dead if he didn't act.

It was enough. He blinked away the pain and his grip found Gordo's shotgun moments before Tug. Quick assessment.

There must have been some synapses still firing properly. Instead of blowing away the man who had killed Si Larson and tried to murder Martin, he pressed the barrel against the dog ripping his arm to shreds, and fired.

Tug screamed a "NO!", the dog's mouth went slack, and Martin scrambled backwards, blood spilling from the teeth marks.

Danni and Nick were on him in seconds. Kneeling on his back, pushing his face in the dirt.

Tug cradled his dog, its final moments ebbing away, its gaze asking him what was happening, its master unable to help.

"You're under arrest," Danni said, "for the murder of Detective Sergeant James Gordon."

Hearing Gordo's full name for the first time almost convinced Martin this was all some awful fever dream. Almost. He said, "James Gordon? Like Jim Gordon? Like in Batman?"

Nick said, "Why do you think we call him Gordo?"

Danni cuffed him as she recited his rights, making no attempt to cushion the free-flowing gouges, but that was okay; he was so full of drugs he was only vaguely aware of the tissue damage anyway.

Nick asked, "What now?"

Danni said, "GSR on his hands, he's obviously tripping. We clean up Gordo's gunshot residue and we got him murdering Dave *and* the guy trying to bring him in. His mates. We overpowered him as he tried to reload."

Martin now viewed everything as if his eyeballs were smeared in Vaseline. As if his ears were plugged with cotton. He said, "What about the dog? It leads to Tug."

Danni said, "You reckon citizen of the year Tug had it chipped? Take its collar, it's a stray."

"She's chipped," Tug said.

Nick threw his hands up. "What? You chipped that fucker?"

"Yeah." Tug streamed real tears. "What if I had to run from the feds and had to claim her later? What if she was chasing some scrote for me and got lost?"

Danni said, "You don't chip a lethal animal like that, you idiot. Well, shit, that makes you a witness."

"Nah, man. I ain't going to court."

"A hero," Martin said, suppressing a giggle.

Tug moved away from the dog. It had died at some point, but Tug hadn't left its side. Its head now thudded to the ground as Tug made his way over to the three police officers.

Martin said, "You're the working class hero, remember?" The river sounded louder now, rushing by, channelling hill floods to the sea. He said, "Walking his dog, stumbled on a commotion, heard a gunshot. Brave working class hero he is, he sics his beloved doggie on the bad man holding a gun on two police officers, having killed two of them. Doggie sacrifices its life in the service of its community. Bad cop goes to prison."

Nick and Danni scanned the scene. Danni nodded agreement first. Then Nick.

"Why you sayin' this?" Tug asked.

"I'm good at it." Martin couldn't keep the giggle in any longer. Blood loss, coke, knowing he was done. "Dog'll probably get a medal from the queen. Post… I mean, postum… what do I mean?"

"Posthumously," Nick said.

Martin laughed out loud. "That's it! Can't form a bloody word now. But that's your one way out, folks. Set me up."

"It'll work," Danni said. "Let's get it sorted now, and—"

"No." Tug swung a boot into Martin's gut. "He ain't goin' nowhere." Another kick, this time the face, cheekbone flaring.

Martin giggled some more. The next blows impacted vaguely upon him, his body growing numb, Tug a dentist applying pressure without pain.

Danni said, "Stop!"

"No," Tug said. "Put him in the hole and bury him. Once he's down, I'll have the boys cement it over like the others."

Others.

"You do it," Tug said. "Or I tell your IA fucks the truth. I'll do a couple a' years, but this cunt ain't gettin' away with murdering Vera."

Vera. The dog's name was Vera.

"What do we use?" Nick said.

"Nothing." Tug gestured to the hole Dave now lay in. "We bury him."

Nick and Danni took a couple of seconds to consider, then shifted Martin to the edge of the hole in which they dumped Dave. Martin still laughed on and off, a giggling fit, unable to stop. Danni uncuffed him so they wouldn't be traced back to her, and besides, Martin couldn't really fight it.

"I *did* kill him," Martin said, face-down, staring over the edge of the pit. "Didn't I?"

Tug glared down at him, Martin glancing up out of one corner of his eye. Back down at Dave, twisted in the freshly-dug pit.

Tug said, "You remember?"

"No," Martin said, calming. His vision cleared, lingering on Dave. His mind settled into a sleepy kind-of clarity. "I think that part of my brain is gone forever. I just can't face it at all. It makes sense now, though."

List, observe, conclude.

"I was a bastard. To Edith, to scrotes all over, to my wife, to my friends. When I gave her permission to hide for a while, she took that chance. She told me she hated me, that she was scared of me, especially after I threw Julie down the stairs. Then you got wind he was leaving town. Callum?"

Tug said, "Batty boy was upset his boyfriend was leaving."

"Edith told me Si was going to take her away from everything. From me. That's what didn't make sense, if we were in a three-way relationship. I mean, if Si viewed us that way, he'd have talked to me about her. But it was only me who thought that. Fucked up as I was, right?"

Tug shoved Martin toward the hole with his foot.

"Then," Martin said, "you convinced me. That night, you got me all riled up, and when we confronted Si here, I couldn't allow him to escape with Edith, and you didn't want to lose that income stream."

Tug tipped Martin over. Martin's stomach loop-de-looped as he dropped, then the wind whooshed out of his body as he collided with Dave.

"Buried him in here," Martin said, wheezing, unsure how long this clarity would last. About to be entombed alive, the puzzle unsolved. "Tell me! It was me, wasn't it? I killed him!"

"Yeah, Rosie." Tug appeared in the dark opening, staring down from the side of the rectangle of wan light. A shovel in-hand. "You strangled him. I tried to pull you off, but you throttled the life outta that smug poofter. You said you'd find the bitch without him." Tug pushed the first shower of dirt over Martin. "But a week after we poured concrete on him, you was feelin' guilty. Wanted to confess to everyone. Get clean, win Edith back fair and square. Tell your wife, yer bitch friend in internal affairs..."

Dirt flew in from two more angles now, Danni and Nick joining in. Clods hit Martin's face, crumbling apart and landing in his mouth. He spat but the taste lingered, clogging his throat.

Tug said, "You wanted to tell Si's mummy and daddy, give 'em hugs or some shit, ask for forgiveness, and hand yerself in with those tapes Dave made of our business."

The soil covered Dave and most of Martin. He spat more grains and globs from his mouth.

He said, "That's enough, isn't it?"

"It's better if we cover you right up," Tug said. "The cement settles better."

Martin shouted this time. "*I killed him! I strangled Si Larson to death! That's what you wanted wasn't it?*"

Nick said, "We don't need your confession, dick head."

Danni said, "Yeah, we were there."

"You helped," Martin said.

"Of course," Danni said. "We were a team. We always helped each other. No matter what. You forgot all that long before you took a swim."

Martin said, "You helped me dispose of Si's body, helped cover it up."

Nick paused with a shovelful of dirt. "Who else would it be, Martin? Of course we did."

"Hah! So that's what they were waiting for!"

"What the fuck?" Tug said. "What who were waiting for?"

Martin dug his left hand out of the dirt, his good one, sat up a far as his aching body would allow. "I wondered what the hell this was all about, but as soon as you killed Dave, I knew."

Danni said, "I'm gonna hit you with my shovel if you don't lie down."

"Doesn't matter," Martin said. "My confession wasn't for you. It was for *THEM*."

The hole filled with white light. *Cracks* sounded, one by one, electrical gunshots careening off the walls. Floodlights burst to life all around the warehouse. The three grave-diggers wielded their tools like weapons, looking this way, then that.

Voices from far away:

"Armed police!"

"Put down your weapons."

"On your knees."

"Hands on your head."

A louder voice, female, over a bullhorn: "You are all under arrest. Armed police are present. Keep your hands in plain sight. Do not reach for anything or you will be shot."

The three of them, silhouettes against the heavenly glow, tossed the shovels aside, and knelt. Hands on their heads.

And Martin Money laughed once again, closed his eyes, and embraced the dark as it descended and consumed him

.

Rooting Out

Martin stirred. Not dead. He smelled disinfectant. On his back, the surface hard, yet squidgy. He felt for a call button. Out of his reach.

He shouted, "Nurse!" but nothing came from his mouth.

A prick shot into his chest. A voice, like, "Clear!" and—

Light blasted Martin's eyes. Air rushed into his lungs and his back wrenched him upright. Adjusting to the glare, he found a needle in his chest, a man in a green and yellow coat patting his shoulder, two men in dark blue uniforms, coppers, holding his legs and his one good arm. He twisted but they didn't budge.

Blurs all around. He blinked.

Not a hospital.

The Shack. He was still in the Shack. The squidgy surface was a gurney. The needle—

"Adrenaline," the paramedic said. "Brought you back."

"We need to know what you took," came a familiar voice. A woman. She stood in front of him. He had to look up to see her face. *DI Cupinder Rowe.* She said, "Martin, what did you take?"

"Pizza Hut," he said. "Do you have a cup of tea?"

"What *drugs*?"

"Oh," Martin said. "The usual. Bit of coke, bit of speed. No smack for a change though. That's something isn't it?"

Rowe said, "You think this is funny?"

"Radio mic." Martin had been trained in the use of those contraptions. Like a handheld radar dish—point, activate, and listen in to conversations from hundreds of yards away. He said. "You got it all?"

Cupinder asked the paramedic about Martin's condition. The paramedic removed the syringe from Martin's chest, shone a light in his eyes and checked his pulse, and said, "He'll be okay for now, but he needs to be in a hospital," so Cupinder told him he could wait over there. Somewhere over there. Martin didn't see where he went.

A second woman entered his field of vision. Helen Cartwright. Side by side with Cupinder, both in trouser suits and flak-jackets. Helen said, "We got it all, thanks. We missed DC Essex's murder, unfortunately, but yes, everything after that."

Martin saw his arm had been bandaged, that hollow sensation echoing again. He flexed his fingers on both hands. Both extremities worked, the right, the damaged one, a tad stiffer. He asked, "Did you ever believe me, Cupinder?"

"No," DI Rowe said.

"She convinced me," Helen said. "She convinced me that this sting would work. I didn't believe you'd stay clean if you went back to that world, especially unprepared, but DI Rowe had more faith in you. Thought you'd be strong enough to lead us here before you dropped back down."

Martin said, "Here?"

Helen swept her hand around. "To Si Larson. We guessed he was either here or in the river. Just needed your confession." She shifted slightly, so the floodlight illuminated her scar. "You accept that you murdered Simon Larson in cold blood?"

A team of white suited scene-of-crime officers hoisted Dave's body from the foundation hole, and set him aside for processing.

Cupinder said, "The footage. We always had the footage you uncovered with Wadaya."

"What sting?" Martin said. "You said the sting wouldn't work. What sting?"

Someone in the bowels of the Shack yelled, "Clear!" and Martin shrugged at the pair of constables holding him. "Is this necessary?"

Helen and Cupinder shared a look, then Cupinder dismissed the bobbies with a flick of the head and said, "Try anything," and placed a hand on her belt where she carried a gun.

The gun Martin helped train her to shoot.

Martin said, "That kit's a little extreme for MisPer."

Cupinder said, "I'm not in Missing Persons."

Martin took it all in—the guns, the jackets, the perfectly executed plan. He felt cold.

She said, "I'm PSD."

Helen grinned on the non-scarred side. Leaned on Cupinder; a movie poster, two cop buddies. Two cocky cop buddies who'd nabbed their man.

Cupinder was Professional Standards.

Cupinder convinced DCS Black to give him the chance to redeem himself.

Cupinder assigned him to Si Larson.

"You knew it was me," Martin said, "but couldn't prove it."

Cupinder said, "You made ground where Khaira and Webster couldn't. You had contacts, even if you didn't remember them. Your instincts came back so quickly, and Tug Jones couldn't resist fucking with you. Yes, you had a change of heart, and Dave came to explain it all after you were stabbed, but we had enough on you, and the rest of that stupid club to put you all away for a decade." She stared at the trio being held by the exit, ready to transfer to a van as soon as it got through the park.

Helen said, "But you had to go down for murder. Or there was no point."

Martin said, "But Dave thought I was going to die, and he was going to jail. That's why he ratted on his mates."

"Informed, Martin," Helen corrected. "We're police. We say *informed*."

"You already knew," Martin said, the pair nodding slowly. "Edith. You knew about her. The baby, the porn parties, you even had the CCTV that me and Wadaya uncovered."

They nodded away, smug as cats. Relaxed.

He said, "But it was still circumstantial. You needed a confession. You needed me to lead you here."

Nodding, nodding. Yes, yes, you're so right.

He said, "But the undercover thing. Didn't that nearly ruin it? When I found out?"

"Not really," said a male voice behind him. *Wadaya*. In his suit and vest, joining Helen and Cupinder, gun on his hip.

"Well," Martin said. "It was actually your idea, wasn't it?"

"Rising star," Cupinder answered brightly.

"Your phone," Martin said. "You traced your phone."

"Tracking device." Wadaya held his thumb and finger a centimetre apart.. "Had you pinpointed to within two metres at all times."

"Not really." Martin felt his legs. They worked fine. His stomach flipped some. "You said 'not really', about Julie pointing me to the undercover thing."

"Yeah," Wadaya said. "That was part of it too."

"Moving too slowly," Helen said. "You needed a push. Julie needed some convincing, refused to see you at first, but then she played her part so well."

"Considering how terrified she was," Cupinder said. "Couldn't believe she even slept with you."

Julie slept with Martin.

Julie planted the seed of 'coming back up'.

Julie was terrified of him.

Julie was part of the sting.

Wadaya said, "She was supposed to say the line as she left, but she bottled it. Said she worried you'd see right through her and hurt her, maybe hurt the baby. Couldn't risk it. So yeah, she shagged you. Even though we heard everything, saw everything, we couldn't interfere."

"I wouldn't have hurt our child," Martin said. "She must have known that."

"It isn't yours," Helen said.

And Martin didn't have to hear the truth. He knew it already.

Helen said, "It's Alan's."

Alan's. Alan Cartwright.

Martin's best friend.

The guy who he fought with so ferociously.

Helen said, "I lied to you. Back on the roof. *We* didn't have the affair, Martin. *They* did. They're the ones who cheated on *us*. That's why we started up together. Drunken revenge shagging. It grew from there and soon it was like we'd all swapped permanently, but then you agreed to try again with Julie. You didn't love her. Just wanted to take her away from Alan. Then you found out they were seeing each other again, that she was leaving you cos she was pregnant with his kid… that's why you threw her down the stairs, Martin. It wasn't your child, it *isn't* your child. She and Alan are living happily together in York, and she was brave enough to confront you. You. The man who tried to murder her *baby*."

"This whole thing," Martin said. "This whole thing—"

"Yes," Cupinder said. "Every detail. Me, Wadaya, Helen. *Devon Carlisle,* he isn't quite the addict he made himself out to be. He knew he had to mention the girl to you. We were surprised you went to Tug so soon, but we guessed by then you really didn't remember anything, or you wouldn't have gone near the man who tried to have you killed."

Wadaya said, "Oh yeah, cheers for leading us to that Hardcastle guy. He was arrested earlier today too."

"Edith?" Martin said.

Helen said, "Edith was happy to help. She knew you'd done something to Si, but when we offered to take her in she said she wanted to play her part. Knew you'd come for her. There were four coppers in the flat next door, waiting for her to utter the safe word if she believed she was threatened by you."

Cupinder bent down so her face was level with his. "But you were so proud of yourself. Getting her step-dad arrested. You know, I almost felt something good for you when that happened. But that isn't you, is it, Martin? Doing that good thing, it was all part of finding redemption or whatever it was."

"No," Martin said. "I was being honest. All that time. All I wanted was to show I'm a good man again. And I proved it."

Helen held up a single finger. "One week. You've been back *one week*, and you are a mess, high on coke and lying in the dirt. You tortured a suspect, you broke a dozen laws, concealed evidence. *One week*, Martin. All you've proved is how you will always return to that place. Your Dead Time *is* you."

"That's not true. I'm Martin. From The Before."

Cupinder said, "Really? Take a look at yourself."

Helen joined Cupinder, her face twisted as far as the scar tissue allowed. "But you'd done those things, Martin. The drugs, the abuse, the murder. They're on you."

"I'm not that person anymore!"

Wadaya's hand hovered near his gun, but no one drew. Yet.

"Doesn't matter," Cupinder said. "That man was gone a long time ago. Your wife's affair, the stress of going undercover for PSD, your misguided loyalty to those friends you made... it took you too far down. You went native and there's no coming back up from murder."

If he'd been on the other end of this, Martin would act the same way as them. A police officer; a drug addict and killer; wife-beater and exploiter of a sexually vulnerable teen; taking bribes; a *conspirator*.

Wadaya said, "Tonight went wrong when Gordo showed up with a sawn-off and killed DS Essex. We'll have to answer for that. But for the most part, the op worked to perfection."

Martin ceased trying to justify it. He stopped pushing that other guy away, the man from his Dead Time. The drugs in his system, his sheer pleasure without guilt of the prostitute last night, and his desire to locate Edith and make her all his again—those things led to a single course of action: surrender.

"Okay," he said. "I'm all yours."

Then the gunshots rang out.

Everyone turned to the sound. Chunks of door splintered inward. Automatic fire rattled beyond the walls. Screaming, shouting. Orders bellowing.

And one man inside yelling, "You pigs are so fucked! You're FUCKED!" Tug Jones. The only person not panicking. Lying on the floor with a grin the size of a bus. "You're all *FUCKED!*"

THE NEW TIME

Showdown

In a way, what happened next was a godsend. Had the operation not gone to shit there, right at the end, as everything was seemingly resolved, no one would have been sacked. Sure, the covert monitoring team had been following Martin rather than Dave, stretched thin by the spectre that commands all aspects of police work—the budget—and so arrived at the Shack later than would have been ideal. Yes, they wasted no time in rigging up the radio mic, enabling the monitoring team to listen in by pointing a device at an open window, but such equipment, even at optimum efficiency it can't be completed immediately. So, once they established a police officer had been killed, it was too late to act, too late to do anything but nail the killer. They did everything else correctly. Dave informed them that things would go down here, in this place, and the floodlights and access points and observation posts had been in position ever since it became clear Martin would not back down from his demand to return to work, and so it was inconceivable to the top brass and, more importantly, to the press that such a well-planned operation might omit the possibility of armed thugs storming the place to free their beloved boss.

The working class hero.

No one took Tug Jones into account. He wasn't supposed to be there.

Never touch the crime.

It should have been Martin, Dave, and the OTT club. It was them who carried out the worst of the crimes. Tug, if anything, was a pawn with delusions of royalty. Manipulated and controlled by Gordo and his minions, he grew to control the community, gave back so much, offered the people who worked for him security and a sense of belonging. The people didn't work for Tug Jones out of fear. They worked for him out of loyalty and ambition, because—as they saw it—he commanded respect, controlled the police, and returned their commitment ten-fold.

He was, without a doubt, a working class hero.

So what happened next would take away the spotlight from Cupinder and Helen.

No one would question, other than in passing, why they failed to properly protect their confidential informant, Detective Sergeant Dave Essex.

No one would launch a blistering article attacking the government's policy on policing or budgets.

The focus, the glorification, would descend on the violence. Because violence sells papers. Violence sells advertising space on news websites. And violence is just so damn sexy, any autopsy of events would hold a lens to the planning, to the West Yorkshire Police's failure to combat chavs and scumbags.

How, the Sentinel would ask, *can people from a poor housing estate afford such weaponry, and learn to fire it so well, and organise themselves so professionally?*

How, the Daily Mail would ask, *did community policing and a soft touch on crime lead to the deaths of three officers, as ten youths fired at the guards outside a building known as The Shack?*

What, the Guardian would ask, *could possibly lead to such a breakdown in trust between the community and the police, that disaffected youths would be willing to take up arms against those charged with protecting said community?*

Who, the Sentinel would demand, *was responsible for allowing ten hooded youths to scatter a dozen armed police as they stormed a supposedly secure building, and freed a violent pimp and drugs dealer from under their noses?*

They would be fair questions too.

Because the police *were* caught unawares. Budgets again played their part, with an armed police unit doubling up, gathering evidence as well as bodyguarding. And it wasn't a dozen, as the papers would say; it was eight. Four patrolling outside, two inside guarding Tug, Danni and Nick, with two out back, ensuring no homeless or other surprises brought up the rear. It was as sound a setup as could be hoped given conventional operational standards. And funding.

It would also emerge later that Tug's key right-hand man, recommended to him by Detective Sergeant James Gordon, spent six years in the army. Six years during which he served his country in Afghanistan and Iraq before landing a dishonourable discharge when a shipment of guns went missing, and his signature was identified on many of the documents.

Admin error.

The cunts.

Some of those guns were awfully similar to the ones wielded by the hooded youths who flanked the Shack that night, opening fire when the flat terrain threatened to expose them. The four armed officers went down, two finding the strength to loose off a few rounds, but it wasn't enough to repel the hoards. Despite their body armour, wounds to their extremities neutralised them within half a minute.

And so the invaders penetrated the fortress, and while Helen, Cupinder and Wadaya took cover behind the Portakabin in which Si and many others plied their trade, the hail of bullets consumed the entire space. The walls pinged and the dirt kicked up. Bullets punched holes in the Portakabins and shattered floodlights.

Through it all, Martin crawled. The adrenaline shot had gifted a high degree of sensation. The grainy soil, hardscrabble flagstones, the bandages, the throbbing bite on his arm. Dirt down his pullover where they'd ripped it open to administer the shot. The whizz of hot metal slowed down over his head as he, for some reason, moved forward, away from Cupinder and Helen and Wadaya, hunkering behind some sort of generator with a dead light stemming from it.

Close enough to Tug to watch as Riccardo, in a full face mask, shot the cuffs off him. Close enough to hear Tug say, "Them too." Close enough to see the bone and brain blow out the back of both Danni's and Nick's heads as Riccardo shot them both in quick succession.

The police guarding them were two of the three who died. Already down by the time Martin reached them. Cops whose names he hadn't known.

"Martin!" cried Helen from her position behind the cabin, her gun drawn on him.

This was the end. He was guilty of all that he'd been accused of, and his future was, basically, a prison cell.

And he had no doubt now; it was a cell he deserved.

But he had also done the training. Firearms. He was good at it. Before this could finally be over, he had more business to complete, a redemption of sorts, but different to the one he'd hoped to attain.

The Glock 17 from the dead officer was already in his hand when Helen yelled at him. He'd already locked the plan down. So it didn't take a lot of thought to roll on his side, and fire once in Helen's general direction.

He fired high, obviously, but it was enough to send her scurrying. A clip of seventeen. Now sixteen.

Outside, the thugs had dispersed, leaving three injured officers and one dead on the path outside, but Martin could not help. Paramedics were on-scene, emerging from cover even as he made the decision to run, to complete his mission.

His final mission. One that, in his own eyes at least, might allow him to sleep peacefully once again.

A Nice Wool Coat

With the medically-administered adrenaline boosting his failing body, Martin took off through the Lille Park toward the city centre, where there would be crowds in which to lose himself, or at least civilisation. Riccardo would not have risked that direction. He'd have taken Tug north or east, toward the industrial estates and wide-open roads. No, Martin had a free run, so to speak.

A forty-something man, jacked on coke, adrenaline, and fear.

Ripped pullover.

Bloody, bandaged arm.

A gun.

He hopped the waist-high fence at the south end of Lille Park and stuck to the shadows. Lots of shadows at night. Drunk partiers, revellers, people out for a good time, they gave him space. The cameras would be out in force soon, the operators scanning specifically for him, for a fortyish white man with the handy unique identifiers of a gun and a bloody arm.

He slunk into a narrow street with four bars, all the size of a sweet shop, all with smoking areas out back. He hid the gun under his jumper and slipped into the first bar without a doorman, a sparse crowd, but enough to squeeze through unnoticed by staff who wouldn't welcome someone who might start a fight at any moment.

Locating the smoking deck, Martin nodded 'hi' to two men who smoked whilst drinking from bottles. One wore a leather jacket, the other a long woollen one. It took Martin, with the help of the Glock, all of ten seconds to part both from their outer garments.

He exited via a fire escape that led to the bins in an alleyway wide enough for a single refuse lorry, and ran up there, donning the long wool coat as he did. He stumbled out into a busy street, lined with restaurants that served sloppy animal organs as delicacies and portions better suited to a sample menu as main courses. He pulled the coat tight, rolled the gun up the leather jacket, and hailed a cab.

Inside, muted from the goings-on of the real world, he gave the driver directions back to his own car.

In the investigation that followed, his robbery would be pored over, and the independent inquiry would conclude it had been a distraction. Correctly, as it would turn out. Correctly, because in the back of the cab, with Martin looking pretty much human in the newly-acquired nice coat, he guided the cabbie the long way round the city centre loop road, the wrong way round the ring road, and eventually to where he parked his car, a ten minute stroll from Lille Park.

The robbery pulled most officers away from their station, away from their search of the industrial estates, and the roads surrounding them, allowing Martin to take back possession of his vehicle, and the money in the boot, and to pay the cabbie—adding a significant tip—before driving away into the night.

What happened next, no inquiry would ever truly uncover.

Payoff

To get any sleep, Martin needed to come down from over twenty-four hours of speed, coke, and an adrenaline infusion that waned a couple of hours after he fled the Shack. Legal pills weren't up to do the job. The stomach cramps ambushed him as he rolled around streets with dark houses and boarded up pubs, but he kept going. He avoided the Bankwell, instead exploring Edith's neighbourhood, and further west where violent crime spiked in summer and the number of junkies needing hospital treatment spiked each winter.

A white lad sat on a wall that surrounded one of those boarded-up pubs. He kept his hands in the pocket of his requisite hoodie, his jeans low-slung even in that position. When Martin pulled up, the kid didn't reveal his face, didn't move. Martin rolled down his window. The night misted cold on his sweat. He said, "Hey."

The young man risked a glance. His stone face lingered on Martin, who was pale and had not bothered to wipe the beads of perspiration from his brow. He needed to look the part. His car screamed Five-O, even with the switched licence plates. He flashed four twenties, which brought the kid ambling over.

He asked, "Whatchu need, grandpa?"

Martin said, "H."

After completing the transaction, Martin drove for as long as he could before his hands shook and his guts ached too much to focus. The district grew unfamiliar, morphing from ring roads into single-tracks lined with trees and the occasional house. Amazing how here, in his home town, he was seldom less than thirty minutes from the countryside. In France, America, almost every other country, it took hours to reach such solitude.

He pulled into a narrow opening, a field with an open gate, and parked behind a wall.

Having already bought a spoon and a lighter, and retaining a fine supply of needles from those he procured earlier, he bent the cutlery and cooked the nasty brew. He injected enough to take the edge off his cramps, to allow him the rejuvenating energy of sleep.

He woke at ten A.M. and snorted two lines of coke to bring himself back to life.

The Bankwell would be crawling with police, but he had little choice. Providing the real owners hadn't yet reported them, the false plates gave him a fair chance, but his photo and his vehicle's description would have been circulated, and since he had no idea how to steal a new car he was stuck with it.

He drove as near to the Bankwell as he dared, then carried his rucksack of money around the neighbouring district until he spotted a cab, flagged it down, and had it drop him two streets behind Rose Grove. He used the cover of the many overgrown gardens and abandoned developments to sneak up on the house, what he and his mates called 'garden-hopping', back when he was a boy. In the back, he crept through the tall grass and weeds, watching the house for as long as his coke-blasted nerves would permit.

The cops could be inside, waiting. If that was the case, they'd be armed. He couldn't just wave the gun and threaten them.

He used the jungle as cover before stashing the bag and crouch-running to the MDF door, possibly galloping like an Olympian, possibly dawdling, it was hard to tell with the buzz he was on. He moved the panel aside in what he believed was silence. Inside, the rotten kitchen was empty. The hallway held the same decomposing stench as before, and flies darted around him as he wandered to the living room. In here, the usual array of lost people lounged around, more flies zipping from person to person, patch of filth to patch of filth.

No Dev Carlisle.

No Callum.

"Hey."

Martin spun to the voice. Callum made a clumsy swing with a baseball bat. Clumsy, but it still hit Martin on the arm and it sent a narrow burn across the muscle. Not enough to subdue him. Martin grabbed the bat in his right hand, hit Callum in the gut with his left. As he wrenched the bat from Callum, the wound under his bandage ripped and the blood dribbled wet on his skin, but did not breach the dressing.

Callum glared out from under his shaggy hair, barely able to catch a breath.

Martin said, "Dev's gone, I assume."

Callum tried to speak. A gasp came out, so he nodded instead.

"Police?" Martin asked.

Again, affirmative.

"He was a CI," Martin said. "He's safe now." He hefted the bat. "This is expensive. Someone leave it with you?"

The nod again, yes.

"One of Tug's guys?"

Callum sat down, back against the door frame.

"You supposed to call him if I show?"

Callum strained to speak. "Yeah."

Martin crouched, his face level with Callum's. "You know what I did to Si?"

Callum's gaze shifted slowly, finding Martin. He said, "I know what you did."

Martin took out the gun. "Make the call."

Callum closed his eyes.

Martin removed something else from his other pocket. The arm should have been agony, but again, the drugs helped. It only hurt like hell instead. The blood pooled inside the bandage, making it soggy rather than dripping. He placed the something in Callum's hand.

Callum opened his eyes and looked at the package. Bank notes.

"Fifty grand," Martin said. "I'm not trying to make up for Si. But junkies always talk about getting clean, starting again. They get some money, but spend it on drugs, never enough to make a break. They earn, they inject. They try to save up, but they're always dragged back in, whether it's shoplifting, burglary, muggings or prostitution, they need to earn, and it stops them getting a place, finding a programme."

Callum's hand dithered, staring at the cash.

Martin said, "Edith managed it, though. If you want to clean up, get out of this life, avoid ending up like Si, get in touch with her. She'll help you. And anyone else you might want to share that with. It's enough cash to kill yourself or keep yourself stocked up for years without working the park. But I hope you make a different choice."

Martin stood up and put the gun away. Callum's gaze remained on the brick of money.

Martin said, "No obligation. It's yours whatever. But I'd really appreciate if you'd make the call."

Stand-Off

There's this myth that people enjoy believing. It involves soldiers. It goes that soldiers, when they've seen action, they become superhuman in some way. You see in movies and TV shows, highly trained agents and combatants, walking down a deserted street or corridor. They stop suddenly, some sixth sense telling them all isn't quite right. It's true that someone experienced in modern warfare might be more attuned to spot *that* glint on a hilltop, or be able to pick a person out of a crowd observing them in a way that suggests surveillance, but near-psychic abilities are simply an invention of writers and directors seeking to elevate the audience's sensation of awe.

It's the same with police. They're trained to spot a liar, to recognise when a suspect is moving with a relaxed gait, overcompensating to avoid suspicion, so an experienced patrol officer will zone in on that person for a random stop-search. But they have no way of scanning a room and picking out a piece of lint that the forensic team somehow missed.

The thing about soldiers, though, it often extends to the soldiers themselves, especially those who feel hard done by. Riccardo, for example, was caught between emanating an air of indestructibility, and surviving.

Out the back of the Blue Pussycat, he and his white, hooded mate, the one with the mafia-sounding name—Pauly?—stood guard. Steel barrels of beer lined up in stages, which would act as cover if anyone came at them, yet there they stood, upright, pacing in front of the door, allowing those under their protection the illusion of security.

Martin positioned himself on the corner of the next street, viewing the men briefly each time they passed the gap formed by the narrow angle of his approach. Occasionally both men disappeared from view. It was semi-regular. And Martin didn't have to wait long for the chance to move.

Up on speed now, he sprinted to the wall and pressed his back against it, six inches from the opening to the yard, Glock pointed upward in a two-handed grip. Listened.

Pacing.

Pauly grumbled about being cold.

Riccardo told him to shut up.

Martin listened to their footfalls.

He calculated their rhythm. Every five back-and-forth circuits, they crossed over one another's path. It was the point at which they made the smallest target, and also placed one of them, briefly, in a blind spot.

Martin counted the steps, depressed his finger over the second trigger on the Glock that would allow it to fire when he squeezed fully. During his training he asked the instructor several times if she was sure there was no safety catch on the pistol, and it took him four hours to get the technique down to make it ready to fire. Once he got it, though, it was difficult to forget.

There.

The cross-over.

Martin levelled the gun in his grip and paced into the yard. Riccardo was closest. Without warning, Martin squeezed the trigger and the gun roared and bucked. Riccardo's chest sprayed red, and Pauly, instead of running for cover, fumbled with his gun. Martin breathed steadily and fired, blowing Pauly's hood down as the bullet erupted out the back of his skull. Riccardo, although staggering hadn't gone down. He swung the Army-issue machine-gun up, but already Martin drew a bead and fired three times, shredding the ex-soldier's chest. Riccardo's gun arm hung loose and Martin fired one more round into his head.

It really was that easy. With no super-human sixth sense, the element of surprise trumps any amount of experience.

Five rounds spent, plus the one back in the Shack. Eleven to go.

He found the door unlocked, ready for a quick retreat if required. This is where it grew harder to predict the future. No way of knowing what lay beyond here.

He peeked inside: a long corridor made the approach a bottleneck. Riccardo, surely would have stationed someone at the end, and the gunshots would have penetrated. Or would they?

The club was all-but soundproofed. They would have heard something, dull thuds perhaps.

Fuck it. Martin swung the door open and rushed in, the Glock in one hand at first, his left, but he quickly brought up his right to support it. The forearm felt stretched and sent a spike into the bone with every squeeze of the trigger, yet it was the only way to shoot.

At the end of the passageway, a lad, maybe nineteen, in an American football jersey, popped into view. His jaw slackened at the sight of Martin gliding toward him, then Martin fired. The bullet gouged into the wall and the kid ran back, yelling, "Feds!"

Martin used the wall as a barrier, robotically covered the interior of the table dancing club, picking out danger points.

The American Football guy ducked into the DJ booth, while two others hid behind the bar. One hoodie lad in the middle tipped over a table, a cowboy imitating those westerns he might have watched as child.

As a child.

The guy had been an actual child until a couple of years ago.

Maybe they still were, these guardians of their hero; it was hard to tell. Riccardo and Pauly were adults for sure, and made their choices on the back of years of living like this. But there wasn't a single person under Martin's gun over the age of twenty. All with weapons, none of them firing. Their faces popped up to see, but no one even drew down on Martin.

"I killed Riccardo," Martin said. "He was a fraud. So's Tug Jones. He's about to die."

One the lads behind the bar appeared, aiming his Sig pistol. Tried to fire, but it jammed. Martin lined him up. The kid froze. The gun in his hand wilted and he shook his head rapidly.

Martin said, "Go," and the kid dropped the weapon, ran from behind the bar, and slammed into the fire exit, daylight slicing into the club momentarily. Martin called out, "It's not easy. Firing randomly at night is different isn't it. Mowing down faceless coppers like they're zombies or Arabs in a computer game. But now, here, up against a guy who's won trophies for shooting. It's not quite that easy."

Shuffling from out there. Repositioning.

Martin said, "You guys were shown how to use guns, how to make them go *bang*, but you've never been trained how to *shoot*. Not properly. I have. For example, I could put three bullets through that table and you'd be dead. Hear me?"

No reply.

Martin said, "I'm gonna count to three, then start shooting."

A shuffle. The guy from the DJ stand yelled, "Don't fuckin' try it."

Martin said, "I have over a hundred hours of firearms training behind me. How many do you have?" He listened for movement, risked peering out. No one had moved. He added, "Hitting even a stationary target with those big boy guns is tough. Imagine how well you'll do when I'm moving." No reply. "So here's the deal.

Anyone wants to go the same way as the last guy, think about it. I didn't shoot him, I won't shoot you. You can stay, protect your boss-man, your local hero, and maybe—just maybe—you take me down. But to guarantee your survival, you have to drop those guns. And go." Martin made a noisy show of unloading the clip and re-inserting it, giving them something to think about. "In five seconds, I'm coming out, and anyone holding a weapon gets a bullet."

The kid behind the table went first. The Sig skidded out and he showed his hands over the rim—ever the cowboy fan—then rose fully. A black kid, wild afro shaped into dinosaur spikes. Martin aimed his Glock and flicked it toward the exit and the kid ran, clattered out through it.

Martin said, "One."

He said, "Two."

The other guy behind the bar, a white youth with pale show muscles under a basketball vest, walked out, gun held between thumb and forefinger, the way some TV show probably demonstrated. He laid it on a table, then calmly swaggered the same way as his pals, eyeing Martin all the way, that *I'm not scared* bravado oozing from him.

When he was out, Martin said, "Three. And bear in mind where you're hiding isn't bulletproof."

He leaned out and aimed at the DJ booth, and said, "Four."

The gun flew over the top of the glass and the lad emerged, hood pulled low over his face. He said, "Fuck you," and ran out the fire exit. He would meet up with his fellow deserters shortly, and between them, if they were typical of their species, they would concoct a story that allowed them to feel like someone else fucked up—Riccardo or Tug—and thus relinquish any residual notions of cowardice to the realms of fantasy.

Now all Martin had to do was locate Tug fucking Jones.

ENDINGS

Another Last Chance

"You knew I was a plant," Martin said, as he opened the door to the porn-party room.

"Gordo did," came Tug's reply, accompanied by cloth on cloth, by soft thumps and footsteps on carpet.

Martin crept into the doorway, shielding enough of himself behind the frame so that only an expert marksman could hit his target area. Tug appeared unarmed. Instead, he stuffed money into the false bottom of a suitcase from a safe built into the wall behind one of the mirrors that opened on a hinge. Laid out on the sofa where Martin shagged a variety of girls was a pinstripe suit, shiny black shoes, and a dark wig. At least four places to hide a gun.

Martin said. "Going somewhere?"

"Got a mate," Tug said. "Works the high-end side of Leeds. Bad ass smuggler. People, drugs, money. You name it. He sorted me out with someone in Paris. He'll help us get out of Europe."

Martin held his aim steady. "Us?"

"Yeah, Rosie, me and you. We both got serious heat now. We got money, though. We even got our falsies, man." He waved a passport. "I ain't armed, Rosie."

"Yeah," Martin said. "You never touch the crime."

"Not until I need to."

"Only ask someone to hold a gun if you trust that someone with your life." Martin revealed himself fully, stalked into the room with Tug in his sights. "You trust me, Tug?"

Tug's mouth pulled back, his off-white teeth bared. "Nah, Rosie.

We never trusted you. Gordo liked fucking with you, though. Saw it as sport. We was all smokin' it up one night, and he was like, 'Let's bring him in, guys. Let's fuck him up. Make him one of us. For real,' and we were all, like, 'Naw, let's keep our heads down and he'll go away.' Not Gordo, man. He was great. Pretty soon, you fuckin' loved it, Rosie. But you couldn't take the big time stuff could you? Si Larson was too much. You hadda go ruin it, go confessin' and shit. Get all catholic priest with your IA twats and go hug his mommy and daddy and tell 'em you're sorry. Well fuck that shit, Rosie."

Tug angled the suitcase with the fake panel upwards. At least five hundred grand. More in the safe.

Tug said, "Last chance, Rosie."

"No," Martin said. "It's *your* last chance."

"I don't fuckin' *think* so."

A *click-clack* from behind Martin sent a cold shiver through his arms and fingers.

"Sorry, Rosie," Caz said.

She glided out from her hiding place by the private bar, pointing a pump-action shotgun square at Martin, looking comfortable with it in her hands.

Never Touch the Crime

"Never touch the crime," Tug said. "I mean I coulda done you, but it's been lucky for me so far. Don't do nuthin' that'll dump me in prison more'n a couple a' months. Started out as good sense. Now it's kinda just superstition. Good luck charm, y'know?"

"I get it," Martin said.

Tug accepted the Glock 17, then threw a fist into Martin's gut. Martin doubled at the waist, unable to breathe. A colourless bile shot up his throat and oozed out onto the floor. The back of his mouth burned, spreading down into his stomach. He coughed. Yacked air back into his lungs, but simply couldn't get enough.

Tug carried the suit, shirt, shoes and wig over to his suitcase and closed the false bottom, piling other smart businessman-type items on top. He said, "All I gotta do at Dover is talk all posh, like a regular fuck, and I'm gone. Caz too, right, hon?"

"Correct, darling," Caz said, all posh like a regular fuck.

"She's comin' down with the rest of the cash, same as me, but separate. They said don't travel together, so, like, we look like we're bankers or managers or some shit."

Martin pushed himself to a sitting position, back against the sofa. He pointed a thumb at the mirror to the side. He managed to wheeze the word, "Camera?"

"Smart, Rosie. Always the smart one. Yeah, had a guy behind there. Full panel, man. No auto shit. Not worth it when you need quality."

The shotgun's black opening stared at Martin. Heavy in Caz's hands, but she coped with it well. No shake.

Caz—the woman who'd trembled in Martin's presence when he first came back from the dead.

Caz, who held both his hands in hers.

Who asked, "Does that mean you don't remember *me* either, Rosie?"

Those words. *Does that mean you don't remember* me *either, Rosie?*

He'd told her he didn't.

Caz, who—in Martin's presence—hid her face when it was bruised.

Who followed Tug's instructions in silence, an obedient geisha.

Who rushed Martin out of her flat, urging him to leave whenever Tug grew tense, whenever it seemed he might snap.

Now, in this room, Tug said, "Okay, Caz, when you're ready."

She inched to the left, a couple of steps back.

Caz, who—that first day Martin came to them in the flat—said, "I'm stuck with him then?"

Now, cowering before her, Martin inhaled as much air as he could and said, "You're not stuck with him anymore, Caz. It's all in your hands."

She said, "I know it is," then turned the gun on Tug, and pulled the trigger.

The shotgun boomed so loud, one of Martin's eardrums snapped. The buck from the discharge jerked the weapon from Caz's hands as she stumbled. Blood trickling from one ear, Martin caught her. The pair spun round to locate Tug, but that was okay.

The spread of the shot had ripped a hole the size of a football in Tug's gut. He pawed at the wound, trying to close it, to hold his bloody, destroyed organs inside. That grin remained static. More blood infused itself into his teeth. His pale face coughed out one of his stupid, cocky laughs.

Caz said, "Something funny, you cunt?"

Martin's right ear had died for the time being, so in order to hear what came next, he had to move closer to Tug, and told him, "Say that again."

Tug said it again, but too softly.

Remembering his own trick used on Gordo the previous night, Martin scooped up the shotgun, racked another round and, still crouching thanks to that punch, he approached Tug. Placed the gun barrel on the dying man's forehead. "Say it again."

Tug had enough strength left for two things: first, he forced that blood-streaked grin wider; second, he raised one hand, the middle finger extended. And then he stopped breathing altogether, and his hand flopped into his lap.

Martin lowered the gun. "It's over."

Caz said, "Did you believe him?"

"Believe what?"

"What he said."

"I didn't hear."

"Oh," she said. "I thought you was just being all macho."

"No." Martin pointed at his bleeding ear. "I really didn't hear."

Once Martin angled his good ear toward Caz. She blinked a few times. Perhaps it would be more accurate to suggest she *fluttered* her eyes.

She rested her arm around Martin's shoulders and said, "He claims it wasn't him, Rosie. Tug didn't order the hit on you."

REDEMPTION...?

A Fresh Start

A man and woman in tracksuits ran side-by-side. The man hadn't shaved but looked okay for it. His slight gut shook with each step, a mere couple of stone or so of extra fat, maybe thirty pounds at the outside. The impact of a sedentary job, sat at a desk, earning good money, then spending a chunk of that money after work in an effort to unwind. Still, approaching forty years of age, it would be difficult to shift.

The woman was trimmer. A larger arse than Martin favoured, but then Martin's taste ventured only as far as girls in their early twenties, and he preferred them even younger. As long as they were legal, it didn't matter to him what in their lives had led them onto the receiving end of a middle-aged man's penis. As long as *he* was satisfied. As long as they put up with his choice of position, his choice of drug, his choice of time; if they took his money or his affection, he did not ask questions. In The Before, that sort of man was ripe for a bag-nabbing, but now, as this woman jogged, her small breasts and wide backside bobbin, all he could think of was a large, firm bed, with a young pretty girl beneath him.

He snorted a line of coke from his dashboard.

No, even though she was younger than him by almost a decade, the jogging woman did not stir him at all. A 'handsome' woman, perhaps, and her husband was clearly punching above his weight, looks-wise, but there were things a person has to accept.

Martin's taste in women was another reason why he could never approach this couple.

The woman pushed a buggy with inflatable tyres. A three-wheeled contraption with a padded bar, a cradle of sorts securing a baby inside, as they ran at a pace more comfortable for the woman than the man. When they disappeared around the corner, Martin started the car, and followed.

The blood had dried in his ear, but pasted his clothes and his neck. Although he cleaned himself up in the Blue Pussycat's loos, he hadn't dared stop off anywhere for wipes, or indeed for a supply of first aid gear. After assuring Caz she should take all of Tug's money that she could carry, he strongly suggested she leave the country on her false passport, convincing her it would be okay to return in six months or so. Then he drove around, thinking hard about what Tug said.

It wasn't me.

One final jibe? Fucking with him one last time? The drug-dealing pimp was dying, and already had ample opportunity to come clean, but at no point had anyone confirmed they had tried to kill Martin. At no point had anyone questioned it, either.

They all thought one of the others did it.

Nobody talked about it, but they all assumed one of their number carried out the hit, the assault, and yet...

The jogging couple rested at a bench on the edge of an urban park. Cars lined the road; BMWs, Audis, upmarket Fords. Children played football in Leeds United kits, in Manchester United shirts, dressed as Chelsea players and Arsenal stars. Younger ones chased one another, and even younger ones whooped on swings and yelled as they whooshed down slides, and screamed as they hung on for dear life as a man in jeans and shoes and a wool jumper spun them mercilessly on a roundabout.

The jogging man with the flabby body lifted the baby and held it in one arm while the woman mixed formula in a Tommy Tippee bottle. The man made goo-goo eyes and slipped his finger into the baby's mouth, and its hands waved around. The woman offered the bottle to the man, and he fed the infant while she stretched, watching the pair constantly.

Her smile was so much like Julie's, the way Julie stared at the pregnancy test kit every time she and Martin made the choice to become parents. After each failed attempt, the urge went back in the box. "What's the point in trying?" she said whenever this happened. Until the next time.

Martin went along with it. After all, it was the thing to do at their age. Maybe they didn't try enough. Maybe they'd have had kids if only they'd put in the effort, and maybe she would never have had an affair with Martin's best friend, and Martin never would have gone undercover; Si would still be alive, Martin would not have been stabbed and dumped in the river; heck, even the police murdered in Lille Park would probably be eating Sunday lunch with their families. But then, in this alternative reality, Edith Long still fell under the thrall of her stepfather, her young sisters becoming victims too; Tug Jones was king of the Bankwell, and Gordo and the OTT club were laughing their arses off, sat on a fortune, untouchable; and, finally, without all that came in the Dead Time, a slightly overweight couple, with a good life and so much happiness to bestow, might not be jogging around a park in matching tracksuits, pausing to gather their breath and to feed a child.

Replaying these events, weighing up each pro, each con, soon the week's verbal exchanges slipped through. The conversations. Conversations that made sense at the time, but in the light of Tug's final words, some of them took on new meaning.

As best he could, Martin mentally listed what they'd said, what everyone he'd met this past week had told him, what he'd seen.

He observed the effects of those things.

And he came to a conclusion.

Scene of the Crime

The box arrived addressed to Edith Long, and a scruffy man delivered it to the Church of St Augustine's chapel at around six P.M., about an hour before evensong. He told the priest that he heard they ran shifts at a homeless shelter, that they would come across Edith. The priest asked why the man couldn't send it straight to Edith.

"I'm a bad person," replied the man with the blood-streaked ear. "I enjoy being bad. Everything a person like me should not do, I enjoy it. I can't stop enjoying it."

The priest said, "Surely if you know you are bad, you can redeem yourself."

"I tried that," the man said. "But it's too deep inside me. Even if I resist, it's still there. One slip up, and I'll go back to it. What's in that box will help people, but it won't make up for the things I've done." The man pulled up his hood and faced the doors, his back to the priest. "I've hurt everyone I cared about. Even though it's gone from my memory, I know it was me. I know it was real."

The priest said, "I'll pray for you, son."

The man did not reply.

Outside, Martin Money had no clue how to refer to himself. 'The man from The Before', 'the man from his Dead Time', or something new, something that emerged from the chrysalis of his Christmas Eve coma. He could have been an alcoholic about to embark on a period of rehabilitation, making amends, confessing all, but it would be empty gestures. Sure, Edith would use the remainder of Martin's corruption money for good, but it was unconnected with the abuse he laid at her door.

Did his actions in removing her step-father from the family make up for the things he did to her?

Again, they were unconnected actions. One didn't necessitate the other.

He took her because he wanted her, because he wanted to *possess* her, and used his authority and power to attain her. Getting her pregnant might not have been the initial plan, but he sure as hell used it to claim her from other men. He scared her so much, though, that she turned to another man, a good man, a *young* man, who lost his life protecting her, and in the end she gave the baby away.

When Martin then discovered what the step-father was doing to her, to her young sister, it should have resulted in the same actions, irrespective of the things Martin had done. It was the right thing to do. He shouldn't be weighing one thing off against the other, as if there was some cosmic karmic scale to balance.

The money, too, shouldn't be seen as repentance. He had money, attained illegally, that should be out there doing good things. Because he hurt Edith, messed up her life, giving her money to work with was the right thing to do.

Yet the money didn't make up for his actions.

Likewise, the others he hurt, he could not begin to atone. No matter what social sins Julie inflicted upon him, she did not deserve his rage, his vengeance.

Helen, whom he hurt so physically and visually and, although she probably didn't want to admit it, mentally too.

Cupinder, his student, the young constable he plucked from the detective constable pool, who listened to his every word, obeyed his commands, and as a result found herself able to intimidate suspects, to voice her ideas to superiors, and to implement her plans with such precision that no one would be surprised when she made DI at such a young age.

Dave Essex, now dead, because back in his Dead Time, Martin felt so guilty about the things he'd done, about murdering Si Larson, that he roped Dave, his *friend*, into helping him.

And of course, the person who stabbed him. That person attempted to kill Martin with good reason, a reason Martin would never have questioned. Had he been the investigating officer, had he learned of the sins the victim had committed, he would find the suspect straight away, but he would be torn as to whether he should arrest him, or simply look the other way.

In The Before, looking the other way was a moral act.

In his Dead Time it was a profitable one.

So he called his assailant and told him to recreate the crime. To do it right this time. To do it properly.

He told his assailant to make the knife a bigger one, or if he didn't want to, that was okay; Martin could supply a gun.

The person accepted.

Asleep

Using the coat's hood, he concealed himself for the benefit of the cameras whose tapes had been wiped once Martin woke up and demanded to return to work. Wiped by PSD or CID because no one could allow Martin to know the truth until he uncovered it for himself. He could not risk some CCTV operator spotting him and putting in a call to have him arrested.

He loitered directly beneath the nearest mast, ensured the scene was all clear. And why wouldn't it be? It was the last place in the world they would expect him to come.

And so he wandered over and waited on the bridge.

The angle of the wound, the strength that was needed, and that the wound is on the right side of your back, suggests you were approached from behind by a right-handed male.

The person approached. A wide-brimmed hat shadowing their face, as Martin had instructed.

You wanted to confess, get all huggy and shit...

The person stopped before Martin, and looked out from under the hat.

Martin said, "I came to you, didn't I?"

The person said, "You remember me now?"

"No," Martin said. "But you're the one person who could have done it. The most obvious suspect now all the facts are out there."

"They questioned me," said the person who stabbed Martin. "For many hours. They knew I did it, but the tape was fuzzy. Couldn't prove it was me for certain."

"I called first, right? All slurred, fucked up. Begged forgiveness."

A mute nod this time.

Martin said, "I met you here, because I could show you the Shack, and when I told you I killed him, I asked you to hold me. Begged again. For understanding. For forgiveness before I turned myself in."

"You were a maniac," came the reply from under the hat. "You really thought I would forgive you. You thought a hug would make this right."

No one stabs you in the back from in front.

"Then DI Rowe told you to play along with me, pretend we'd never met."

On Martin's first day back on the job, this person told him, *Now we have no hope. Except, maybe, justice.*

"It was hard," the person said. "So hard. But they promised to make my charges go away if I did what I was told. Now you bring me here. To do it again. This is not a trick?"

"I won't fight you. You deserve this. But please know, I am genuinely so very sorry for what I did to everyone, but especially for what I did to your son."

No one stabs you in the back from in front. Unless you're hugging them, making a left-hander look right-handed.

"Good," said Aamon Larson, and Si's father felt in his coat pocket and produced a new knife with a seven-inch blade and a serrated top edge. He drew back his arm.

This could never make up for the man's loss, but it was the right thing to do.

The After

The spinning is the worst. No—it's the hope. Hope I might survive, might crawl out of this when, really, I'm underwater, hurt, wrapped in wet ice, my arms and legs shooting into spasms, and now the water...

Inside me.

I try to cough. More water sluices into my mouth, my throat, my chest.

I taste mud and copper.

My nose stings, as what little air inside me leaks out, the razor-sharp bubbles a new category of torture.

Then darkness.

My feet hit the sludge at the bottom of the River Aire, and plumes of muck swirl. The current grips again, and the spinning resumes. I try to pivot, but swimming up, swimming down, it's all meaningless, even if I could have taken a breath.

Spinning.

Up.

Down.

Gulps of muddy water...

Fighting on was futile.

Only pain lies ahead if I do.

So, to end it all as quickly as possible, I simply open my mouth, breathe in hard, and—

THE END

Acknowledgments

Thank you primarily to my wife, who accommodated my personally-imposed, ridiculously tight deadline by basically reverting our house to the 1950s where she did all the work while I sat on my bum. To be fair, I was sat on my bum creating this novel rather than watching wrestling but you get the picture—she stepped up so I could (mostly) relinquish my usual share household responsibilities.

To my beta readers, as always, I thank you for pointing out many obvious strands I should have spotted and quite a few smaller details that I don't feel so bad about, and my highly-skilled and very reasonably-priced editor, Zoe Markham, who eradicated the errors my fast fingers caused.

My cover art is the work of Adrijus at RockingBookCovers.com who is exceptionally talented and patient enough to guide me away from too many dumb ideas of my own. Trust the professional, folks!

Finally, thanks to all the generous authors out there in various mediums—blogs, forums, podcasts and, most of all, the one-to-one exchanges that have made the experience of my second novel feel far smoother than the first.

You all made this a much stronger story and a far more professional novel.

Newsletter

If you made it this far, I'm going to assume you enjoyed Three Years Dead at least a little, so thank you for that.

I just wanted to remind those who read the section at the beginning, or tell you for the first time if you skipped that page, that I have a newsletter.

Although this is only my second book, over the next 2-3 years I will be growing my list of titles, and if liked this one – or my debut novel, *His First His Second* – you might be interested in forthcoming work too. Plus any freebies that will be exclusive to subscribers. When I've written them, of course.

I am planning a number of short stories over those years, and even some novellas, which will cost money on retail sites, but will be free to those who sign up at www.addavies.com/newsletter.

I guarantee not to pass on your details anywhere ever, and I won't spam you constantly with sales pitches or irrelevant nonsense. Thank you for taking the time to read this, and I look forward to talking to you later.

HIS FIRST HIS SECOND – out now

HIS FIRST HIS SECOND

A. D. DAVIES

Meet Detective Sergeant Alicia Friend. She's nice. Too nice to be a police officer, if she's honest.

She is also one of the most respected criminal analysts in the country, and finds herself in a cold northern town assigned to Donald Murphy's team, investigating the kidnap-murders of two young women—both strikingly similar in appearance. Now a third has been taken, and they have less than a week to chip away the secrets of a high-society family, and uncover the killer's objective.

But Richard—the father of the latest victim—believes the police are not moving quickly enough, so launches a parallel investigation, utilising skills honed in a dark past that is about to catch up with him.

As Richard's secret actions hinder the police, Alicia remains in contact with him, and even starts to fall for his charms, forcing her into choices that will impact the rest of her life.

REFLECTED INNOCENCE – *summer 2015*

Ex-private investigator Adam Park is hired by an old mentor to locate his troubled niece, missing for over two weeks. Using his vast experience, Adam tracks her to Paris, then to onward to South-East Asia, and a violent network for whom human life is just a commodity.

For updates on this and more, sign up at
www.addavies.com/newsletter

Printed in Great Britain
by Amazon.co.uk, Ltd.,
Marston Gate.